KINGDOMS

KINGDOMS

Book 3 of
The Frencolian Chronicles

Carolyn Ann Aish

Horizon House Publishers
Camp Hill, Pennsylvania

Dedicated:
To my daughter, Deborah

Horizon House Publishers
3825 Hartzdale Drive
Camp Hill, PA 17011

ISBN: 0-88965-093-4
LOC Catalog Card Number: 92-70181
© 1992 by Horizon House Publishers
All Rights Reserved
Printed in the United States of America

92 93 94 95 96 5 4 3 2 1

Cover illustration © by Karl Foster

Scripture taken from
THE AUTHORIZED KING JAMES VERSION.

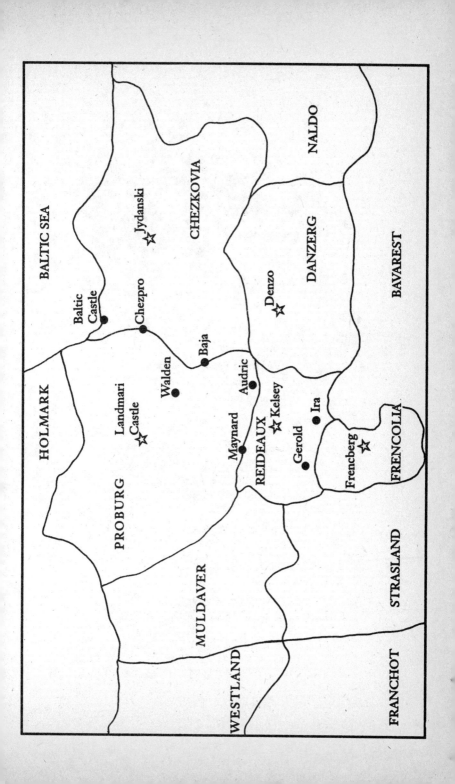

1

Princess Jobyna Chanec's face was flushed from the heat of the kitchen chamber. She was in her element, rolling out the spicy dough on the freshly floured board. To be occupied as such was something that had not changed; it ignited happy memories forever cherished in her mind. The manor house oven emitted captivating aromas that made one's mouth water in anticipation.

King Luke Chanec unobtrusively entered the bake house and stealthily slipped his strong arms around his sister's slender waist, hugging her closely to him. Prince Konrad, from the kingdom of Proburg, had been following Luke, and he now stood sheepishly in the doorway, amused by the king's boyish antics. As Luke released Jobyna, she swung around, waving the rolling pin. In mock consternation, she shrilled, "Luke Chanec! If you don't . . ." The reprimand halted abruptly as her fern-green eyes locked with Prince Konrad's sparkling blue pools.

Snatching two gingerbread bears from the cooling rack, Luke tossed one to Konrad as he pushed as much as he could into his own mouth.

"If I don't . . . what?" the king queried, his voice muffled by the delicious, warm gingerbread.

Embarrassed, Jobyna turned and continued rolling the mixture. "You shouldn't talk with your mouth full!"

Luke promptly pushed the remainder of the tasty morsel into his already overloaded mouth and grabbed another cookie.

Jobyna spun around, remonstrating, "Dinner is to be served later in the dining room; you'll spoil it." She pouted, "Anyway, I wasn't expecting you for a few hours yet, and I made just enough mixture for 60 gingerbread bears. Now I'll be short. I'll finish these and then I can come and greet you properly, if you please, Your Majesties." The princess dropped a mock curtsy and returned to the dough. She was upset because Luke's early arrival had spoiled the welcome she had planned for him.

Snatching two more cookies, Luke flipped one to Konrad. The brother muttered, "We shall go outside then, little Sister, and await your welcome." The two young men ambled from the kitchen.

Jobyna discarded her apron and turned to Daisy, the kitchen-maid. Daisy glared at her mistress with great consternation in her large, muddy-brown eyes.

"Yes, I know. My brother is the king, and I should not talk to him as I do, *and* in the presence of Prince Konrad! Please finish these Daisy. The children will come for them before the hour is up." The princess rushed upstairs to her bedchamber, where Chrissy had set a dress at the ready.

"Cor, 'n they're here already, Miss." The chambermaid fetched a wide-toothed comb while her mistress sponged her floury face. Somehow between the two, they made short time of Jobyna's dressing. Chrissy managed to fix a green bow in her mistress' hair, but was still arranging the coppery tresses as Jobyna descended the stairs.

The king and Prince Konrad waited in the garden beside two crosses, erected to mark the place where Luke and Jobyna's parents were buried. Luke explained to Konrad how Sabin, a servant, had helped Jobyna and him escape to Litton from the wicked self-appointed king, Elliad John Pruwitt.

"We had not been in Litton very long when a loyal knight, Felix, arrived. He said that he was on duty on the wall when my parents were killed in the garden here. Evidently it was very sudden. Father had wanted to try to reason with Elliad, but . . . ." Luke's voice faltered, as he recounted the story.

"Felix said Father . . . embraced Mother, and the knight Berg, at Elliad's command, thrust his sword . . . up through Mother's back, into Father's heart.

"According to Frencolian law there were supposed to be papers signed regarding the . . . execution. Also, the bodies should have been officially identified, preferably by a relative, but this was not done for . . . obvious reasons.

"Felix left his post and rode to Litton to warn us that Elliad wanted to capture us and rid the country of all Chanecs. I was the last threat to the throne, being related to the late King Leopold. As Elliad had already poisoned Cousin Leopold, and disposed of any who questioned his authority as king, I suppose my parents' murders meant nothing to him. Ours would have touched his conscience even less."

The orphaned king shook his head, trying to dispel the overwhelming bitterness he found creeping over him at the memory of his parents' deaths. "The only consolation is that Father and Mother were believers and will be in heaven. I will see them again."

Luke turned away, concealing his threatening tears and tenderly opened the large book which lay in a glass case. "This

Bible contains some books transcribed by Father's hand. The book of Luke was copied by Mother."

The two young men were interrupted by a group of noisy children skipping around the house to play on the lawn. Konrad spoke to one small boy, who looked up sharply at the thick accent of the prince's deep voice.

The boy answered the foreign prince's question, "We are waiting for the princess to come. She gives us gingerbread bears to eat while we listen to a story from the Gospel Book."

A little girl spoke in a loud voice, "Princess Jobyna is reading us the story of Joseph. He has been sold by his brothers and taken off to a far away country."

Jobyna hastened from the front of the house. Moving over to Luke, she curtsied. "Forgive me, Brother Luke. You are very welcome. I apologize that I did not greet you formally, but I was not aware of your early arrival."

He took her hand. "You will have to forgive me, Jo, for being early. I told the guards on the gate that I wanted to surprise you." His handsome young face broke into a smile and his warm blue eyes filled with laughter. "Uncle Dor is always at me for not keeping to our schedule. We, that is, Konrad and I, were anxious to see you and to know how you have settled in here at Chanoine."

"Oh, it is wonderful," she said smiling, but the smile quickly faded, to be replaced by a frown as her green eyes beheld the Gospel Book in the glass case. "Apart from Mother and Father and . . . other things. I miss you, too, Luke."

A small boy interrupted the siblings, calling the other children with excitement in his high-pitched voice, "It's King Luke Chanec! It is true!" The lad cautiously approached Luke, bowing. "We were going to welcome you with the princess, after our story, when you arrived. We have a special song to sing for you, King Luke."

4

Gathering the youngsters to her, Jobyna asked them to wait in the courtyard until all the children congregated. She would then escort the king to them and they could sing the song. After introductions, they would have the cookies and their story.

When the children had moved away, Luke asked softly, "So, little Sister, how are you? Tell me truthfully."

"I am very well, thank you. But I do miss you," she replied. Hanging her head, she added wistfully, "I miss Papa and Mother so very much. I hate to think how they . . . died. . . . "

"And the nightmares? Do you still wake up in the night?" he asked, watching closely for her answer.

"Not for the past week. I have prayed every night before going to sleep, and I have had peaceful rest, thank you. How have you been?" She turned to include Konrad. "And Prince Konrad?"

Luke spoke first, telling Jobyna about some of the matters at court. He turned to the prince. "Konrad is teaching me about mountain climbing. We are planning to climb the cliffs by Frencberg and will climb down into the valley."

Jobyna drew a sharp breath at the thought of such risk. She hoped she would not be asked to witness such a dangerous activity. Already, in her imagination, she could see these two swinging precariously down the sheer face of those rocky gray crags. Unwittingly, she felt her eyes drawn toward the blue gaze of her brother's new friend. The blue eyes seemed to be laughing at her and she drew another sharp breath, this time in dismay, not knowing why this prince left her feeling so stirred.

A boy came whizzing happily around the corner. Bowing to Luke, he spoke excitedly to Jobyna first before addressing her brother. "We're all here, Princess Jobyna. And we are ready for you, King Luke."

Sweet sincere children's voices sounded out, chanting the 23rd Psalm. Then at Jobyna's direction they sang:

You are welcome here,
We are fam'ly here,
In God's fam'ly we are one,
You are welcome here,
We are fam'ly here,
All because of God's dear Son.

The boys bowed, the girls curtsied and one of the lads gave a short welcome speech. Jobyna suggested Luke and Konrad go in the house where light refreshments would be served and they could make themselves comfortable and rest. She would hasten the story along and join them soon. However, the two young men would not be brushed aside and remained in the garden, sitting with the children on the small grass lawn.

"Would you like to read today, King Luke?" Jobyna asked her brother. She was disturbed by the two young men sitting quite relaxed, looking as eager as the children.

The brother shook his head, saying, "No, it will break the continuity for the children. Go ahead. Don't mind us."

Jobyna began to read, but she did mind them. Every time she looked up, she beheld Konrad's distractingly blue eyes gazing at her, totally absorbed in her reading.

The longer Prince Konrad remained in Frencolia, the more thrilled he was by all he saw. Luke had shared the outline of his program to teach the people of Frencolia about God's Word, to show them the difference between good and evil and to encourage the people to choose good.

Prince Konrad was from the country of Proburg in the north. He was the youngest of four sons of the absolute monarch of the kingdom, Prince Gustovas. His father did not accept the Gospel Book but sought to destroy the books if he could discover them, and he would harshly punish those who possessed them. When the evangelist had come to Proburg, Konrad believed the message he heard preached. That had been six years ago, when he was 12. Since then he had come to love God's Word greatly and was the instigator of a plan to make hand-written copies, replacing those his father destroyed. Konrad was known as the "Crazy Prince" because he would rather climb mountains than be in court with his father and brothers. This title served as a cover for his activities in copying the Gospel Book. To be considered "crazy" allowed Konrad to please himself in what he did with his time and where he went.

Luke's blue eyes were warm as he listened to his sister's expressive reading. She paused here and there, explaining the Egypt of the Bible and describing how prison would appear to Joseph. Jobyna eloquently answered the children's many questions. The king was reminded of his mother's readings.

His father, Louis Chanec, (known simply as "Chanec"), and his mother, Elissa Chanec, had believed the message of the evangelist who visited Frencolia before his visit to Proburg. Baron Chanec had been converted from atheism to the Christian faith. Chanec had been a senior knight, first cousin and closest friend of King Leopold of Frencolia. To become the father he believed God wanted him to be, the baron had resigned as a knight. King Leopold reluctantly accepted his cousin's resignation, commanding him to surrender his sword, dismissing him from court and restricting him to the district of Chanoine.

The king had been prepared to let people believe as they wished, so long as they paid their heavy taxes. Chanec continued believing in the Gospel Book and began to make hand-written copies so that others in the kingdom could have the Gospel Book for themselves.

Daisy arrived with the tray of gingerbread bears. Luke took his dagger from the sheath on his belt and cut a dozen of them in half.

The young king gazed at his sister as she distributed the

gingerbread bears. He was happy to know she was home, safe in Frencolia. The past six weeks had disappeared quickly and they had spent little time together. Luke hoped his sister would agree with his plans to change this.

He watched as the sun gleamed on her long curls, showing off the coppery highlights. She was extremely beautiful, fair as the summer's day, but her being radiated far more than simply a pretty face. No wonder the children came to listen! The words of the Gospel Book came alive on her tongue.

The sister smiled impudently as she handed Luke one of the cookies. He reached around to grasp another off the tray but she anticipated his tomfoolery. Evading his hands, she held the tray to Prince Konrad, then distributed the halves to the smallest children. Satisfied, the young congregation dispersed, some of them hugging her, some bowing, but all promising to come again the following day.

2

Tender roast duck glazed with honey, accompanied by a variety of roast vegetables, sliced beans and peas made up the main course of the meal that evening. Sabin joined Luke, Konrad, Moritz (the Proburg prince's personal friend and bodyguard) and two dozen other men to eat the dinner Jobyna had helped prepare. Scrumptious desserts were served; Jobyna had ordered her brother's favorites.

The knight Ruskin and his wife Sabra also dined with the visitors. Luke had commissioned Ruskin to accompany Jobyna to Chanoine as her protector. Other knights and soldiers were also stationed in and around the manor house and village as extra security, though told to be unobtrusive. Jobyna had been surrounded by guards from the time she had been captured by Elliad's men until she returned to Frencolia, and she needed to feel free, not cooped up or tied down.

With the incentive of 2,000 gold pieces reward, Prince Konrad had been worried that some of Elliad's soldiers would journey from Chezkovia to Frencolia to recapture Jobyna. Luke could not discount this possibility, and the thought had become more disconcerting over the past week with reports of numerous strangers arriving in Frencolia. All the well-known border passes into Frencolia were monitored; lists were compiled of those who moved in out of the country, their purpose for entry or exit also being recorded.

Luke had no intention of upsetting Jobyna or causing her to be fearful, but with his uncle's advice, he had ridden here today to hasten her return to the safety of King's Castle. Travelers arriving to buy the prized Frencolian lamb's wool could well be enemies in disguise.

"We need you at court, little Sister," Luke told Jobyna seriously. "We are to be visited by kings, queens and princes from other countries. It has been decided that chief dignities from the countries to which we sent the contract against Elliad will meet here in Frencberg to decide the matter once and for all." Jobyna was silent, so the young king continued, "I would like you to stand with me and greet these royal people when they arrive."

"Who is coming?" the princess asked with interest.

Luke extracted a piece of paper from his jacket and read, "From Strasland, Their Royal Highnesses King Willem and Queen Anstice."

Jobyna drew a deep breath, remembering Ellice, the woman Elliad had kidnapped, branded and rendered a mute slave; she had been stolen from Strasland. She closed her eyes, wondering how Ellice was faring, a slave-prisoner in Chezkovia.

Luke continued, "From Zealavia, Crown Prince Dietrick, the eldest son of King Dionysus; from Bavarest, His Supreme Highness King Jarvis, and son, Crown Prince Haroun; from Danzerg, Their Majesties King Thurlow and Queen Saline; from Chezkovia, His Imperial Highness Czarevitch Kenrik—

whom you have met, Jobyna—accompanied by Doctor Sleven; from Proburg, Crown Prince Gustav, who is Konrad's oldest brother; and from Muldaver, a representative named Lord Stansfield, who will be ambassador for the king and country."

Jobyna was trying to take it all in. "What about Reideaux?" she asked.

Luke looked across the table at Konrad as he replied. "King Kelsey has requested Prince Konrad, although from Proburg, to represent him; he is also sending two of his knights who are known by Konrad to be with us. So you can see, little Sister, with all these visitors I need you. Minette will need help with the arrangements for the womenfolk. Each country will be sending their entourage and all will bring members of their courts, plus servants and militia."

"Are all these people coming to discuss Elliad and his pretense as the czar of Chezkovia?" Jobyna asked, amazed at the thought.

"Not entirely. We have asked that the alliance matter of the kingdoms be discussed. But then, apart from Muldaver and Proburg, every other country has been plundered and raided by Elliad. And there is no doubt that we must be prepared for him to utilize the many thousands of troops he now has at his immediate command."

"Did Elliad raid Zealavia, in the south?" Jobyna asked. The extent of his plundering seemed unbelievable.

"Yes," Luke replied. "Before Elliad was king here in Frencolia, he would go on raids to neighboring countries, pillaging and destroying manor houses and castles. We are checking out reports that he sold Frencolian children in Zealavia as slaves. The man is mad! It is alleged that he stole the slaves back and sold them to another kingdom!

"The king of Bavarest wrote to me, warning that if it were not for the high mountains and the knowledge of the skills of the Frencolian knights, they would have declared war on Frencolia long ago. Elliad has a lot more to answer for than our parents' deaths, Jobyna. I have written to King Jarvis, deeply apologizing on behalf of Frencolia, but stating Elliad was responsible and as he had terrorized in Bavarest, he had done the same in his own kingdom here. It shames me, though, to think our country helped produce such a monster." He folded the paper and looked into his sister's wide green eyes. "So, what about tomorrow morning? Do you think you can be ready to come with us?"

The princess had difficulty in switching her thoughts so quickly and hesitated momentarily. "Such short notice!" she exclaimed, thinking of the eager children returning for the story the next afternoon.

Konrad also remembered the children promising to come again, and he spoke up. "Jobyna has to complete the story of Joseph for the children." He turned to the princess. "Will they be able to come earlier so we can journey back before sunset?"

"Yes, that's possible. I can ask Sabra to put the word around when she goes to the market in the morning. I'm sure the children could come as soon as they have completed their lessons. Then if some of the children do miss, it will be a good opportunity for those who heard the story to recount it in their own words." Jobyna sighed, then said, "Actually, in some ways, I will be happier to go with you to Frencberg. This place holds too many strange memories. I have learned that time and circumstances change some things beyond repair. . . ."

Sensing there was more, Luke asked, "What do you mean, Jo?"

"Well, there is a different atmosphere in Chanoine; it's hard to explain. Many of the people we once knew have moved away, like Shepherd John and Jane—but you told me they had gone. Then again, no one will speak of them. . . . When I ask questions people shy away from me as though they are afraid or there is something to hide! No one wants to speak of Papa or Mother; it is as though they never existed. . . ."

She paused and wiped a lone tear as it made a track down her cheek. "One day I visited a home with one of the children. The plates in the wall-rack were the ones Mother used for special occasions, here in the manor house. I knew them because it was the set Mother said was a wedding gift from King Leopold. It is strange to think how people had taken our home apart and then forgotten so quickly."

She paused again, a catch tearing her breath. "Then the other day I saw a little girl carrying a doll. It was the doll Father carved so carefully for my ninth birthday. I called her 'Martha.' It was my doll, Luke! I remember telling Father I would look after Martha forever so that one day my own little girl could play with her. You remember my doll, Luke!"

The princess bit her lip and hung her head. "There are so many memories in Chanoine. I saw your dog, too. . . ." The sister's voice trailed off and her eyes met those of Konrad, then Moritz. This should have been a private conversation! She stood suddenly, her voice low and full of emotion, "You won't want to know . . . who has Shadow, Luke."

With extreme effort she composed herself and curtsied. "Chrissy will help me begin packing tonight. In the morning we will finish, and I shall bake jam tarts for the children. I will be happy to go with you. I have learned to put the past behind me and to look forward to the unclouded future. I'm not sure whether I want to come back here again. . . ." The princess turned away to leave the Great Hall.

"Just a moment, Jobyna!" Luke's voice was insistent. "Who's got Shadow?"

His sister hesitated, remembering when the beagle mutt had been given to Luke as a gift from their father. "The man who betrayed Father and then recognized you at Westbrook when you were captured—Tod!" She shuddered at the thought of Tod, remembering the way his eyes seemed to gleam with triumph every time he saw her. "I know you said he had begged your pardon, Luke, but . . ."

She did not complete this statement, aware of the many other listening ears. Instead, she tried to be positive and spoke quickly with false brightness, "Tod is living with his wife and family in the village. He leases a plot of land and grows vegetables to sell. The children come to listen to the stories and sometimes Shadow comes with them, but he always leaves with them and it seems they are treating him well." She forced herself to smile, saying, "I feel glad to see the children, and I pray the Gospel Book will make them wise."

Luke did not speak; he just stared at her, his blue eyes glistening with pent-up emotion. He knew she had been through enough and should be protected from facing these unnecessary emotional encounters. Her earlier words were wise; to drag up and mull over the past would do nothing for the present, nor would it enhance the future.

Standing suddenly, Luke moved to embrace her. He rested his chin on her head and held her close, speaking as though to comfort her, in tender tones. "I do not want you to be apart from me any more. We need each other. You need your cousins, too. Maia asks about you about six times a day, wanting to know when you are coming back to Frencberg or when she can visit you in Chanoine. Sometimes I see her and think it is you, Jobyna, and then realize it is not. Maia is Maia, and there is only one of you, dear Jobyna. Uncle Dor and Aunt Mindy said to tell you how much they miss you and want you to return. We almost brought Maia and Charles with us, but they have lessons in the mornings. Their mother said they are behind in their reading program so they could not come. Charles is presenting his first reading in the main square tomorrow morning. I told them you would be home at our castle for dinner tomorrow night. The children are to dine with us as a special favor." Grasping her

14

hands, he pushed her gently from him, "Go and do your packing. We shall celebrate at King's Castle tomorrow. Maybe you could teach the children there to sing songs and you can bake them some cookies. There are two big boys here who like your baking as well!" Kissing her cheeks, he murmured, "Good night, little Sister."

The children came at noon the next day and Jobyna gave them two jam tarts each to eat while she finished the story of Joseph. At the completion, a boy spoke up. "I am glad Joseph and his brothers were back together for the rest of their lives. It is good how God works things out."

A girl, about age six stood up and shyly said, "It's just like Princess Jobyna and King Luke. You were apart for a whole year, but God has brought you back together, forever."

Jobyna was about to add to this statement, but an older boy stood up and cleared his throat, quoting words he had memorized. "We want to thank you, Princess Jobyna Chanec, for reading from the Gospel Book and explaining to us the stories. We have enjoyed your cookies, too." He turned and beckoned (using the length of his whole arm) to a girl hiding around the corner of the manor house. She approached timidly, carrying a parcel wrapped in green cloth with a rose tied on top with yellow ribbon. The boy said, "We all wanted to give you something to remember us by, and my father just finished it this morning. We hope you will come back and we can sing with you some more."

Jobyna untied the bow and carefully opened the cloth. "A Noah's Ark! Look at all the little animals! Your father made it, Leon?" she asked, tenderly fingering the intricate carvings. The ark's roof was hinged and inside were beautifully carved animals of every species, all contained in neatly formed cubicles. Four men and four women figures stood beside small sacks of grain. Around the walls on perches were tiny carved birds.

"My father read about it in the Gospel Book. He has just learned to read in the last year. He thought you would be able to use it when you tell the story of Noah."

"This is wonderful, children! Thank you all so very much." She turned to Leon. "I will write a note to your father, Leon, to thank him. I will come again, but I don't know when . . . not for some weeks. My brother, the king, will be keeping me busy in Frencberg. Sabra is going to read to you each afternoon and I know you will all come to hear the stories." She walked among the children, hugging them, some of them tearfully exclaiming that they had just met her and she was going away, leaving them.

She gathered one tiny tot, a girl, in her slender arms and as she stood her eyes met with Konrad's concerned but warm expression. "I hate to interrupt, Princess, but if we do not leave very soon, your cousins will be disappointed and waiting at the banquet without us."

Jobyna, sitting sidesaddle on Brownlea, drank in a final glimpse of the manor house before turning the corner toward Frencberg. Her feelings were so mixed and muddled. She knew it was important to give up all bitterness toward past events and keep one's mind on the present. One day was enough to deal with at one time.

Urging Brownlea on, she wondered if they would catch the cart carrying her trunks before it reached King's Castle. The cart had left that morning and the trunks contained the new dresses Sabra and the servants had helped sew while she had been in Chanoine. It had been fun, even though they worked long and hard; they had talked and laughed and shared as they stitched. The dresses were simple, plain and very necessary because when she had arrived back in Frencolia she had no luggage at all, not a stitch of clothing to call her own!

Fifty soldiers rode in the company, and as they came to the "Y" fork in the road, Jobyna's eyes lifted to behold the cascading waterfall to their right. She remembered this hidden entrance very well. Beyond it was the valley where she and Luke had hidden from Elliad. So many haunting memories! Shuddering, the princess urged Brownlea into a gallop, directing him to the side to overtake the soldiers ahead. Luke drew in behind her and when they were clear, he coaxed Speed to pull ahead. Breathless, they slowed, waiting for Konrad to catch up. They laughed, remembering the many times in the past when Speed had outrun Brownlea.

"One day, Brother, Brownlea will win! He's so much younger than Speed," Jobyna promised Luke.

3

Your dress is soiled!" Minette scolded Doralin. Turning to Doralin's nursery-maid, the mother requested, "See if you can sponge it off, Beth." Charles stood patiently awaiting his mother's inspection. Minette straightened the lace collar of his shirt. "Now, remember the word *slow—s-l-o-w*. If you keep reminding yourself to read slowly, then all you say will be clear and people will hear you. You must not rattle it off like a bolting horse, 30 miles an hour."

"Yes, Mother," Charles said while his mother picked a piece of fluff off his lush, green-velvet jacket. "No, Mother. I'll try not to rattle."

Elissa giggled. "You don't rattle, Charles; Father says you boil over!"

Maia joined the conversation. "I wish Father could hear Charles read. It's not fair he has to be so busy."

"Now, now!" Minette cautioned, "Luke will be back tonight

and Father will be less tied up. Maybe he can come with us next week when Charles reads again. Luke and Jobyna may both be able to come."

The young mother beckoned her children closer. She warned, "Listen up, all of you. You must stay together. You each have a special friend of your father's watching you, a *minder*, he called him. Remember?" Minette's light-brown eyes passed across each face, reassuring herself that they were listening and taking in what she was explaining. "These friends will make sure we all stay together. Elissa, if you wander off I will send you home." The big brown eyes of her five-year-old stared seriously into Minette's probing observation.

The four children with their mother, Princess Minette, would proceed to the main square in Frencberg to listen as Charles read from the Gospel Book. He had practiced the 10 chapters from Proverbs over and over for weeks. The Gospel Book was read throughout the day in the main square, from one hour after sunrise until one hour before sunset. Young men all over the city were encouraged to take part and Prince Dorai had agreed for Charles to take a turn.

Great numbers moved through the market place to the square which was already over-crowded. Minette's eyes surveyed the immediate surroundings, her eyes meeting those of the various knights, "minding" her children. She told herself to stop worrying, and her eyes fixed on Charles as he stood on the platform. The reading began.

"Mother, can I stand by Constance?" Maia asked.

Minette turned to view Constance standing with her mother over by their shop frontage.

"Yes, dear, but mind you stay with her." Minette cautioned.

Constance's mother returned to the shop as a customer entered, and Constance whispered to Maia, telling her about her cat, Blossom, who had given birth to six kittens. Maybe they could snatch a quick look at the little babies while Charles read? She would like her friend to have one when they were old enough. The princess could have first choice. Maia looked across the square. Charles would be a long time and she could be back well before he finished. Eager to view the kittens, Maia followed her friend down the alley beside the house-shop. The sound of a firm footstep following reassured Maia that father's friend was close behind. Prince Dorai had insisted each of the children have a special "guardian" when they were away from the castle.

A cold, clammy hand slipped silently around Maia's face, and a thick cloth slid over her mouth and nose, as a black cloak fell between the princess and her friend, Constance. Terrifying thoughts flew through Maia's mind. *I should have stayed with Mother!* was the one plaguing impression which would remain with her for weeks. A myriad of brilliant colors flashed in her eyes, and she realized, too late, that everything was wrong! For a few moments, Maia struggled against the blackness that threatened to engulf her. The harder she fought, the tighter the cloth gripped her face! Before long, Maia could no longer struggle and knew nothing but darkness.

Minette turned as she heard a scuffle by the shop front. A man lay on the path, and people were gathering to see what had happened. She looked for Maia, but the crowd was too dense for the anxious mother to see the slight form of her daughter. Charles hesitated for a moment, but catching his mother's determined nod, he continued reading. Minette saw Mattheus, her own bodyguard, run to the shop front, pushing fiercely through the throng. (Minette could not remember the sequence of events from that moment on; it was as if a fog descended on her mind). She promptly forgot words Mattheus yelled to her.

The knight rushed back to the mother, gesturing wildly to Charles' bodyguard, who ran to Charles and halted the reading. Confused and mindless, Charles and Elissa were unceremoniously herded back to King's Castle. Minette looked back desperately for Doralin and Maia. She tried unsuccessfully to shake the knight's firm, shepherding grip from her arm. Mattheus, still issuing orders, left Minette surrounded by a group of castle guards and soldiers. He sent for Prince Dorai, and Minette found herself ushered through the castle foyer and into the front reception room together now with Charles, Doralin and Elissa. The two little girls were in tears and it was enough for the mother to comfort them.

After the space of about seven long minutes—a time that seemed to be hours—Crown Prince Dorai came rushing to his wife's side. "What happened? Where is Maia?" he gasped, and grabbed her hands frantically, staring into her face for an answer that did not come. Releasing her quickly, he hastily inspected each of the three children.

"I . . . I don't know what happened. . . ." Minette found her voice and cried as her husband rushed away, along the corridor, through the foyer and out the front doors.

Prince Dorai entered the small living room where Constance lay on the couch. Maia's bodyguard, Ruben, lay stretched out on the floor; both were obviously unconscious. A doctor was in attendance, pacing between the two prostrate figures. Mattheus, kneeling on one knee beside the couch, gingerly handed the crown prince two thick pieces of cloth, instructing him to inhale the fumes, but from a safe distance, not too close to his nose!

"It contains some sort of drug, like powdered poppy seed or such. Ruben was overpowered by the shop front, and Constance in the alley. There is another piece over there also. It was discarded in the alley." The bodyguard looked hesitantly at the prince. "Doctor Paul says they may be unconscious for an hour or more."

Prince Dorai spoke, and his voice broke, "And . . . Maia?"

Mattheus stood, bracing himself, to face his master, "We have dispatched soldiers to every part of the city, both on foot and on horseback. I have ordered roadblocks to be set up. Do you want us to close the borders, Sire?" Dorai did not answer. Shock and grief began to surge into the father's consciousness. "Sire?" Mattheus queried. "What are your orders, Sire?"

Dorai struggled with the angry knight inside himself. How could this happen? Such criminals would only understand one thing—his sword! He heard a strange voice—Maia's father's voice—commanding, "Mattheus. You are in charge from this moment on. Have the borders carefully monitored. Everyone must be thoroughly checked before leaving Frencolia. Do all you can. You have total authority in this matter. I will speak to the senior knights and they can contact you." Dorai knew that he had a duty that he could not neglect. "I must go to my wife."

Mattheus saluted and bowed. "We will do all we can to bring Princess Maia back, Sire."

Frencberg took on a fiery glow as the retiring sun sank into a flaming orange sky. The royal party from Chanoine rode toward the south entrance of King's Castle. The moat bridge was heavily guarded and Luke was instantly surprised. Guards carefully monitored the party through the gates but Luke held Speed back and spoke to a knight, inquiring the reason for the extra guards.

"Prince Dorai has bad news, Sire." The knight saluted and bowed. Luke knew by this curt announcement that he would have to glean the facts from his uncle. He rode Speed right up on the front steps, handed the reins to a waiting soldier and hurried into the castle.

Jobyna and Konrad rode on toward the stables, not recognizing the abnormal security; they were unaware of anything unusual. Jobyna could see the empty cart near a side door and was glad to see it had arrived safely. Konrad stood ready to help her off Brownlea—not that she needed help. Her eyes met his as he helped her dismount, and she felt disconcerted by his intent gaze. She was glad Luke had found a close companion in Konrad, but as for her, she wanted to keep a safe distance. He was Prince Konrad from Proburg and she had no ideas of becoming too friendly with a prince, no matter who he was! Now if he were a farmer or a trader and would live an ordinary, simple life, then she might find him attractive, she thought. Yes. Smiling once more into the friendly, warm eyes, she knew he was a young man whom she greatly esteemed, appreciated and felt a kinship toward. Remembering his princely title, she lowered her sparkling green eyes.

A soldier led Speed past them to the care of the grooms. Jobyna wondered where Luke had disappeared so quickly. Konrad escorted Jobyna to Minette's apartment, where Jobyna had stayed the last time she was at King's Castle. He told her he would come back for her in less than 30 minutes as dinner would be served then. Princess Minette did not like the children to be up much after sunset, he explained.

The apartment was deserted and dark. As Jobyna moved through the silent rooms, she felt most surprised. Not a soul was there to greet her! Aunt Minette must have dressed and gone ahead to dinner. The bath was drawn, but no servants were to be seen. Jobyna lit the lamps and the gloomy apartment was instantly transformed into friendliness. She saw that one of her evening dresses had been laid on her bed so she bathed quickly and dressed, brushing her hair until it crinkled and crackled with bright life of its own. The princess was ready, but there was no knock at the door. Prince Konrad did not come. She sat on the couch, listening; wondering again where Minette was. She did not want to go ahead lest she spoiled the children's surprise for her, so she sat patiently for some time, reading idly here and there from the book of the Psalms of David. After a long period,

Jobyna, having paced back and forth from the door, began to fret a little. She hoped her family, namely her brother and cousins, were not playing a trick on her. This was the week of the celebration of her 15th birthday and she had wondered if they had planned to surprise her, somehow. Luke had told his sister that her true birthday was actually six weeks before the recorded birth, as she had been premature and not expected to survive the first few weeks. The doctor had predicted that if she lived until the date she should have been born, then she would continue to live, but he had given little hope. Their mother named her "Jobyna" and had written down her birth date as being six weeks after the actual event.

Why didn't Konrad come? The princess decided to make her own way to the dining room, and as she descended the stairs, she felt a little hurt that no one had greeted or welcomed her. Where was Aunt Minette? Or Uncle Dor? What about the children? She hated the way her imagination speculated the unknown. Smiling she said to herself, "A monster has *not* devoured them all or carried them off into the secret tunnels!"

The dining room door was unattended and she pushed it open gingerly, half expecting Luke to jump out, startling her, scaring her, then laughing. The chamber was totally void of life; there was no surprise—nothing! The Great Hall dining room was in complete darkness, but she could see the tables were set ready for the evening meal. This was getting past a joke. Where could she go next? Following the corridor, she descended the stairs to the front of the castle. Sentries and attendants at the door bowed and gazed up at her. Recognition on their grave faces was instantly replaced by great concern.

"Where is everyone?" she demanded, sensing the reality of there being something wrong. A guard pointed wordlessly to the front reception room. Jobyna headed toward the room and the castle attendants bowed and held the door open for the princess to enter. Minette was sitting on the edge of a couch, dabbing her red-rimmed eyes and Dorai was pacing back and forth. The couples' personal attendants stood conspicuously against the walls. Prince Dorai started as the door opened, and upon recognition of the visitor, he rushed to his niece's side.

"Jobyna, you're here!" Stating the obvious, he hugged her, holding her close. Perceiving her uncle's disoriented attitude, Jobyna realized that something was definitely very wrong.

"What is going on?" she asked. Silence greeted her question, and all eyes stared as though she had uttered something abhorrent. Dorai moved away and sat down with his head in his hands.

"Where are Luke and Konrad?" Jobyna questioned, turning to Minette. "There was no one in your room, Aunt Minette." Her relative's stricken tear-filled eyes stared, lingeringly. Jobyna saw Minette begin to tremble uncontrollably, shaking and crying. She sat beside her aunt. "What is wrong?" Jobyna asked compassionately. Minette cried harder into the already saturated kerchief. The niece was silent for several minutes. She asked cautiously, "Where are the children?"

Minette, between sobs, managed to reply, "In . . . their rooms. All but Maia. Oh, my poor Maia!" Her sobs grew louder and Jobyna put her arms around her, looking searchingly at her uncle for an answer. Jobyna always had an eager imagination. It was easy to think the worst, and she was consciously trying to prevent her mind from working too fast. Facts! She needed the facts! Soberly quiet, she listened to Minette crying for some minutes before she pushed her gently away and stood to her feet.

"What happened?" Her voice was barely a whisper and she moved close to her uncle. He drew her to a couch in the corner of the large room and sat with her, recounting all they knew of Maia's abduction. Jobyna asked why he wasn't out looking for Maia.

"I want to be here with Minette when we get word."

"What are you expecting?" Jobyna whispered, instantly regretting verbalizing such a question.

"A ransom note, for sure," Prince Dorai said with hope in his deep voice.

Jobyna asked where Luke and Konrad were, and the uncle said that he thought they had joined the search.

Drowning out Minette's now sedate sobbing, a crying, screaming, wailing sound came from the corridor. The somewhat artificial commotion grew louder as the offender drew closer and closer. A woman servant entered carrying the noisy culprit, Elissa. Charles and Doralin followed sheepishly behind their sister.

The woman curtsied. "I'm sorry, Your Highness. . . . Ma'rm, the children would not sleep without seeing you, and . . ." Her voice cut off as Elissa wriggled, struggling to get down.

"Maia!" Elissa screamed.

"Maia?" Doralin ran to Jobyna who stood, speechless, returning the hug as Elissa rushed over to join the embrace. Doralin pushed herself away, "No, it's Jobyna, not Maia! Papa, where is Maia?" She began to wail, "I want Maia! I want Maia!"

Charles joined the concerned chorus, "Have you found Maia yet, Father?"

Jobyna's eyes met her uncle's and knew he had the same thought as she. His grim face was drawn, distressed. The girls, at first glance, had thought she was Maia! Jobyna did not want her personal assumptions to stay in her head! Turning to the children, she said brightly. "Luke and Prince Konrad and all the soldiers in Frencolia are out looking for Maia, and God will help them find her, I feel sure. Charles, please take me to your rooms. We will have some stories while we wait. I have a surprise to share with you." She watched as the children kissed their parents, Elissa patting her mother's cheek, wiping the silent tears with her forefinger. Then the princess-cousin ascended the central stairs

26

with the youngsters. She sent a servant to fetch the Noah's Ark.

"Joseph was stolen away to Egypt and he was there for years. God used this time for a very good reason." Jobyna recounted to the children her favorite Bible story.

"Do you think Maia will be away for years and years?" Doralin asked.

"No! God is going to bring her back! Tonight!" Elissa's tone was final.

Jobyna thought of how much Maia looked like herself. "God may allow Maia to be taken a long way away, but whatever happens, we must remember that He is in control."

"What's 'control'?" Elissa asked. Jobyna looked at Charles, her eyes seeking the lad's input on their conversation. So far he had been sullen and silent. She waited.

"It means God won't let anything happen that He doesn't want." Charles answered his sister's question.

"Then why did Maia get taken at all?" Doralin queried. Silence reigned in the bedchamber for a few moments while Jobyna thought deeply. New revelations entered her mind.

"You all know that I was captured and was taken from Frencolia for a whole year. Well, I learned things that I could never have learned if I had not been away."

"What things?" Doralin asked seriously.

"Like trusting God. I mean really trusting, even when I was sick and lonely and wanted to come home. And I learned to pray for my enemies," the princess added, remembering Berg. "And do you know God made me strong so I could love them and not hate?" The children looked at her soberly, their eyes wide. She continued, asking them, "And while I was away, what did you do for me?"

"We prayed." Elissa replied, eagerly, "Every day, too."

"Then what did God do?" Jobyna persisted.

"He answered our prayers! You are here!" Doralin smiled. "We must pray for Maia, that she will be strong and trust; but I want to pray she comes home soon, like tomorrow!"

Delight and excitement filled the children as they played with the animals and the ark. Charles fetched a Gospel Book and read the story of the building of the ark from the book of Genesis. Once the novelty of the new toys wore off and the children's tiredness came to the fore, Jobyna read, sang and prayed. One by one, the girls fell asleep and she beckoned to the watching servants to carry them to their respective beds. Charles, the persistent one, solemnly declared he would never sleep again until his sister was safely home. Jobyna promised to come and wake him if there was any news, or else she would bring Maia to see him. Reluctantly, he climbed in bed, allowing her to tuck him in and sit with him. She read from the Gospel Book, making her voice as monotonous as she could. His eyelids grew heavier and heavier until he could fight to stay awake no longer, and he, too, fell fast asleep.

Descending to the front reception room once more, Jobyna realized how late in the evening it was and how hungry she felt. Her uncle sprang to his feet as she entered the room; she gave them the good news that the children were all asleep. Minette continued to pace back and forward, wringing her hands.

"No news?" Jobyna asked her uncle softly, as she sat on the couch. He shook his head sadly.

"We have had some reports back. They reveal nothing; no signs anywhere. No messages. . . ." His voice trailed off and he dropped, exhausted, to the couch. His face hung in his huge hands and he rubbed his eyes vigorously, as though trying to erase the invasion of a bad dream.

"There won't be a ransom note, Uncle." Jobyna's tone was decisive. The prince closed his eyes when he heard these dreaded words, only to open them as his niece continued, "Whoever abducted her thinks Maia is me." She hung her head, and her

28

long locks hid her face. Speaking as though to the floor, firmly forcing any tears from forming, she said, "I wish it had been me! You would have been spared all of this. . . ." She looked up at Minette, who had ceased her pacing and was stone still, staring at her niece. A strange light entered Minette's red-rimmed, light-brown eyes.

The aunt moved to sit by the sorrowful girl. "No, you're wrong Jobyna. It would be the same." Minette shook her head, trying to gain her regal composure, realizing what this moment meant to Luke's sister.

Prince Dorai interrupted, "Minette's right!" He paused, thoughtful for a moment, then finished, "In fact, we would probably feel worse if it were you, Jobyna. You mean as much to us as Maia. And Luke . . . you are all Luke has." Jobyna hugged both her relatives and they wept together. A new bond entwined their hearts, uniting them strongly together.

Prince Dorai stood, speaking to the attendants, "Bring us something to eat. Yes. We will eat something now."

Many miles away, to the east of Frencberg, a party of four men on horseback arrived at the border, their horses bearing great packs of lambs' wool. Two of the men led an extra horse, each animal heavily loaded. They drew obediently to a halt as they were challenged at the border pass. A small keep had been built on this path in the past year. This was the exact place Elliad had exited from Frencolia carrying all the kingdom's treasures, including Jobyna.

"We came in a week ago to purchase lambs' wool and are returning to our master in Danzerg," the man lied. "Cormick, Edsel, Lester and Welby. If you check the paper, you will find recorded that I said we would be bringing my sister from

29

Samdene with me. Her name is Lana Cormick."

The knight on duty directed the torch closer to his list. Turning back two pages, he said, "Yes, here it is, Sir Cormick, and Edsel, Welby and Lester." He perused the men, evaluating each one. His eyes moved back to the spokesman, who had a large cloak tied around his body, with a head of curly fair hair showing.

"My sister is asleep. We have had a long day and did not get away as soon as we thought." Cormick murmured, his voice a monotone. He brushed his fair hair back from his face. The beady eyes watched as the knight looked from Maia's hair to that of the supposed "brother."

The knight motioned for them to pass, wishing them a good journey. On later reflections, he remembered feeling amazed to see a girl so sound asleep and traveling in such a fashion. Also the hour was so late; but there was no legal reason to detain them. So well was their trickery planned. The blond wig successfully disguised Maia's distinctive copper-brown hair.

Luke and Konrad arrived at the border with 30 soldiers, four and a half hours behind the Chezkovian-bound party. The knight and his men were dozing but roused quickly at the sound of hoof beats. Luke and Konrad studied the records carefully. They were unsure whether there was anything of significance. But Luke's gut feeling told him there had to be. He ordered the knight to enter the keep and make them a copy of the record: names, dates, entry and exit. Cormick, Edsel, Lester and Welby—and the sister, Lana, who had supposedly exited from Samdene.

"There is no point in further pursuit tonight. They have too much of a head start," Luke told Konrad. "We are not equipped for a long journey either, and if they have Maia, there are sure to be men waiting for them somewhere out there."

Day was breaking when Luke and Konrad rode back over the moat bridge in Frencberg. Luke was met by Sir Keith, a senior knight, and Mattheus, who reported their efforts as also fruitless. The king gave them the paper and ordered a search to be mounted in Samdene for the home of a woman called "Lana Cormick," who supposedly had a brother in Danzerg, named Sir Cormick.

"I want you to go to every house, even if it takes all day. And when you find who this woman is, report back immediately. Also, these four men—I want the name of the inn they stayed in, whether in Samdene or Frencberg, and I want a report about every move they made," Luke commanded. The king's knights bowed, moving off instantly to carry out the royal orders.

Luke and Konrad found Prince Dorai, Princess Minette and Princess Jobyna, all sleeping in the front reception room where they had remained all night. Dorai was stretched out in a chair, a footstool under his feet; the two women lay on separate couches. Minette roused the instant the door swung open, Dorai just seconds later. Konrad gazed intently at Jobyna, who was still sound asleep. He too realized that Jobyna was the one supposed to have been kidnapped; Maia had likely been abducted by people who believed she was the older girl. While the emphasis had been on protecting Jobyna in Chanoine, no one had suspected such a terrible mistake could take place. They spoke in undertones, and when Jobyna suddenly opened her eyes, her brother had to retell the happenings of the night.

"I shall write to Elliad and tell him I will exchange places with Maia. He will send her home!" Jobyna proclaimed when Luke told her what he feared.

"Those are the most unthinkable words we have ever heard!" Prince Dorai's voice vibrated with astonishment that Jobyna could conceive such an idea. "Then he would have both of you! There will be no such talk! We will never bargain with a madman!"

4

Maia tried to rouse herself. A desperate cry formed in her throat but would not surface from her dry lips. The young princess tried to pull herself out of the darkness of drug-induced slumber, but her struggles were in vain. Soft cloth bonds tied around the princess' wrists would not yield against her weak efforts to repel them. She was hot, thirsty and sick; a vile taste sat at the back of her tongue; strange feelings surged like waves over her and a prickly sensation ran through her body making her feel hot—much too hot! Hearing her heartbeat pounding in her head, Maia tried to wake from the horrific dream. The acidic odor of a stranger's perspiration was overcome by a sweet sickly smell which would not go away; she was breathing her own exhaled air, but her head felt too heavy to lift out of the fabric that surrounded her face.

Remembrance of the journey was never truly clear to Maia. She could recall the carriage ride clearer than the journey on horseback. At a special rendezvous point on the smoother roads of Danzerg, Maia, still heavily drugged, was placed in a carriage. Once, while only half awake, she drank thirstily of some liquid offered her and promptly vomited. The woman traveling with her gave her small sips after that, speaking encouragements in a language Maia could not comprehend (nor did she want to). Sleep. The princess just wanted to be left alone to sleep, but there was no rest.

A message had been sent ahead to the Chezkovian capital, Jydanski, and Brian, Elliad's chief bodyguard and counselor, brought the good news to him. "Czar Kievik, we have word! The Princess Jobyna has been captured for you, over a week ago, and is in fact being brought here. She will arrive in two or three days." Brian did not know the details—who had abducted her or how—but he did know that she had been taken from the capital city of Frencolia.

Elliad was elated. The loose ends were being tied. He was looking forward to seeing his "treasure" again. He had nicknamed her "Sparrow," because Jobyna had been so sickly and thin when he first met her. A doctor from Jydanski had been paid handsomely to restore her to good health—Doctor Sleven, who had changed her from a "sparrow" into a "swan." Elliad greatly regretted his past neglect of her; the missing treasure had become more valuable, more desirable, by the long absence. He had grown tired of Czarina Terese, whose idle chatter and illogical conversation contrasted sharply to his memories of the submissive, quiet, sensitive, Jobyna. Czarina Terese was fast becoming another loose end, but Elliad was sure he could take care of her very quickly when the time came.

Elliad enjoyed the autocratic power he had in Chezkovia even more than the great treasures he had stolen from Frencolia, more than the wealth, treasures and splendor of his newly captured czardom. As czar, he was worshiped, his every whim obeyed without question. Those closest to him who had helped him become czar welcomed and revered him with unfailing loyalty and affection. With their advice, he had grown his hair and beard the same length as the czar's, curling and blackening it to match; it had been streaked here and there with silver-gray. Of slighter build than the czar, Elliad wore extra clothing and larger shoulder pads so the difference would be undetected.

Due to the unrest created by Chezkovians defecting to Proburg in support of Czarevitch Kenrik, the czar's elder son, Elliad had made several public appearances and was acclaimed and cheered. A decree, stating his son Kenrik had committed treason against the crown was to be issued and the czarevitch would be banned from entering Chezkovia; Kenrik would be disclaimed as heir. Extensive lists were being compiled of emirs and their men who were loyal to Kenrik. Execution orders for these "traitors" were being written. Kenrik's brother and sister, Cynara and Kedar, were being held as prisoners in Baltic Castle, an impenetrable fortress. Elliad would like to add Kenrik to this collection.

Elliad watched eagerly from the palace balcony as the carriage entered from the oval courtyard, under the massive marble archways, and into the palace courtyard itself. His captive had arrived at last! She would not escape him this time! Smirking, he watched as she stepped down from the carriage. His eyes narrowed as he saw her struggle persistently with two soldiers. He had known her to be submissive and controllable. A little bit of freedom had taught her bad habits! The small distant figure continued to struggle, her long copper-brown tresses, tangled, blowing in the wind. The soldiers dragged the unwilling princess toward the front steps and they soon disappeared out of sight under the great palace frontage.

Elliad had ordered that Borena (known as "Boey"), the woman who had cared for Jobyna before, and Ellice, the mute slave-girl, look after his "treasure" when it arrived. She would be taken into the care of the chief chamberlady, Sofia Vievers. The pretender-czar decided he would wait until later in the day to confront his captive. He was sure he had Jobyna safe in his clutches and she might need a few hours to compose herself, especially from the hysterical type of behavior he had just witnessed. Oh, how much he hated childish tantrums! He had thought Jobyna had grown out of that stage, if she had ever suffered such childishness! He frowned at himself; the picture in his mind must have been an ideal, not a reality!

Maia continued to fight against the soldiers. She created such a fuss that they had to carry her up the stairs to the rooms where Boey and Ellice waited expectantly. It was unheard of for soldiers to enter the women's quarters, but the big soldier toted her right into the apartment, dumping her roughly to sprawl on the couch. Maia's hair fell over her tear-streaked face, and Boey rushed to her charge as the door was slammed soundly by the departing soldier.

"It ain't any good to make such a fuss, Princess," Boey chastened the sobbing girl. Ellice was looking at Maia strangely. The slave-girl knew instantly that something was wrong! The princess looked too little, too short, altogether too small! How could Princess Jobyna shrink? With large, velvet-brown eyes that were wide with fear, Ellice stepped cautiously toward the new arrival.

"Leave her be for a while. She'll recover soon," Boey murmured as she moved into the bathroom where she sprinkled rose petals on waiting bath water, stirring them and mumbling about the princess' wasted tears.

Ellice poured fruit juice into a silver chalice and gently tapped Maia on the shoulder. The princess pushed her untidy hair back and took the proffered receptacle, drinking thirstily. Her brown eyes met Ellice's sympathetic stare. Ellice's fears were confirmed;

this girl was *not* Jobyna, the princess to whom she had been close for a year. The mute moved quickly to Boey, urgently tugging the servant's arm. Bringing her back to view Maia, she gently pulled the hair away from the captive's face. Boey's eyes did not detect anything amiss; her simple mind was preconditioned to the fact that this was Princess Jobyna. Boey scolded Ellice and ordered her to help the princess bathe and dress.

The servant spoke to the motionless captive. "Czar Kievik has requested you dine with him tonight, Princess."

At Boey's words, Maia perked up. Someone knew she was here! The czar! As though in a trance, Maia moved to the bathroom and allowed Ellice help her bathe. Succumbing to the fragrant, tepid waters with a resigned sigh, she could not remember how long it had been since she had enjoyed this usually ordinary occurrence. The warm water engulfing her felt like a beautiful lost luxury. Ellice dressed her in one of the gowns from the collection prepared for Jobyna. The dress was too wide, too big and much too long. Boey stared at her, trying to comprehend the difference, seeking to work out who Maia really was, not wanting to think what this terrible mistake would mean to the czar. She could now discern the differences in Maia's features. Her oval face and hair were the same as Jobyna's, but her nose was a different shape, her eyes smaller, more slanted. There was no doubt that she was beautiful, but she possessed a different beauty than Jobyna. Boey suddenly remembered Jobyna's unusually large green eyes; this girl's were brown. She looked at Ellice and knew the slave-girl had been trying to tell her previously about the difference.

"Well why didn't you say so?" Boey felt put out by Ellice's "I tried to tell you" stare.

"Who are you?" she demanded of Maia, who sat on the couch with her arms folded defiantly. Maia was desperately hungry and very tired. If only they would leave her alone. She haughtily scrutinized Boey, a large, pleasant woman, obviously a servant, and wondered who she was. What right did she have to ask questions of her? But at least they were speaking the same language.

"Where am I?" Maia asked.

"You are in the palace at Jydanski," Boey answered.

"What country is that?" she asked, then answered the question herself. "Chezkovia?" Boey and Ellice nodded.

Boey was facing a dilemma. She was not used to making decisions and knew it was not up to her to question this girl. The servant walked to the door and pulled twice on a thick silk cord. The door promptly swung open.

"Tell Sofia she must come. It's *very* urgent-like!" Boey told the woman attendant.

Sofia entered the room after a few minutes. "So, we have the Princess Jobyna with us once more." She spoke to Boey, not seeing past the large women to where Maia sat. "What do you want?"

"She ain't the Princess Jobyna. She's someone else," Boey informed Sofia.

Sofia pushed past them and stared briefly at Maia. "Well that's *very* obvious! What idiot brought *this* child?" She turned to Ellice. "Go and get her some clothes that fit. I will have to work out how we will tell the czar. She cannot be presented to him as Princess Jobyna Chanec!" Sofia turned to Maia, "What is your name, girl?"

Maia felt somewhat relieved that she had been mistaken for Jobyna. Somehow this revelation cleared up the reason for her abduction; the puzzle was slowly fitting together in her mind. Little snatches from conversations at home came back to her, but the children had been protected from the story about Jobyna, except that she was still being sought by the czar of Chezkovia. That had been one reason Jobyna went to live in

37

Chanoine, Maia thought.

"I won't tell you my name!" Maia answered defiantly as she folded her arms tighter across her chest.

Sofia slapped Maia forcefully across the face, gripping her shoulders and shaking her roughly. "You had better change that attitude, and fast, girl! Czar Kievik will have your tongue if you speak to him like that." She pushed her violently backwards on the couch, speaking severely, "Loosen your tongue, child, and be ready to answer the questions you will be asked." Sofia pulled the cord and the door was opened. Without looking back, the austere woman left the room. Maia noticed, fearfully, as the door slammed shut, that there was no handle on the inside!

Boey spoke, "Miss, you better mind what Sofia says. You must tell them who you are and answer all the questions you are asked. If you keeps up fighting, you'll only be worse off in the end."

Brian received Sophie's note. He could not believe what he read. "The maid who was brought in is not Princess Jobyna Chanec. We do not know who she is. She refuses to cooperate and won't give us her name."

Brian sent two soldiers to tell Sofia to send the girl with them. He would meet them down in "number one"—one of the palace interrogation rooms where the czar's prisoners were first taken for questioning before consignment to the dungeons or elsewhere.

Maia entered the small room, a soldier on either side of her. Brian was waiting. He scrutinized the captive and saw how easily she could be mistaken for Princess Jobyna. Brian spoke to the soldiers in a language Maia did not understand. The soldiers pushed her firmly into a chair, locking her arms and wrists to the mechanisms, adjusting the bands tighter to fit her slim limbs. She struggled but realized there was no release; she was held fast. Her breath came faster as she felt the palpitations of her heart.

Brian walked around the chair slowly, looking at Maia. He

could see she was terrified. "If you behave and answer my questions, I will have the bands unlocked. Tell me your name, girl."

Maia trembled with fear. She had never been treated with violence before and her heart thumped so hard that she felt its pounding in her head. She wanted to defy these people, but her cheek was still smarting from Sofia's slap. What would she gain by not speaking, she wondered?

Brian grabbed her hair, pulling her head sharply backwards to meet his angry eyes, "Your name! Tell me your name!"

Maia gasped at the pain of his careless grip. Her fear suddenly changed to anger. She yelled, "If you let my hair go, I'll tell you!" He complied, slowly. She pulled her head down so she could look straight ahead and not at her interrogator. "I am Princess Maia, daughter of Crown Prince Dorai, and I am first cousin of King Luke Chanec of Frencolia."

Brian walked right around the chair, staring at her, surprised but satisfied. He barked, "You are, are you? You look like Princess Jobyna; how is this?"

"Jobyna's mother and my father are brother and sister; I mean they were. Father says I look like Jobyna's mother and so does Jobyna." Maia rattled on the bands, hissing at him through her teeth, barely restraining her anger, "You said you would undo these things!"

"One more question, Princess Maia, daughter of Crown Prince Dorai and first cousin of King Luke Chanec of Frencolia." Brian wanted to make sure he had her title correctly memorized. "Where is your cousin, Princess Jobyna?"

"She was staying in Chanoine. But the day I was taken . . . she was to come back to King's Castle." Maia answered truthfully.

Brian put his face close to hers. "Czar Kievik will want to speak to you, Princess Maia. You will help yourself greatly if you answer his questions and refrain from an angry disposition. Do you understand?" He unlocked the bands as she nodded at him, and fear once more invaded her brown eyes. Brian spoke to the soldiers and they left the room.

He then addressed Maia. "It would be better if you behaved like a princess of Frencolia and you will be treated like one, Princess Maia." She was silent and he continued, his voice snapping at her. "You must speak when spoken to and answer the questions you are asked!" Maia still retained a defiant set to her face. Brian paced up and down trying to form the words he would join together to inform Elliad that this princess was not Princess Jobyna after all.

A loud knock boomed on the door and Maia's tense nerves caused her to jump. She was still sitting in the chair, feeling too weak to stand, not sure what she should do. Four men entered the room, followed by the two soldiers. The small chamber was now crowded. The men bowed to Brian, staring triumphantly at Maia.

"Tell these men how old you are, and your title, Princess," Brian encouraged her. He flicked his shock of red hair from his eyes and smiled cynically, showing his uneven white teeth.

The kidnappers were waiting to be presented to the czar, to receive praise together with the 2,000 gold pieces reward. Maia looked fearfully at them, faint recollections stirring in her confused mind. She obeyed Brian's command and said, "I am 11 years old and my name is Princess Maia, daughter of Crown Prince Dorai; I am first cousin of King Luke Chanec of Frencolia." The men were silent, glancing anxiously at each other, each wanting to accuse the next, but knowing they had all made the same mistake.

"How old is your cousin, the Princess Jobyna?" Brian asked her, his angry face close to hers. The smile had gone.

"She is 15."

"And are you the same size as your cousin?" He asked, his face moving closer.

Maia sank further down in the large chair and laughed nervously, "No, of course not. She's tall and . . . and really grown up. I will probably be short like her mother. My aunt was . . ." her voice cut off as Brian turned in frustration to the kidnappers, waving for them to leave the room. Although unable to understand the language he spoke, she could still hear his voice screaming at them after he had slammed the door. Maia looked at the two soldiers who stared back at her, unmoving. They stood to attention, on alert guard. She did not like this place or these people, but Maia made up her mind she did not want to get slapped again or locked back in the chair. When Brian returned, he ordered the soldiers to escort the captive back to the women's quarters to Sofia's care.

Brian sheepishly entered the czar's council chamber. Elliad was discussing urgent developments with some of his counselors. This was one time Brian regretted being close to Elliad. He would rather have someone else tell the man of great power his findings than to have to face him. Brian almost felt pleased that the session took so long; it prolonged the dreaded moment of truth.

One by one, the counselors bowed, backing from the chamber. Elliad stood and systematically collected the papers, handing different sheaves to the various scribes. When they had left the room, Brian bowed and moved closer to him, still wanting to put off the words he had to say.

"Your Imperial Highness, Czar Kievik," Brian used the title, having switched totally from calling Elliad by his real name even when he was alone with him, for the sake of the guards, attendants and servants almost always present. "I have something very disconcerting to tell you."

"Nothing could be worse than this ridiculous letter Kenrik sent me today." He went into the details of the letter which stated that Kenrik believed him to be an impostor, that he must surrender the throne to his true father or turn it over to him as his father's heir. Brian let him exhaust the letter's contents and explain what he had dictated to be sent in reply. For a moment Elliad was silent, then remembering Brian's initial statement he demanded, "What is it then? Did Princess Jobyna escape again?" He laughed, but this was cut short as he digested Brian's serious look. With a swallow, he barked, "What then?"

Brian told him about Maia, expecting him to rant and rave. Elliad sat, a statue, cold and still, until Brian finished. "So, Dorai is the boy's uncle, and the boy has made him crown prince! Are there other children?"

Brian replied nervously that he did not know any more; he had thought the czar would wish to question the girl away from the listening ears of the guards and soldiers. Elliad was pleased with Brian's discretion.

"Have this Maia maid brought to me. Let's see . . ." Elliad was thinking out loud. "Tell her that Czar Kievik is sorry she has been brought here by mistake; the czar would like to ask her some questions and then she may be allowed to go home. Make arrangements for me to dine with her in the Green Room. And Terese . . . she can be there, too." Brian bowed and would have moved off, but Elliad continued, "Tell the men who brought her here that they will receive a reward, but not as much as they expected. The czar will see them tomorrow. The czardom has a further task for them!"

5

Gripping Princess Maia firmly by her arm, Sofia escorted the captive back to her room. Maia did not struggle this time but sat limply on the couch, sobbing. Ellice wanted to comfort her, but Boey stood aloof, devoid of the slightest show of sympathy. Maia hungrily ate of the food Ellice placed in front of her and did not resist when led to the bedroom where she was tucked into the large, comfy bed. Reminded of her bed in King's Castle at Frencberg, Maia slept soundly in spite of the turmoil she felt.

The young Frencolian princess was awakened some hours later. She was not used to being up at night and could well have slept until the morning, but Boey and Ellice were persistent and patient, helping her dress again and arranging her copper hair. Sofia reiterated Brian's words, adding, "Just remember to behave the way you have been brought up, and you may find yourself on your way back to Frencolia." Ellice rolled her eyes doubtfully as Sofia said these words, but no one caught the slave's disdainful expression.

The knave made the introductory announcement at the door of the Green Room, a small private dining chamber. "Princess Maia, daughter of Prince Dorai, first cousin of King Luke Chanec of Frencolia."

Maia entered the room, recognizing Brian. She curtsied to him, eager to please. Her arm placed on his, she was escorted to the table where Elliad and Terese stood waiting.

"Her Imperial Highness, the Czarina Terese." Maia curtsied to the beautiful woman wearing an exquisite, sparkling, golden crown. Brian turned to Elliad, "His Imperial Highness, Czar Kievik of the Czardom of Chezkovia." Maia curtsied. Elliad extended his hand to her and when Maia put her hand on his, he kissed it. His piercing icy-blue eyes stabbed deep into her wide velvet-brown pools. With a sweeping motion, he indicated that Maia sit and Brian placed the chair for her, then stood behind Elliad as he too sat. Servants brought the meal and the two wearing the Chezkovian crowns began to eat in silence. Maia's appetite was suddenly revived. She enjoyed several helpings of the sumptuous chicken served in creamy apricot sauce.

When the desserts were presented, Elliad said to Maia, "I hope you are feeling better after the long journey. You have been treated well, have you not?"

Maia quickly cleared her mouth, swallowing hard, "I do not remember very much about the journey, I think they put something in my drink. But I feel much better now, thank you."

When they finished dining, the czar stated that they would retire to the small adjacent lounge. Maia discreetly concealed a yawn, trying to appear wide awake. The servants handed Elliad and Terese a silver chalice each, pouring wine for them. Elliad asked Maia if she would like milk or juice. She declined the offer of either beverage. The captive gazed with unveiled admiration at the glittering, jewel-encrusted, golden dome-shaped apparition Elliad wore on his head. Her eyes then examined his incredible gem-encrusted garments. Maia was overawed by the czar's appearance. She decided she would tell him anything he wanted to know. This magnificent emperor-king must have the power to allow her to go home.

Questions began to fly from the pretender's lying lips. He wanted to know intimate details about her father and mother, and he encouraged Maia to talk freely about her home life. Terese stifled a yawn, bored; she felt like a chastened child because Elliad had strongly cautioned her to speak only when spoken to. (In spite of her position, Terese did not dare disobey his commands.) Elliad asked Maia about Luke and his kingship; the charlatan questioned her about life at King's Castle in Frencberg. She answered all his questions, telling him more than requested, chatting idly on like a normal 11-year-old.

The impostor asked about Jobyna, "Does the Princess Jobyna talk about her stay in Chezkovia?"

"Not very much. I haven't seen her for a long time, over a month. She has been living in Chanoine. Luke rebuilt the manor house there, but she was moving back to Frencberg. They did not think it was very safe for her. . . ."

Maia's voice tapered off; she remembered it was the czar who wanted to capture Jobyna. She frowned, staring at her interrogator. Confusion took hold of her childish mind.

Elliad noticed her self-confidence and the direct way she met his gaze. "You have a question?" he encouraged her.

"Why do you want Jobyna, Your Highness?"

Elliad ignored this query. Instead he asked her the one question which may give him the information that had been haunting his mind for weeks. "Did Princess Jobyna ever speak of . . . me?"

"No, I don't think so." Maia felt encouraged again, and she asked a question which had puzzled her, "But if that Elliad man was executed, why do you still want Princess Jobyna, Czar Kievik?"

Elliad breathed an internal sigh of relief, as his whole being relaxed. If this girl did not know the truth about him, then maybe Jobyna had kept the revelation to herself—but for what purpose, he had no idea. His dagger-sharp eyes scrutinized Maia and he realized the girl was only 11 years old. It was very unlikely that Dorai's children knew the whole truth. The longer he conversed with the childish Maia about Jobyna, the more he longed for the return of his "treasure."

He watched and listened as Maia chatted happily about her close friendship with her cousin Jobyna. Maia's glowing copper-brown hair was the same as Jobyna's; the soft, creamy skin of her face and rose-colored cheeks were duplicates. They were identical in the coloring of these features, alas for the difference in their eyes! How restful and attractive were Jobyna's unusually green orbs! Maia's brown eyes seemed ordinary and plain by comparison.

Elliad also noticed the significant differences in character and personality; Maia was so much more forthright, childishly naive and frank. When Maia was 15, she would probably be less like Jobyna than she was now; she would be more her own person, stronger and more dominating than her beautiful cousin. Yes, Maia was still very much a child.

How completely boring, he thought. Children made him nervous and unsettled; they asked the most ridiculous questions and had no sense that he could understand! This child's unguarded answers proved just how stupid these "lesser beings" could be! In every simple sentence she uttered, Maia was giving away the secrets of her kingdom without realizing she was so doing.

Elliad's memory wound backwards as he allowed the child to ramble. He remembered Jobyna when he first saw her, sick, thin and childlike. It had taken him more strategy than that necessary now with Maia to learn from Jobyna the whereabouts of the

Frencolian treasures—but she had finally given in. And for what? Just a few worthless Gospel Books!

Jobyna had trusted him as "Doctor John" and he had reveled in their strange friendship. Her initial trust in him was something he could not get out of his mind. She had been the first woman he ever wanted to please. Elliad was deeply mortified when she had fallen and dislocated her kneecap. He recalled the night Jobyna had been announced into the Chezkovian throne room, following Terese along the ruby-red carpet. His "treasure" had been so surprised to see him sitting on the czar's throne that she had fainted! The counterfeit czar had been tremendously pleased to see her! How much she had changed in that last year; and she was submissive and under his control. It was a sour turn of events when she escaped! He wanted so much to possess her now!

Elliad sighed audibly and Terese turned to look at him in perplexity. He smiled at the czarina, realizing she, too, was showing submission. Terese had recently given him many wonderful compliments; she had compared him with the true Czar Kievik and said how much more regal, powerful and generous he, Elliad, was. Kievik had been a hard taskmaster and Terese told him that the czardom would be so much better off to have Elliad ruling with his goodness to all the citizens. Recently, on a tour of the city, they had thrown thousands of coins to the cheering crowds.

Elliad's blue eyes narrowed as he scrutinized Terese; he was thinking how much better it would be to have Jobyna at his side.

The hour was late when Elliad finally completed his numerous questions. He learned that Prince Konrad from Proburg and Doctor Sleven from Chezkovia had been with Jobyna when she arrived at King's Castle, and men from the Chezkovian cavalry had accompanied them. On further subtle questioning, Elliad learned that Sleven's sons were involved. The other valuable item of news was the conference planned in Frencberg, with all the kings, queens and princes from outlying kingdoms invited to be present. He learned the names of those who had accepted the invitation. Maia did not know the full purpose of the conference, except that it was for "friendship." She had been practicing the royal titles with her mother so she would correctly address the visitors at the appropriate moment of introduction. Elliad was pleased to observe Brian inconspicuously jotting the names down as Maia reeled them off. He questioned Maia about Konrad once more.

Her defenses were completely gone by this late hour, and she thought the czar was a very nice man. Stifling another yawn, she said carelessly and in a deliberate undertone, "I think Prince Konrad is in love with Jobyna. He couldn't wait to go to Chanoine with Luke to bring her back to Frencberg, but I don't know if she likes him very much. Luke said that she is always slow to make up her mind, but I expect she will marry Prince Konrad. Jobyna once told me she wanted to marry a farmer, but that's not a very good idea for a princess is it?" When the czar did not reply, Maia innocently continued, "I think Prince Konrad will be asking Luke if he can marry Jobyna soon! I wonder where they will live? I hope they stay in Frencolia. . . ."

Elliad allowed a yawn to escape unhindered. With his true feelings struggling wildly to surface, his self-control was about reaching its limit! His ability to act was stretched as far as it could go. Standing suddenly, he drew Maia to her feet by both hands. The light shining on the glowing red tones of her hair drove his anger back into his self-control.

"It is late! I am tired! Tomorrow we will talk about sending you home, Princess Maia. You must sleep as long as you can in the morning." He kissed her small hands and released them.

"Thank you, Czar Kievik." Maia curtsied, then turned to Terese, "Good night, Czarina Terese." She curtsied again and Brian accompanied her from the Green Dining Room.

6

The next day introduced many changes. Maia was sent in a closed carriage to Baltic Castle. She was to become a prisoner with Cynara and Kedar. Boey and Ellice sat on either side of her on the bumpy journey. Numerous mounted soldiers accompanied the small black vehicle. Maia believed she was going home and eagerly looked forward to the end of the journey, impatient for a reunion with her mother and father.

Elliad ordered Brian to send soldiers out to Doctor Sleven's home and to the abodes of Doctor Sleven's sons. The soldiers' reports came in one by one; each was the same. Doctor Sleven's sons, who were constables in the Chezkovian cavalry, had fled the country taking their wives and children with them. Elliad was furious when informed of these escapes, and he realized how serious the division of ranks in the cavalry had grown. Reports all gave Proburg as the traitors' destination. The pretender-czar immediately decided to draft another letter to Prince Gustovas.

To Prince Gustovas of Proburg, my friend and counselor:

It is with grave concern I write this letter. My son Kenrik has turned against the throne of Chezkovia. He has misled many of my trusted and loyal cavalry. I must insist you do not provide shelter for Kenrik or those who support him, but send them back to Chezkovia so our family can be united and work out our problems and differences in the privacy of my palace.

How would you feel, my trusted friend, if one of your sons turned against you and tried to wrestle your throne from you, naming you after some impostor? Then act for me as I have for you in the past. I want our countries to remain allies, so work with me to solve this serious rift. (Signed)

Your lifelong compatriot, Kievik.

Elliad was careful to consult counselors. He carefully studied copies of other communications with Prince Gustovas to make the letter totally authentic. Often, when Kievik had written to Gustovas, he had used the pronoun "I" rather than the royal "we." Elliad copied the style and mood of these letters and he used Kievik's ring to imprint the sealing wax. The document was dispatched immediately, and Elliad calculated its arrival at Landmari Castle to be soon after nightfall.

The charlatan met with the four men who had kidnapped Maia: Cormick, Edsel, Lester and Welby. He commended them for their courage, expertise and speed.

"It was a good exercise, a successful practice run! Now I command that you organize and act on the real thing! You know what the Princess Jobyna looks like, and I have seen to it that you will not be able to make the same mistake twice!

"I have here 1,000 gold pieces for you to share to cover the costs for capturing Princess Maia and to help organize a return trip to Frencolia. You are to set up headquarters in Frencberg and send weekly reports to me of all you see and hear. I am canceling the offer of 2,000 gold pieces to all others for Princess Jobyna, and recalling those who have been working on the project. The 2,000 gold pieces will be yours if you can capture and bring Princess Jobyna, unharmed, to me. If, however, you succeed in capturing King Luke Chanec, I will give you the 2,000 gold pieces because I am sure the sister will exchange places with her brother."

Elliad communicated in intimate detail about the extra Frencolian people they would need to hire and the tremendous care that would have to be exercised for them not to be detected or caught. They would need disguises, name changes, new identities, personnel who could forge documents, etc. . . . The list went on and on. He cautioned the brigands that if they were caught, he, the czar of Chezkovia, would disclaim any responsibility of knowledge or part in their mission.

The four men left the palace eager to set about returning to Frencolia, happy to feel their purses bulging with Frencolian and Chezkovian gold pieces, their tongues wagging about the intrigue of new abduction plans as ideas emerged from their cunning minds.

After the carriage was monitored through five awesome sets of imprisoning gates, Maia arrived at Baltic Castle. Wearing the beautiful, crimson-velvet cloak which Boey told her had belonged to Jobyna, she traversed the numerous walkways and steps to find the cold stone monstrosity looming ominously about her. Elliad's knights, Julian and Hagan, accompanied her and before she had time to resist, she found herself locked in a reception room to the side of the castle foyer. Boey and Ellice had gone on ahead with the trunks to prepare the room for Maia. The young princess still believed this to be a night's stopover on the continuing journey to Frencolia.

51

Prince Gustovas had just finished dining in the Great Hall at Landmari Castle when the second letter arrived from "His Imperial Highness, The Czar of Chezkovia." He politely excused himself from the conversation with his three sons and Kenrik, and moved to his study to read the document. Gustovas was flooded with grave concern for his friend and their alliance. The monarch summoned his eldest son, Gustav, and five of his closest counselors. After close deliberations, they all agreed that Prince Gustovas should send a message to the czar first thing in the morning, leaving soon thereafter with Gustav, the crown prince, to travel to the palace at Jydanski. They would arrive shortly after noon. Surely the two old friends, discussing the matter face to face, could work the problem to a logical, happy conclusion! Czarevitch Kenrik was to be confined to the castle at Landmari until the matter was resolved.

Kenrik was furious when informed of the contents of "the czar's" latest letter. The earlier communication was bad enough, but to know that Prince Gustovas was showing support for the pretender made Kenrik's heart turn to stone. How dare an impostor confine him and his men to Prince Gustovas' castle! Kenrik noticed extra guards positioned around the stronghold; every door was guarded. The czarevitch had swiftly become Proburg's prisoner!

Kenrik pleaded with Prince Gustovas' third son, Prince Mayer. "The impostor is so clever, he will likely convince your father that I am a traitor to the throne of Chezkovia. I must escape until I know which way your country will finally move. Your father, like mine, has been a close friend of Elliad; maybe he will accept Elliad's pretense. Will you help me escape, Mayer?"

The prince nervously darted his eyes sideways, unsure of what to do. Trying to remain in a neutral position, he answered cautiously, "You were planning to go to Frencolia for that conference. Why don't you ask Father if he will let you go? He can tell your father that you left before he could stop you. Father will be relieved to have you off his hands. Send and ask for an audience, now."

Princes Gustovas and Gustav met with Kenrik and debated long into the night. They finally agreed to let Kenrik travel to Frencolia, and they would send word there about the outcome of the meeting with the czar. Kenrik must leave with his men before first light in the morning. The czarevitch was urged to send communications ahead to inform Reideaux and Frencolia of his arrival and formally petition the two kings for the right of refuge and sanctuary.

"You realize of course, Kenrik, that if my son and I agree with your father's judgments on this matter, then you will not be free to return here to Proburg?" Prince Gustovas' face and tone expressed the extreme gravity of the situation.

Kenrik's mind began to think of the ramifications. It was equivalent to being forced into exile. He almost laughed at the irony of being exiled by an exile! Controlling his surfacing emotion of fierce bitterness, he answered, "If the so-called Czar Kievik (he dare not say again, 'the man who calls himself my father') wants the crown of Chezkovia, then he can have it! Tell him that one day it will be mine! The truth will surface! I will wait until then."

Prince Gustovas tossed and turned sleeplessly the whole night. Thoughts of the czar's letter and his planned journey on the morrow circulated around in his mind and the prince tried to put himself in his compatriot's place. The czar's heir was not insane, but the young man was definitely acting negatively against his father! Well, tomorrow the matter would be settled once and for all! It was absurd, impossible even, to imagine the czar being anyone other than the czar!

Gustovas and Kievik had been boyhood friends, just as Kenrik and Mayer were close companions. This visit to Jydanski would prove that Kenrik was out of line!

Gustovas was sure there would be many advantages by being eyeball to eyeball with his friend, Kievik, to discuss this whole ridiculous situation the father and son had locked themselves into. Once face to face, the disagreement would prove to be a misunderstanding and it would almost certainly diminish in its intensity and intrigue. The czarevitch would eventually come to himself and accept Gustovas' word: Elliad had been executed. And Kievik the father and Kenrik the son would be reunited. Yes, that is how it would be! Kievik always did have a hot head and a quick temper ready to flare and jump to false conclusions! Kenrik, unfortunately had inherited his father's chief failings!

One thing was for sure; the exile, Elliad, had not benefited the czardom one iota, and providence could be thanked that he had met his demise before real damage could be done!

Sunrise saw a great company depart from Landmari Castle in Proburg. Prince Gustovas, Princess Rhaselle and their son Prince Gustav, with their extensive entourage, headed east toward Chezkovia.

Czarevitch Kenrik, his cavalry men, Doctor Sleven and hundreds of soldiers dressed in red and white uniforms pointed their horses south toward Reideaux and Frencolia.

Elliad had received the note Brian brought him with great consternation. Letters were one thing, but a confrontation! He felt sure Czar Kievik's old friend would instantly discern the physical differences and recognize his true identity. Elliad himself, many times in the past, had met with Gustovas. They were of kindred spirits in many of their philosophies.

The impostor's nervous system tingled, challenging him with

apprehension, and he paced back and forth with Brian, awaiting the prince's arrival. Elliad wanted to believe that Prince Gustovas would accept the truth of his conquest when viewed in the light of his immense power. If, however, Gustovas and his son Gustav did not accept him in Kievik's place, then Elliad would change his plans to turn the ill-timed confrontation into a personal advantage. Yes! This day could mark a terrific triumph for the czardom of Chezkovia! Brian had alerted and briefed all their Frencolian cohorts, now dressed in the Chezkovian uniforms, to be on duty. Those Chezkovians who knew Elliad's true identity yet remained loyal to him as czar were also briefed and installed in strategic positions.

To the leaders of the cavalry, the "czar" lied, informing them of a volatile situation. Prince Gustovas was coming to challenge him, and Proburg's confrontation would mean trouble for the czardom. The cavalry must be ready to contain the military escort from Proburg if and when the occasion required such intervention.

Elliad left no stone unturned in making sure every likelihood (and every exit from Jydanski) was well covered if the longstanding alliance between Chezkovia and Proburg was to be shattered that day.

Prince Gustovas, Princess Rhaselle and Prince Gustav were welcomed in front of the palace by an elaborate guard of honor. Elliad had key Chezkovian men in charge who knew the protocol, right down to the most minute detail. Everything appeared to be exceptionally normal and functioning like clockwork! The royal visitors from Proburg were announced into the Oval Throne Room where Elliad sat, as czar, upon the Chezkovian throne.

So meticulously accurate was Elliad's disguise that Princess Rhaselle, curtsying, and Gustav, bowing, breathed enormous sighs of relief, both positively sure that it was Czar Kievik who wore the Chezkovian crown and sat upon the throne. The fact that Czarina Terese sat beside him added to their peace.

Elliad had spent much time on his elocution, working on his accent; but Gustovas knew the instant the royal figure spoke that he was not, in reality, Kievik, but Elliad. The Proburg monarch did not divulge this knowledge immediately; he was tortured in his mind when he realized how easily deceived he had been, and now he was left unprepared for this twisted reality! The man's audacity was unbelievable!

When he drew nearer to Elliad and noted the dictatorial arrogance projecting out of sky-blue eyes, Prince Gustovas was unable to contain his overwhelming anger and bitterness any longer. Keeping his voice as even as he possibly could, he stated, "Kievik and I prided ourselves as boys about our matching brown eyes. You have done very well for yourself, Czar of Chezkovia!"

Such a denouncement Elliad had expected to hear, and with a very small but definite gesture of his hand, a quick warning was communicated to Brian.

"So what does the great Gustovas of Proburg think he will do about the matter?" Elliad snapped, his senses heightened and his mind on full alert.

The son, Crown Prince Gustav, slightly baffled by the cryptic conversation, stared first at his father, noting the familiar brown eyes, then at the czar who sported brilliant-blue orbs. The Proburg crown prince became uneasy and he spun around as he heard movements on the other side of the huge doors. Red and white uniformed men entered the chamber silently, and with their swords extended, began closing in from around the back wall.

"My dear Czar, I cannot believe you have successfully lived this facade for so long—and it was so very strategically planned! It is obvious I have played right into your hands, along with my wife and son. I hope your mind is not closed to negotiations on this matter?" Prince Gustovas' heart beat fast; he knew he was walking a tight-rope. One false move, one callous word spoken without thought would plunge them into oblivion; the white marble floor of this Chezkovian throne room would most certainly be stained with their blood.

The Crown Prince Gustav of Proburg saw the matter differently. He had met Elliad a few years ago. It was hard to believe that this was the same man. How dare such an impostor wear the Chezkovian crown! Gustav's savage aggravation was ignited as he realized all Kenrik's accusations were true! The Frencolian girl, Jobyna, had not fabricated a fantasy after all! Gustav was enraged, indignant; he would not let this atrocity continue!

As though to be sure of the so-called czar's depravity, Gustav asked, "Do you mean to say, Father, that this is Elliad?" The crown prince's uncertain voice echoed loudly in the silence of the royal chamber.

"Hush, Son! This is the czar of Chezkovia." Gustovas gestured silence with his hand, not taking his eyes off the "czar."

Gustav, used to the freedom of voicing his own adult opinion, decided he would not keep quiet. "I'll not hush before an impostor!" Turning to Elliad, he yelled a string of curses, denouncing him as a degenerate despot. As the czar stood to his feet, Gustav looked around and his face paled. He suddenly understood his position and panted, "Where are . . . our men . . . ?" His voice faded as six swords, preceding six red and white uniforms, closed in on him.

"The czar of Chezkovia is not an impostor!" Elliad shouted, his accent more noticeable as his agitation grew. "This man, Gustav, has spoken against the crown of Chezkovia! Stay the swords from this, my royal sanctuary! A good taste of the lash and a few days in a cell will change his mind!" The soldiers bodily dragged the fighting, yelling and cursing Gustav from the room.

Princess Rhaselle would have fainted in fear had Prince Gustovas not supported her, his strong arm about her narrow waist.

"Do you still wish to negotiate with the czar of Chezkovia, Gustovas of Proburg? You may change your mind if you so wish." Elliad smiled, knowing he had won a battle against Proburg with no bloodshed so far!

Still supporting his trembling wife, Prince Gustovas bowed his head. The prince spoke submissively, "We are at your service, Your Imperial Highness. I would like to think we can talk as . . . as friends. The power is obviously in your hands."

Elliad beckoned to Brian, "Show the prince and princess to their quarters." He spoke severely to Gustovas. "You are to stay in your suite. I will not be responsible if you attempt to leave. I have a few matters to attend to and then I will have you join me for dinner."

In the room to which they were escorted, Princess Rhaselle lay upon the couch as though in a drugged stupor. The chamber was similar to the one in which Maia had been confined; there was no handle on the inside of the door. A Chezkovian woman attended Rhaselle, but the princess was too distressed to be bothered with refreshments or conversation.

Prince Gustovas sat at the small table, his shoulders drooped and his head was supported in his hands. He wondered where his entourage was: knights, soldiers, counselors, scribes, attendants and servants. The prince thought in despair of his two sons in Proburg, Warford and Mayer, with their wives and children. He had not agreed with Konrad's trip to Frencolia, especially when he discovered his son's reason for the journey: to escort the escaped princess home. But he now felt encouraged to know that Konrad was safe in Frencolia.

Tormented thoughts filled his mind as he remembered the way he had treated Czarevitch Kenrik, sending him south, when in fact he needed him and his troops right now! "I don't have any wisdom . . . not a scrap!" the prince told himself. Gustovas was not comforted by the fact that he had avoided, so far, informing Elliad that Kenrik had left Proburg.

The captive monarch of Proburg strove to compose his muddled emotions. He must try to face the truth of this dreadful situation; he needed to piece together exactly what he would say and do. His heart felt heavy, as though death sentences had been passed upon him and his family. Gustav was not aiding his family, nor the kingdom of Proburg. His rampant rage would get him nowhere but dead, and rapidly, too! The monarch of Proburg realized they were prisoners of this fraud acting as the czar of Chezkovia. Elliad held ultimate power over their fate!

Recapping the times he had spent with Elliad, he remembered the boastful stories the man had told him of those he had savagely executed. Gustovas shuddered and a chill crept through his veins. The deviant was completely unexplainable and unpredictable. He would leave suspect Frencolian knights in dungeons for his enemies to rescue; he would brutally murder innocent women and children; yet he would work and pay to save alive the maid Jobyna.

Sleven, a reputable doctor, had believed the girl's story and had pleaded uselessly with Gustovas, explaining that Elliad had captured Czar Kievik, and that the news of Elliad's execution was a carefully concocted lie. Sleven's words had sounded like little more than a far-fetched fairy tale. Elliad as czar? The impossible was true!

Gustovas continued his musings, plunging deeper into despair. Where was Kievik? How, and why, had the traitor achieved such unbelievable fame? Maybe Elliad was trying to prove something to himself. Yes, that was it! To conquer! To reign! Ultimate power over others! He had to have everyone in total submission, and then he would feel he had won. Gustovas shook his head. Power and control could only be maintained by being responsible! Any blue-blooded child knew this!

The new czar was diabolical, completely devoid of true human compassion and feelings. Such a ruthless being was in control of Chezkovia—and the czardom!

7

The days following Maia's disappearance were full of upheavals for all at King's Castle in Frencberg. King Luke and Prince Dorai, upon consultation with their counselors, dispatched messages to the outlying kingdoms informing them of the dreadful kidnapping of Princess Maia and warning them against sending their royal dignitaries due to the danger and uncertainty existing. The conference would go ahead as planned and representatives from the different kingdoms would be most welcome to attend, but choice of the ambassadors attending was to be at the entire discretion of each individual kingdom's council.

Replies arrived intermittently. The king and queen from Strasland would still attend. The crown prince from Zealavia planned to visit in person, but representatives only would be commissioned from Bavarest, Danzerg and Muldaver. The next week a reply arrived from Proburg, stating that Prince Gustav would travel with Czarevitch Kenrik and Doctor Sleven to represent Proburg and Chezkovia. This communication was sent just a few days before Prince Gustovas departed for Jydanski.

An urgent summons arrived from Reideaux for Konrad. Luke noticed the blank expression shadowing his companion's face as he read the communication.

While the two young men walked from the royal suite where Konrad occupied a guest room within Luke's apartment, Konrad confided in his friend, Luke. "King Kelsey has fallen seriously ill and his doctors have requested my presence with him immediately. He has no family and we have grown very close. I will leave today, Luke."

The prince slowed his pace, saying, "There is one matter I would like to take care of before I leave, Luke. I would like you and your uncle to consider giving me the hand of your sister, Princess Jobyna, in marriage." Ignoring Luke's unveiled surprise, Konrad continued seriously, "I was going to leave it until all this unpleasantness was over, but I do not know how long I will be detained in Reideaux. I hope King Kelsey sends an ambassador for the conference in case I do not return in time to represent him.

"There will be the matter of the dowry to consider and the length of our betrothal, but we can discuss that sometime in the future. I am very much in love with your sister; she is the most wonderful woman on earth to me, and I hope, Luke, you will allow me the honor to take care of her as husband." They had stopped walking and Luke leaned nonchalantly on the castle wall as he listened to Konrad's earnest confession. "I loved Jobyna from the first moment I set eyes upon her."

"I have noticed your attention to my sister." Luke smiled at this "would-be" suitor. The idea—his precious sister marrying Prince Konrad—it was very pleasing!

Luke spoke as in confidence, "Jobyna needs a husband like

yourself, Konrad. Uncle Dorai and I are her sworn protectors and we would continue this protection even after she marries. However, our father promised us when we were young that we would not be betrothed by our parents, but they would guide us to choose suitable partners for ourselves. They did not like the current ideas of young people being victims of 'mismatch-making' to suit the ends of those using the dowry for their own gain." Luke was thinking out loud, "But things are different now for Jobyna and me. . . . And you, Konrad—no one could be more perfect for Jobyna! I must speak with Uncle Dor first. I'll go now, while you gather your men to make preparations for your departure. I will miss you, Konrad of Proburg."

Prince Dorai gave instant approval to Konrad's offer, and he urged Luke to settle the matter before Konrad departed. Luke, however, was not willing to make a final decision without speaking to Jobyna. "How can I just tell my sister, 'you are betrothed'? She must be involved in the decision." The uncle did not agree; women were subservient and therefore needed no such consultation. However, he suggested Luke seek Jobyna out immediately, then the prince could leave with assurance. That Jobyna would agree without question was accepted by these two royal males.

The young king's search for his sister led him to one of the castle kitchens. The king was not bothered that his sister loved to cook, but he caused unprecedented bewilderment when he, the king of Frencolia, swung open the doors and wandered calmly through the kitchens, flanked on either side by his bodyguards and followed by an attendant and a messenger boy. Servants all around the chambers bowed or curtsied, some dropping bowls and utensils in confusion. Luke drew near when he saw Jobyna and was pleased to note that the mixture had all been used and final trays of cookies were almost filled. Ignoring the obeisance about him, the king distributed warm jam tarts to Loran and Granville, to his scribe and to the messenger boy.

Jobyna pretended not to notice his theft of the children's cookies ("After all," she reminded herself, "he *is* the king!"). She sidestepped, curtsying to her brother and smiling. "The king in the kitchen! No wonder everyone is in such a dither! Just when my friends here are getting used to me, you turn up and cause chaos!"

Luke kissed her hand, greedily licking a piece of uncooked dough and jam from her fingers. The young princess grimaced in disgust and struggled to rescue her hand from this unwelcome treatment. Frowning deeper, she wiped her hand dramatically on her apron as though to remove a stain.

He whispered, "I have to talk with you, urgently." Immediate concern rose upon Jobyna's transparent face. Luke said with a broad smile, "It's *good* news! *Very* good news!"

Jobyna followed her brother through the maze of warm kitchen chambers. Pulling her apron off as she walked, she handed it to an attentive maid. "Have they found Maia?" She was speaking to the king's back; to her consternation, Luke kept walking.

Once out in the corridor, he spoke carelessly over his shoulder, and increased his pace, "We need to talk privately and I want you to prepare yourself not to be ornery, little Sister!"

"Luke Chanec!" Jobyna stopped walking, her hands on her hips, but her brother kept his pace up. She ran after him, calling indignantly, "What do you mean, 'ornery'? I am not 'ornery'!" Annoyance gathered on her fair brow, causing her usually open, happy face to appear more formidable. The princess did not appreciate the manner in which Loran and Granville stared at her, as though daring the maid to answer their king back in this un-royal way. *It is my sisterly privilege!* Jobyna thought, still perturbed.

"Yes, you are too ornery!" Luke called again, over his shoulder. "At least to me you are. I'm the king; I should know." He broke into a run, ascending the steps, three at a time, rushing along the corridor and hiding around a corner. As he anticipated, Jobyna raced after him, and he leapt out at her, scaring her half to death, both of them doubling up with laughter.

Konrad strode purposefully along the corridor from the other direction, wondering how such a commotion was going unchecked; castle guards should be intervening and restoring peace and order! He had no idea that the king of Frencolia was in the middle of a war with his "little sister"!

Luke held both of Jobyna's hands tightly to stop her from cuffing him; they struggled as though in the throes of a great battle, his laughter and her squeals of frustration resounding and echoing in every direction. The prince from Proburg stood intrigued, then amused, watching for some minutes before either of the combatants realized his observation. Luke released Jobyna and she sought to compose herself, trying to tidy her hair where it had fallen loose. The word *ornery* still raced in her mind. Luke motioned his attendant to open the door to a small office, and he bowed for Jobyna to enter. Konrad, catching his encouraging wink, waited outside.

Jobyna turned to face her brother, "I promise not to be 'ornery' if you promise to hurry up with this 'good news'."

"Well, sit down and I shall tell you." Luke commanded with a smile. As soon as she sat, he explained without ceremony, "Prince Konrad of Proburg has asked me for your hand in marriage. We, that is, Uncle Dor and I, think it is a marvelous idea."

Jobyna inhaled deeply through her nostrils, her shoulders rising stiffly at the astounding, unexpected, "marvelous idea." She stared wide-eyed at Luke as though he was a stranger. Words rose into her mouth, but the word *ornery* burned in her mind and she choked back her retorts. She slowly released the pent up air from her lungs, allowing an audible catch to escape from her constricted throat.

"It does not please you?" Luke was surprised at her reaction, but he spoke quietly, closing the door between Konrad and the office. Jobyna stared at the floor in silence. "Jobyna . . ." He sat and waited, watching her.

At last she felt she could trust her voice and spoke, but she was unsure, almost pleading, "I don't want to get married, Luke. Not yet, anyway."

Luke narrowed his eyes, thinking she was, indeed, being ornery. He said firmly, "It won't be right away! Konrad reminded me that there is the matter of the dowry and the length of the betrothal to decide." Luke saw her eyes swelling with tears, and was puzzled. "Don't you like Konrad, Jobyna?"

Jobyna struggled to pull back the flood of tears that threatened to burst. She hung her head, answering, "It's not that I don't like him, Luke. I do . . . I mean . . . but marriage!" She felt afraid, but could not admit this to her brother. Jobyna tried to stall such a life-binding decision and said, "I haven't been home in Frencolia very long. . . . I scarcely get any time with you, my own brother. . . . And I feel I hardly know Uncle Dorai . . . and Minette . . . and the children. . . ."

Luke walked around the desk and stood in front of her. His words were reassuring, and Jobyna felt like a small child; Luke was so much more mature. She listened as he explained, "Marrying Konrad would not mean you do not have us, Jo; it would be like extending the family. You would have a husband who loves the Gospel Book and I would have a brother." He could see the blank set of her face, and he sighed. "You need time to think about it, don't you?" His voice was gentle. Luke remembered from the past how his sister hated to make decisions on the spur of the moment.

The brother explained the haste for the sudden need of a commitment, "Konrad has to leave for Reideaux in a few minutes, and I don't know when he will come back. King Kelsey

66

is very ill and his doctors have urgently requested Konrad's presence. Luke paused for a breath. "Konrad is very much in love with you and it will be difficult for me to tell him that you are not pleased with his offer."

In a very small voice, Jobyna said, "You didn't tell me he had to leave so soon!" She tried to reason within herself why Konrad's sudden departure should change anything, and realized then that she did not want him to go away. "I must speak to him," Jobyna said, determined. "You remember Father telling us we could marry when we were ready and not before?" Luke nodded and Jobyna asked, "Then does my king allow me, his sister, to have a choice?"

"Yes, Jobyna, but please, be gentle! You may not have realized it, but Konrad is deeply in love with you. I love you, too, little Sister. Do you think I would want you to marry just . . . just anyone? Konrad is special. You must be kind to him!" He noticed Jobyna's face soften, and the brother opened the door.

Konrad looked first at Luke, then Jobyna, as he entered the office. The mirth of moments before had vanished, replaced now with expressions of glumness.

Jobyna curtsied to Konrad, while Luke sat once more behind the desk. She said, "My brother tells me you have to leave Frencolia, Prince Konrad. I will pray for a return to good health for King Kelsey and ask you to remember me to him." Jobyna beheld Konrad's blue eyes searching deep into hers.

Like a stab to her heart, an unwilling question flew to her mind. *Is this love?* Jobyna felt confused. She faltered as a new revelation tried to surface; she cared deeply about this prince. Trying to choose her words with kindness, she spoke softly, "Luke has also told me of your offer of marriage, and I hope you will understand my reasons for postponing a decision, Prince Konrad." She saw his whole countenance drop suddenly. His sad, doleful expression deeply dismayed her. She wanted, so much, to see him smile at her. Reminding herself of Luke's words, she continued, her voice softer still, seeking to soften the blow that she also recoiled from now.

Jobyna sought to explain, and her honesty caused her to bare her heart which was pounding in an unusual fashion. "I need time to think, and pray. My confession is that I am such a child that I have not seriously considered marriage. Marriage, to me, is for when I am older, more mature. . . . You will have to forgive me. I have scarcely adjusted to my life in Frencolia with my brother and my uncle. . . ." She blushed and looked away, feeling his hurt again, and a strange sensation flooded over her as it dawned on her mind just how much her heart truly cherished this prince. Once again, she wondered, *Is this how love feels? How can I ever know?*

Konrad took her hands, kissing them, causing her mind to compare Luke's brotherly action in the kitchen; this was entirely different! But the prince was speaking. "I accept your words, Princess Jobyna. There is no one else?" It was more a statement than a question. She instantly shook her head. "Then I ask you to consider me, and I promise I will love and cherish you as the Gospel Book teaches a man to so love his wife."

Jobyna gripped his hands and tears sprang to her eyes as she remembered the way this handsome prince had defied his own father and helped her in the dangerous escape from Elliad back to Frencolia. In a manner contrary to her character, she blurted out, "I shall always consider you to be the first prince in my life, Prince Konrad." She hung her head, "You will be a wonderful husband, I am sure. . . ." She would have said more had there had been time, but Konrad bowed to her and left the room, followed by Luke.

Jobyna sat, pensively, thinking about this disconcerting turn of events, Konrad's unexpected offer. Was it so unexpected? She scarcely knew him, did she? Then she thought again of the protective way he had escorted her on the journey from Proburg. How much he loved and encouraged the reading of the Gospel Book! He loved her too, this was obvious; his love was shining appealingly from his blue eyes. What more did she want in a husband? She herself had been battling against their friendship, her weapon an image in her mind of the "perfect" farmer-type husband. If Konrad had been a farmer, she would have shouted, "Yes, I will marry you!"

What if God did not want her to marry a farmer? How could she flaunt a childish whim in the face of this young man who believed in her God and who trusted her enough to believe she cared? She hung her head in prayer. Such an important decision as the choice of a life's partner must be surrounded completely with prayer. Yet in her heart, Jobyna already knew that God had planned for her to meet Konrad; it was no aimless mistake. These past three months, she had missed out on his friendship because of her own stubbornness! Konrad had been there, steadfast, watching and waiting patiently for signs that she cared about him, but she had ignored his slightest hint of friendship. Now he was leaving! She may not see him for months! How could she let him go away believing she did not care for him? Taking herself to task, Jobyna suddenly desired to change her answer to the prince.

The princess found herself running down the stairs, along the corridor, racing around the courtyard, only to collide with Luke and her uncle returning from farewells to the Reideaux-bound party. Upset that she was too late, Jobyna thought frantically of the road to Reideaux; and to the surprise of those in her way, she raced back into the castle, climbing up and around the narrow spiral staircase, up, up, up, and out on to the northern battlements. She knew Konrad would be disappointed that she had not been there for the farewells, and she watched eagerly for him to come into view, out beyond the orchards. Jobyna felt sure he would look back at the castle. She had seen him turn his horse often, to view the way he had come. Focusing her eyes upon the empty stretch of road, her mind was filled with thoughts of the dashing Prince Konrad. To imagine him as her husband! The faster beating of her heart was not all due to the hurried ascent of the stairs.

Jobyna had thought of Konrad as a brother—like Luke, she mused. Asking herself what she thought a husband should be like, she struggled to find an answer. Perhaps a man like her father, mature, older (and her child-mind had been set on him being a farmer, not a prince). But Konrad did not act like a prince, at least not in the fashion of Jobyna's past limited concepts of a prince's behavior. Then, Luke was scarcely the truly over-bearing, "royal" king, was he? Kings and princes could be ordinary people! *I am a princess, and I'm very ordinary*, she thought humbly.

Her thoughts jumped back into reality when she beheld movement of horses. The men all wore brown uniforms, but she knew Konrad by his fair curly hair. He rode out in front with Moritz at his side. In a short while, the company would turn into the hills and out of sight. As Jobyna expected (and hoped), Konrad turned his horse fully around, facing the way he had come, letting the other men pass him. She waved her blue shawl as high as her arm would extend. Her long hair, now loose, was blowing playfully in the breeze. Even from this distance, atop the castle, Jobyna sensed Konrad's blue eyes light up as he recognized her, and she returned the warmth of the wide smile she imagined upon the prince's face.

Wishing she could let him know that she loved him, she put both hands to her lips and threw kisses to him. Konrad pulled his hat from his head. Throwing the head-covering carelessly in the air, he deftly caught it and waved. Placing it on his head once more, he copied her action and threw her a kiss which, to his men, appeared akin to a salute.

Luke had followed Jobyna's passage, wondering to where she was running. He now witnessed the exchange with great happiness on his face. His sister was always slow to make up her mind, he thought. Peeling his jacket off, he waved it vigorously, as he walked along the rampart to join Jobyna. Embarrassment glowed from Jobyna's face at first, but when Luke did not tease her, but kept waving to Konrad, she joined him, waving the blue shawl once more. The rest of the company had disappeared and Konrad turned his horse around twice in full circles, waved his hat again and was gone.

8

Prince Konrad arrived at Kelsey Castle late the next night, having left the saddle only to change his horse and eat hastily. Messengers awaited them at Ira Castle, just past the Frencolian border castle, to communicate the sad news that King Kelsey's condition was now critical and he was not expected to live many hours longer. The company ignored their fatigue and pressed on to the Reideaux capital.

Count Ira and his wife Celia greeted Konrad with grave solemnity at the front entrance of King Kelsey's castle. They spoke to Konrad of the king's seriously failing heart. He had suffered two attacks that very day, and each time the doctors thought he would not begin to breathe again. King Kelsey drew each labored breath in the thin thread of hope that Konrad's arrival was imminent.

Candles flickered somberly in the dim room. Konrad was announced, and doctors and attendants stood back as the prince took King Kelsey's hand and knelt beside the bed.

"Our Prince . . . Konrad. . . ." The king's voice was rasping and faint. "At last . . . you . . . have come."

As though on cue, four old men entered the room and one of them placed the simple gold crown to the kingdom of Reideaux in King Kelsey's trembling hands.

"Speak . . . for us . . . Lord Jarman." King Kelsey struggled painfully to expel these few words.

Lord Jarman moved from the foot of the bed to where Konrad knelt. "The royal commission of Reideaux agrees with the final command and will of King Kelsey that we appoint Prince Konrad of Proburg to be king of Reideaux. We claim the verse from the Gospel Book that "By God kings reign, and princes decree justice" (Proverbs 8:15), and we ask the Divine Ruler to bless Konrad from heaven, that he may reign long with justice and equity."

All voices in the chamber spoke in unison, as though one, "So be it."

Lord Jarman helped King Kelsey's faltering hands place the crown on Konrad's head. Konrad, his head bowed, kissed the dying king's hand. "So be it," he said simply. The prince was otherwise speechless. He knew this deathbed was not the place, nor the time, to question King Kelsey's wishes.

The fading king lingered between life and death for the next day, but finally, while Konrad read words from the Gospel Book, Kelsey peacefully became breathless, then still, succumbing submissively to the waiting valley of death. With a smile upon his wrinkled face, the king passed into the sunshine beyond, in the secure belief of the Good Shepherd's presence with him. Konrad had told him during the night of Jobyna's prayers for him and he had smiled knowingly, saying she would make a good queen. The 18-year-old had agreed. With his face close to King Kelsey's ear, he assured his listener that he was working on it.

Konrad dispatched a message to Luke and Jobyna of the king's death, writing that he would join them for a short while after the funeral. He did not write about his being crowned king of Reideaux, but that there were state affairs in Reideaux which he had been charged to take care of.

The royal commission met with Konrad, confirming his ascension to the throne. The official coronation, as simple as it was, had taken place when the reigning king placed the crown on the head of his chosen heir. Konrad perused the short list of those who might have ascended the Reideaux throne. All were old men and had voted unanimously in support of King Kelsey's choice.

The population of the kingdom of Reideaux had been depleted greatly by the black plague, and the commission showed Konrad documents in which King Kelsey had named Prince Konrad of Proburg as his successor over two years ago, when Konrad gained the adult age of 16. The men had agreed with the nomination, not expecting King Kelsey to die so soon or so suddenly, although he had lived to the good age of 63 years old.

Luke and Jobyna received the news of King Kelsey's death with sadness. Jobyna remembered telling King Kelsey she would like to bring her brother to visit him; Kelsey had requested that she do so. When she repeated to Luke his words of invitation, he agreed that there was no reason why they should not go to the funeral as representatives of Frencolia. King Kelsey's body would be embalmed and lie in state for 20 days to give people time to make the journey and pay their last respects.

Prince Dorai, however, would not hear of Jobyna riding to Reideaux. With the conference coming up in just a few days, he argued, there was enough activity, and no time to spare to deal with this. "The kingdom should not have the worry of Princess Jobyna being kidnapped!" he said, and made his niece give her solemn promise to remain within the walls of King's Castle. Jobyna, not wanting to be an added burden, reluctantly surrendered to his demand. Both Luke and Jobyna knew that their uncle loved them fervently and was as protective of them as if they were his own children.

Prince Dorai listened to Luke's feasible deliberations and agreed for Luke to make a brief visit after the conference to meet the new king, whoever he may be. Great importance was placed upon keeping Frencolia's alliance with Reideaux. Prince Dorai had met men of the Reideaux royal commission and he believed that one of these men would be chosen to ascend the throne.

Konrad, wearing the king's crown, sat on the throne in the Reideaux throne room. The bier was placed close by. All kingdom lords, counts, knights and officials had passed through the chamber, confirming Konrad's acceptance as king of Reideaux and pledging their loyalty.

"The king is dead! Long live the king!" The announcement was made in Reideaux. The people held their breath in anticipation, eager to greet the new king of the kingdom of Reideaux. The new monarch would be revealed as they passed through the throne room.

A castle guard was announced to the throne room with a message addressed to King Kelsey, carried by the foreriders to Czarevitch Kenrik who were waiting at the city gates requesting exile in Reideaux and Frencolia. Reideaux soldiers held the people back while Czarevitch Kenrik was announced to enter the throne room.

Kenrik's surprise was unmasked, and he bowed, speaking with irony in his voice, "Congratulations, my friend, *King* Konrad! You who were not a likely heir to ascend a throne, have obtained one, and I who am supposed to be first in line, have been banned from my own country, supposedly by my own father." Despondent, Kenrik mentally questioned his own credibility regarding whether or not Elliad was truly alive and was in reality posing as the czar.

"I have not set eyes on Father since before he ordered that I be thrown in prison for speaking against Elliad who was dragging up case after case of so called treason against me. It just does not figure in my mind that Father would have executed Elliad so suddenly after listening to his counsel, then left me, his son, chained and flogged in a palace dungeon!"

"I believe Princess Jobyna's word that Elliad sits on the throne of Chezkovia! She saw him with her own eyes and he gloated to her that it was he," Konrad said in defense of Kenrik's fears. "You must continue on to Frencolia and take Doctor Sleven for the conference. The kingdoms need to stand together against such an impostor or all our thrones will be at risk! It is not ultimately the throne that I worry about, Kenrik, but the unjust treatment of the people by a diabolical, despotic ruler such as Elliad!"

Kenrik informed Konrad that Prince Gustovas and Princess Rhaselle had traveled to Chezkovia with Prince Gustav, and they planned to return soon. The czarevitch requested refuge in Reideaux until he had word from Konrad's father, Gustovas, as to his findings regarding his own father.

Konrad explained to the czarevitch that he, himself, was required to spend the next seven days and nights in the throne room, beside the body of the deceased king, leaving only for short times to walk and eat. This was to be an ordeal he would not remember with joy, but having accepted the appointment of king of Reideaux, he was prepared to fulfill his duties as sovereign. The new king urged Kenrik to discuss his needs with the royal commission; they would judge whether or not the czarevitch would receive sanctuary in Reideaux. As king, he, Konrad, would recommend to them that Kenrik be given refuge and all assistance and support to regain his rights in Chezkovia.

The royal commission did agree to give Kenrik refuge, judging that his mission was for the peace of Chezkovia and thus spoke of peace for the surrounding kingdoms. To shelter and assist the czar's son would also be profitable for the future alliance between the two countries, when Kenrik eventually became czar of Chezkovia.

Later, when Konrad left the throne room to dine, he urged Kenrik to learn about the God of the Gospel Book, for it was He who appointed kings to reign and princes to rule. For the first time, Kenrik did not pass Konrad's remarks off as being "religious rubbish from the crazy prince."

Communications arrived from Proburg, written by the hands of Princes Warford and Mayer, Konrad's brothers. The letters stated that their father, Gustovas, was enjoying his stay with Czar Kievik and was having "a whale of a time reminiscing over the past." A feast that would last more than a week was being enjoyed. Their mother was well, and Gustav had decided not to bother with the conference. Elliad the traitor was indeed dead and Frencolia should get on with its own affairs. "Stop worrying about business belonging to other kingdoms!" The letter received by Warford and Mayer had been written in Prince Gustovas' own handwriting and was sealed with their father's royal seal ring.

"There seems nothing to arouse suspicion," Mayer wrote to Konrad and Kenrik. The very fact that Mayer wrote this, about there being nothing to "arouse suspicion," caused Konrad some anxiety. Their father was not one to be beguiled easily, and surely he would know the real czar from the trickster Elliad.

The more Konrad deliberated about the whole affair, the less sense it made. He wanted to dismiss Chezkovia from his mind and forget about Elliad, but he knew ignorance would not cause a disappearance of the problem. The new czar of Chezkovia was fooling everyone, and Konrad dared not think why his own father, Gustovas, was supporting the charade, or . . . ? Konrad switched his mind off Chezkovia. He had enough to take care of right now! One day at a time, he reminded himself.

Konrad sent a gift with Kenrik for the Princess Jobyna—a complete copy of the Scriptures. He knew she would enjoy sharing the writings of Paul the Apostle with her brother Luke. Referring to a particular verse in the book of Romans, he reminded Jobyna that "God is always in control in the lives of those who are His children." He further wrote to her of his appointment and acceptance as king of Reideaux, asking her to seriously consider becoming his wife. Konrad did not write "queen," knowing the title would most likely stir a negative reaction in her active mind. He remembered she had disliked the title "princess," and he hoped the aversion to royal titles would not put her off him for good! He closed the letter with the words: "My love is yours, forever. Affectionately, your friend, Konrad."

Princess Jobyna stood beside Prince Dorai and Princess Minette at the base of the dais of the Frencolian throne when "His Imperial Highness, Czarevitch Kenrik of Chezkovia" was announced. Kenrik entered, followed by Doctor Sleven and two of his sons, Michael and Adolf. Jobyna's heart was glad to see the doctor again, this kind man who had called her his daughter. She could not believe how much grayer he was; how old he seemed now, his face so lined and drawn.

The reading of the book of Romans greatly thrilled Luke and he ordered his scribes to begin making copies of all the new writings now in their possession. The book of Acts and Paul's writings had not been read before. Jobyna and Luke together memorized the verse that Konrad had written in his letter: "All things work together for good to those who love God, to them who are the called according to His purpose" (Romans 8:28).

" 'All' means ALL—not just the things that we choose, not just the circumstances that suit us. This means the bad as well as the good," Luke said to his sister, not knowing that they would both recall this conversation and this verse would bring them comfort when all seemed to be against them, when all was going wrong and the very courses of their lives had fallen dangerously apart!

The day of the conference arrived. Furniture in the large dining room of King's Castle had been rearranged to cater for the seating requirements. King Luke Chanec sat at one end of the tables which had been positioned to form a large rectangle. On his right sat Prince Dorai and on his left, Lord Farey. Kenrik, Doctor Sleven, Michael and Adolf sat alongside Prince Dorai. The senior knights sat on benches along the wall behind Luke and Dorai. Czarevitch Kenrik's counselors were positioned behind him. King Willem and two of his knights sat at the table, Queen Anstice and their counselors behind. Prince Dietrick from Zealavia and ambassadors from Bavarest, Danzerg and Muldaver made up the rest of the group seated around the table.

Jobyna and Minette sat with Queen Anstice to counterbalance there being only one woman present. King Willem had informed Prince Dorai that he required his queen's advice, as he discussed all matters pertaining to their kingdom with her and she was always involved in decision-making. That he considered his wife most wise was a great compliment!

Each country had scribes, sitting at desks behind their appropriate dignities. The room was a mass of royal activity.

Luke opened the conference with readings from the Gospel Book. He commented upon the verse, "Where no counsel is, the people fall: but in the multitude of counselors there is safety" (Proverbs 11:14). Luke verbalized an earnest prayer to "the One and only true God—our wise Creator who made heaven and earth." To the young man's relief, there were no other petitions for prayer to any of the pagan gods which were worshiped by some of those present. Had such a requisition surfaced, Luke told his uncle that he would decline such prayers and proclaim the existence of the one and only true God. In Frencolia, prayer would be made to the Lord God alone!

Kenrik spoke first, explaining that Prince Gustovas and Crown Prince Gustav were absent due to a trip to Chezkovia. The czarevitch sat, sheepishly, not wishing to divulge that the prince of Proburg and the czar of Chezkovia were possibly in agreement against him!

King Konrad's letter of apology was read; his words stating Reideaux would do all they could to support the decisions made at the conference were noted.

Each kingdom which had suffered at the hand of Elliad and his attacks, read documents of evidence describing the raids.

Kenrik gave testimony, stating he believed Elliad had imprisoned or murdered his father and was posing as the czar of Chezkovia, having been joined and supported by his stepmother, Czarina Terese. He expressed the fears Konrad had regarding the safety of his father, Prince Gustovas, his mother, Princess Rhaselle and his brother, Crown Prince Gustav. They hoped to receive word, even while this conference was in session, that the monarch of Proburg had returned safely to Proburg.

Princess Jobyna was called to recount her experience in witnessing Elliad wearing the czar's crown, sitting on the throne in the Chezkovian throne room. She testified that she had dined with him and the czarina immediately following, and he had gloatingly acknowledged his charade.

The rest of the day was filled with listening to proposals as to how the countries could join in ridding Chezkovia of the menace and thus prevent the spread of the reign of the power-mad tyrant. Everyone agreed that Elliad would not ultimately be content to remain peacefully in Chezkovia.

The troops at Elliad's disposal, Kenrik estimated, were 80,000 to 100,000 men. A pensive silence filled the chamber when

Kenrik voiced these figures, all realizing that even if all the kingdoms joined together, without Proburg's help they would not outnumber Chezkovia. If Elliad gained Prince Gustovas' support, another 50,000 soldiers would be joined to the enemy.

Luke verbalized the thought they all had in mind, "If only there was a way to expose Elliad or terminate his reign without having to go to war."

Jobyna secretly thought, *If he is given enough rope, he will make a wrong move and hang himself.* Just what that "rope" was to be, the princess had no idea.

The kingdoms divided, retiring to separate rooms to discuss their final proposals for presentation the next day. Prince Dorai advised the representatives before they separated that time was limited and their vote must be cast as soon as possible.

Two days passed before all were ready to meet in the dining hall again to discuss the final decisions. Luke asked first if any country was remaining neutral, for it would only be just if those representatives spoke up and moved out, while the others deliberated on such confidential information. Lord Stansfield from Muldaver rose to state he was choosing at this stage to stay neutral, but wished to know the decision of the conference. He would then discuss with the king of Muldaver, and if Elliad made movement from Chezkovia of war against any other kingdom, then they would join the alliance by sending troops. It was agreed that Lord Stansfield could remain to hear the decision.

The outcome of the conference was the signing of a final mandate against the man "Elliad John Pruwitt." A list of his crimes included the murder of the previous king of Frencolia, Leopold Friedrich; and it was alleged that he had imprisoned or murdered Czar Kievik of Chezkovia, and was currently acting illegally as czar. Elliad was accused of holding as prisoners the Czarevna Cynara and the Grand Duke Kedar. The responsibility of Princess Maia's abduction lay at his feet. Other countries had submitted names of those murdered by Elliad, and the extensive list included Luke and Jobyna's parents, Baron and Baroness Chanec of Frencolia.

The pretender was granted seven days from receipt of the mandate to surrender and be tried for the said crimes (though no one in the conference room believed Elliad would surrender). Copies of the accusations were being written and would be dispatched to every city and town dignitary in the country of Chezkovia as Kenrik believed many emirs were not aware of the accusation of the charade being lived by their "czar." The mandate should cause the cavalry to rally and check out the personage of this so-called "Imperial Highness." Hopefully, many from the cavalry would join Czarevitch Kenrik in the battle to regain the throne for his father.

The closing statement on the mandate was: "If Elliad John Pruwitt will not return the stolen crown to the rightful czar, then the listed countries will mobilize their troops in war against the pretender and those who support him. This mandate is not against the czar or czardom of Chezkovia, but against one despot, namely, Elliad John Pruwitt."

Over a week had passed before the documents were completed and signed. One by one, the kingdoms' representatives were given formal farewells. Czarevitch Kenrik left first to return to Reideaux where he would be closer to receive news as it came to hand from Chezkovia. Doctor Sleven bade a fond farewell to Jobyna and she in turn sent affectionate greetings to Brenna, the doctor's wife, who was now living in Reideaux. Jobyna penned a brief letter to Konrad, encouraging him in his new role and stating that she was praying earnestly regarding his offer of marriage. She wrote that God would most surely work all things out for their good. "God is faithful, who promised," she added, closing with, "Affectionately yours, Jobyna Chanec."

King Willem and Queen Anstice were the last dignities left at King's Castle; they requested permission to stay for another week, sending the documents back to Strasland with their knights. Jobyna questioned the queen about the slave-girl, Ellice, who had been kidnapped from Strasland, but the queen was unable to give any information as to which part of the country she would have been taken from, or any enlightenment as to who she really was. Jobyna was horrified to know the extent of the raids for which Elliad was named responsible. Not since the time of the Barbarians had the kingdoms experienced a more peaceful style of life, but Elliad's rampages had revived the terror. He had rarely taken prisoners and never left witnesses to his horrible crimes.

Luke prepared for his journey to Reideaux. The Frencolian king would finalize with Konrad projected locations for troop bases and lists of supplies and equipment that Frencolia would transport to Reideaux, together with those from Danzerg, to build bases for the troops that would gather. Prince Dorai commanded uncompromisingly that Luke must be back in Frencberg before Elliad received the mandate in approximately five to seven days' time. While Luke was in Reideaux, Prince Dorai would be amassing the Frencolian army.

Jobyna wrote a letter to Brenna, and another to Konrad, thanking him again for the Gospel Book and stating she would take her brother's and uncle's advice and accept Konrad's offer of marriage.

She wrote, "I must tell you, King Konrad, that I am also listening to the dictates of my heart. When you left Frencolia, after having declared yourself to me, it was then I realized that I do love you. I believe it is God's will for us to be married, and I believe He will bless our lives. Luke suggested that the betrothal take place by proxy, but I would like us to make our vows together in the sight of God." She did not write how much she was struggling with the awesome thought that Luke had brought to her mind, that when she married Konrad she would be the wife of the king of Reideaux and would likely be given the title of "Queen Jobyna."

Luke and Jobyna bade each other a fond farewell, neither dreaming the incredible events which would come to pass in the next days. To Jobyna, Reideaux seemed as safe as Frencolia, but then she did not know of Elliad's men stationed in Frencberg, who were watching, waiting, listening and planning with careful and meticulous mastery!

9

King Konrad, his counselors, Czarevitch Kenrik, Doctor Sleven and sons, with their various counselors, all stunned and disbelieving, gathered for an emergency meeting. Guards, attendants and soldiers from Proburg had deserted Landmari Castle and absconded to Reideaux bearing a devastating declaration.

Prince Gustovas had arrived at Landmari Castle with the czar of Chezkovia, and the staid Czar Kievik had claimed the Proburg throne! Prince Warford, his wife and children, and Prince Mayer, together with Prince Gustav's wife and children had all been transported to Chezkovia as crown prisoners. The assumption was that the monarch of Proburg, Prince Gustovas, was also a prisoner of the czar, and had been forced to obey the czar's orders. They did not know that Prince Gustovas had pleaded to die before he was forced to return to Proburg and betray his sons and his kingdom, but Elliad had needed this prince's presence to authenticate his arrival at Landmari Castle.

The prince was given no choice in the matter, and Chezkovian men, wearing Proburg uniforms, escorted the unwilling monarch to his own royal carriage. He traveled with one hand bound to ropes, which also secured his feet and legs, seated beside the czar. Elliad forced his captive to wave his free hand as they passed crowds which were kept at a safe distance by their extensive escort. To the people, the royal procession spoke of the unity between the two countries. Knights of Proburg and emirs of Chezkovia waved enthusiastically as they rode through villages and towns.

Once Elliad and his men were inside the castle, the takeover was relatively simple. There had been bloodshed, but most of the resistance ceased when royal wives and children were presented as the czar's prisoners, accompanied by death threats if Gustovas' two sons did not surrender. The hostages were conveyed immediately to Baltic Castle. To Elliad, his fortress on the Baltic cliffs was the ultimate prison and his captives were as good as dead, but he would decide their fate sometime in the future. Royal people were worthy hostages and he felt while he held their lives in the balance, he displayed supreme power— power over life and death. Uncooperative castle personnel who were unable to escape were "terminated"; useful prisoners were incarcerated in the Landmari dungeons for interrogation and reorientation.

Mayer's wife, Princess Ordella (who was away from court visiting her family), and Konrad were the only two of the royal family that Elliad had failed to capture.

After two days, Elliad left Landmari Castle in "Prince" Brian's control and returned to Chezkovia, leaving several thousand Chezkovian troops to guard his new conquest. Messages had been posted all over Proburg proclaiming that Prince Gustovas had been deposed; Proburg was now part and parcel of Chezkovia. Knights and soldiers of Proburg were expected to be loyal to the new Prince Brian, under the jurisdiction of the supreme ruler, Czar Kievik. The slightest indication of uprising would be swiftly and permanently dealt with.

Proburg knights, soldiers and families in the hundreds escaped to Reideaux, where Konrad was faced with the huge task of organizing and accommodating them. As far as Konrad and Kenrik were concerned, war had been declared and Elliad had less than two days left before he would receive the mandate, which had now become surplus to this open display of treachery. It was too late to retract passage of the documents which were in the hands of messengers and already moving across borders and on to Chezkovian soil.

King Kelsey had not been enshrined, and Luke was two days overdue in his arrival at the Reideaux capital. Konrad sent a small company in Moritz' charge, to the Frencolian border, and they arrived back the next day with a strange and mysterious problem for the new king to solve. The Frencolian border castle was secured completely, displaying the appearance of a state of siege. Moritz and his men had counted guards with loaded crossbows, on the battlements, some wearing the green and gold of Frencolia and some wearing the red and white of Chezkovia. Konrad wondered fearfully if Frencolia had been invaded and captured as well.

He sent his men to the border castle further to the west, and awaited their reply with trepidation. The men were commanded to divide if the border was open, and Moritz would bring word back to King Konrad. The rest of the company was to continue on down into Frencolia if they could traverse the border, otherwise journey further west and keep trying until they could make a successful entry. Once over the border they were to report to King Luke Chanec, if he was there, or to Prince Dorai in Frencberg.

10

Elliad's artful agent Cormick had arrived at the Frencolian border castle with two knights and 30 soldiers. He presented himself scrupulously dressed as a Frencolian knight. The uniforms were ones he and his men had taken with them when they had left Frencolia with Elliad over a year ago. The bottom part of the embroidered "E" had been carefully removed to revert the embroidery on the uniforms to the original "F."

Cormick had studiously compiled documents, and his scribes had fastidiously forged signatures and seals in the pretense that they were a special party sent ahead of King Luke Chanec by Prince Dorai to inspect the border guard and assure that the king's company progressed into Reideaux without incident. Cormick's company had chosen names and disguises identical to authentic Frencolian men and they hoped the role-play would pass without question or close scrutiny. They required just a few minutes without detection and they would be halfway to their goal of kidnapping King Luke Chanec!

Felix, who had been on duty at the border castle when Jobyna had returned to Frencolia, was again on duty the night Cormick and his men arrived. There were no warning signs apparent for him to suspect trickery. Knights of the kingdom were to be trusted! Felix took Cormick—now named "Sir Stacy, from Bruis"—to his office, chatting about all the visitors who had traversed the border in the past days. He gave Cormick a drink while he carefully checked the papers. Cormick's men used less than 10 minutes to secure the border castle, locking the few men who were still alive in one of the two dungeons.

When the sword-waving Edsel and Lester burst in the office door, Felix was so shocked, he almost suffered a heart attack. On learning they were "representing His Imperial Highness, the czar of Chezkovia," Felix asked Cormick to thrust the sword through him right there and then because it was too much to bear. Cormick was tempted to comply, but had him thrown in the dungeon with the others. The speculative traitor decided to kill all the soldiers and save the knights and captains alone as hostages. A dead knight was not much use, he thought. Sir Felix had more value alive at the present! Cormick's remaining 24 men removed the dead bodies, closed the northern exits and prepared for King Luke Chanec's arrival, scheduled first thing in the morning.

Luke had spent the night at Valdemar. He planned to leave before daybreak, arriving at the border castle around dawn. The remainder of the day would be spent in the saddle, traveling to Kelsey Castle. Luke looked forward to seeing Konrad and to spending some 60 hours in the capital with his friend, the new king of Reideaux. Prince Dorai had agreed that such a visit would help seal future relations.

The portcullis was raised at the border castle, and Sir Keith, riding with Luke, asked for Sir Felix. Cormick explained the knight's absence by concocting the lie that he had been taken sick. The pretender gave the name of one of Felix's captains, "Etam." The fraud had disguised himself to look similar to this man who had been thrown in the dungeons. Sir Keith felt uneasy, but his curiosity was not raised enough to detect that they were in the hands of ruthless, murderous enemies. As King Luke and Sir Keith were ushered royally with Cormick to the office, the leader signaled for those delegated to move into action as planned. The gate was secured behind the 50 men traveling with Luke and before the king's company had time for any counteractions, all were prisoners within the walls of the border castle. The felons found the final stage of the kidnapping relatively simple. Using Elliad's tactics, they seized Luke and Sir Keith first.

Luke entered the small office, followed by Sir Keith. Loran and Granville had remained in the courtyard. What danger could threaten their king, in this fortress, surrounded by knights and guarded by fellow Frenc troops?

From behind the office door, two men overpowered Luke, holding a dagger at his throat. Sir Keith very quickly surrendered his weapons, and the pair were bound and led out, to be presented as hostages to force the company to surrender and lay down their weapons.

"Who will be responsible for King Luke Chanec's death?" Cormick yelled out across the courtyard waving a short sword. His men appeared from all corners of the walls with drawn swords. Sir Valdre tried to sum up the situation. He realized, although outnumbered, the invaders were deadly serious. The knight could not be sure whether the king was to be murdered or taken as a hostage. He knew he must not call their bluff and hasten his king's death, so the senior knight threw his sword down, followed by the clatter of those around him.

Luke's greatest anguish was for these men, loyal to him and to

90

the kingdom of Frencolia. They were herded to the dungeons which became crowded beyond their capacities. Sir Keith was imprisoned with them. Cormick and his other three chiefs divided into two groups. The leader traveled in charge of the captive king, taking Lester and four men with him leaving the border castle in Edsel and Welby's control. The victory of the kidnapping and the heist of the border castle gave Cormick extra thrills, as he knew the czar would be most pleased.

Cormick rode east the rest of that day, planning to rendezvous with Elliad's waiting Chezkovian troops. Luke's heart felt as though it was stuck in his throat when the young king heard his captor command that a company ride back to the Frencolian border taking provisions. Fifty men were commissioned to maintain possession of the castle; the rest would convey Frencolian prisoners to Chezpro, one of the Elliad's lesser strongholds. Cormick told them the czar would send orders as to the prisoners' fates.

Valuable papers had been confiscated by Cormick from Luke, Sir Keith and Sir Valdre. One was a letter written by Princess Jobyna to King Konrad of Reideaux, and another with her signature to Doctor Sleven's wife, Brenna. A copy of the mandate and other documents for Konrad were also preempted. The prize documents gave locations of proposed troop bases, weapons and equipment, and Cormick perused these with ecstatic triumph.

Luke was dazed to realize how swift and final his capture had been. With his arms bound behind his back, he bounced precariously on Speed. Cormick controlled the horse's reins causing their two mounts to travel close together. Luke was jogged dangerously over the rough paths, and Cormick reluctantly slowed the pace to compensate. His valuable captive needed to be intact upon arrival in Chezkovia. An advance patrol was far ahead and Cormick expected a carriage to rendezvous with them on the Danzerg border. His plans moved as smoothly as the flowing hourglass and he congratulated himself for being so well organized. Once Luke was hogtied and tossed to lie helplessly on the floor of the carriage, Cormick stretched out on the seat, making the most of the now-luxurious journey to catch up on lost sleep.

Chezkovian constables Michael and Adolf, in their red and white uniforms, with four men in the Proburg brown and two wearing the dull blue of Reideaux, arrived at the King's Castle in Frencberg, escorted by Frencolian knights and soldiers. Those on duty at the border castle north of Leroy were horrified at the news that their king had not arrived in Reideaux and that the Valdemar border castle was closed and under Chezkovian control. Troops were immediately dispatched to investigate the matter from the Frencolian side.

Prince Dorai, dining with Minette and Jobyna, King Willem, Queen Anstice and some of the senior knights and their wives, was interrupted by Sabin and told of the foreign dignitaries waiting in the front reception room. Sabin announced quietly to Dorai that the men had said the matter was of grave importance to the kingdom, one of life or death.

Jobyna did not learn of her brother's disappearance until the next day. Her uncle had not returned to finish the meal with them, and other senior knights had been called to an urgent meeting. During the night, the news came through from exhausted riders that the Valdemar border castle was indeed in a state of siege and was in the hands of men from Chezkovia. Prince Dorai could scarcely believe this was possible. How could Elliad's men have gained control of a border castle? The border castles were impregnable! Days of ramming would be required to batter a hole in the walls and could cost hundreds of lives.

Dorai worried whether Luke was being held prisoner there, but he suspected his nephew had been conveniently conveyed elsewhere. The prince hoped for a message—a ransom demand, perhaps. However, he had not received any acknowledgment of Maia's presence in Chezkovia, so there was no knowing if they would send information about Luke. Dorai spent the evening planning the mobilization of the troops, consigning extra soldiers to make sure the Leroy border castle was kept open and free to be traversed. If this fortress were captured, the two northern routes out of the country would be rendered immobile and ineffective by the enemy, who appeared to be one step ahead of them all the way.

Eva, Minette's servant, woke Jobyna before dawn. She told the sleepy princess, "Prince Dorai requests that you have an early breakfast with him." When Jobyna had dressed, she found Minette waiting for her. They walked in silence, both wondering what the bad news from the previous night had been.

The prince paced back and forth, waiting in the small breakfast room, his hands clasped characteristically behind his back. He kissed Minette tenderly, turning to Jobyna, and holding her close to him. With an arm around each of their shoulders, he told them to sit and eat breakfast, then he would talk.

Jobyna could not eat. Her uncle's countenance was so grim; the young princess thought he seemed more distressed than when Maia had been abducted. Dorai had always been so strong, so very composed, determined and brave. This morning he appeared drawn, afraid—and Jobyna tried to fathom the depths of the fear she saw in his eyes. As though her scrutiny was painful, the uncle would not meet her gaze, but looked at her hair or at the wall behind. The adjective "defeated" caused Jobyna to drop the bread roll and sit back to wait for his promised "talk." Prince Dorai, not eating either and catching his niece's discerning expression, stood to pace once more.

"It's very bad, isn't it, Uncle?" she asked him.

"Yes, Jobyna—very bad," he replied. "I wish I could make it

easier for all of us, but the longer I leave it, the harder it is becoming for me to find the words. I have to leave this morning, within the hour, for Reideaux." He paused while Minette drew in a loud, resigned breath. The prince stood up, pacing to the window. "Jobyna, I want you to hear what I say. It appears—it is not proven yet, but . . . it appears that your brother, Luke, has been captured."

Jobyna was still, as if she had turned to stone. "How?" She managed to expel this word with a simultaneous gasp.

Prince Dorai unfolded the news as it had been told to him. Jobyna's first reaction was to demand that she go to Reideaux with her uncle, but she knew he would not allow this and would make her promise to stay in Frencolia. Dorai said the whole situation was becoming increasingly complex and more complicated by the minute. The longer they took to move against Elliad, the more ground, literally, he was gaining. Not only had he seized the throne in Proburg, but he had kidnapped Luke, and he now had a base on the very border of their own kingdom, a strategic military position between Reideaux, Proburg and Chezkovia!

The farewell was tearful; Jobyna was still in shock. She thought of Konrad and longed to be with him. Her last words to Dorai as he sat mounted on his horse were, "Uncle, there must be so much I could do to help Konrad. All the refugees from Proburg—there must be cooking and sewing, organizing . . . just say the word and I will come." She saw the negative answer in Dorai's eyes and pleaded, "Please tell Konrad I miss him and will come if I can be of use."

Jobyna returned with her aunt to the confines of the castle, determining to give her uncle a few days' start, then she would follow. She felt she had to be in Reideaux when news of Luke arrived.

Ruskin had been commissioned to be in charge of King's Castle. All over Frencolia plans of siege were being made. The country was at war. News that King Luke Chanec had been taken captive by the evil Elliad was passed on and soon the whole country knew the terrible truth. Prince Dorai told Lord Farey and Ruskin that if neither Luke nor he returned, the throne of Frencolia would go to his son, Prince Charles, with the direction of the lords and senior knights until he was 16, when he would be king in his own right. Sobering thoughts filled Crown Prince Dorai's mind as he traversed the Frencolian border. He turned his face away from his men lest they see the tears falling unbidden down his cheeks. Luke had become so very dear to him and if he could give his life in exchange, he would.

Ruskin secured King's Castle, leaving only one gate open for those allowed to enter and leave. Jobyna fantasized of traversing the secret tunnel in the throne room, but realized it would take two to trigger the mechanisms, and then she would not have a horse when she exited. She fretted and paced and for some hours was unable to find comfort.

In contrition, Jobyna remembered the help that was available to her, a believer in the Almighty God. She prayed and begged God to save Luke. "God, you can do it, and without my help, but I am certainly here if needed! Please give me patience to allow you the time to work. Please protect Luke and return him safely to us."

Time was the enemy; time would have to pass before any news of Luke would come. Jobyna struggled to submit to the knowledge that God gives patience in trials. She decided to occupy every moment—talking cheerfully to Minette, playing exciting games and reading with the children, and going to the kitchen to bake when she needed the therapy of the dough between her fingers. The Noah's Ark was set out to remain on permanent display, and the children enjoyed living out the story with the carved animals. They brought in copious amounts of soil from the castle gardens and built a Mount Ararat. Rainbows made from colored fabrics were draped around the room and Charles hung prisms at the castle window to capture and reflect the sunlight in the brilliant colors of the rainbow. Reading from the Gospel Book, Jobyna found the words were passing her eyes uncomprehended, so great was her concern for Luke. She knew real empathy with her brother, feeling his past trauma when she had been a captive of Elliad.

Luke entered the Oval Crown Room in Jydanski, escorted by Cormick and Lester. His arms were still bound behind him and his shoulders were stiff and drooped.

"King Luke Chanec of Frencolia" the announcement rang out. Luke had no option but to walk along the red carpet toward the figure sitting on the throne of Chezkovia. He was forced to his knees at the base of the throne dais, then pushed to lie prostrate. A foot pressed upon him, brutally constricting his neck for several moments. Finding himself dragged again to his feet by his captors, his eyes beheld the infamous "czar." Elliad descended from the throne and congratulated the men, commanding that they cut Luke's bonds.

"I am sure the king of Frencolia will behave himself in the presence of the great czar of Chezkovia." Elliad spoke in Frenc, switching suddenly as he commanded his guards to move closer.

Cormick handed him the sheaf of documents and Elliad flipped through them with interest. His eyes narrowed as he read Konrad's copy of the mandate, addressed to "King Konrad of the kingdom of Reideaux." The pretender had received his own copy just hours before. News of Luke's coming had superseded the making of plans regarding the mandate.

"Make the king of Frencolia *un*comfortable in one of the interrogation rooms—number six will do." Elliad spoke in

German to the guards, "I will be down later." Once Luke had been hauled from the great room, the pretender turned his attention to Cormick and Lester, telling them he had more assignments for them involving more personnel; greater risks would need to be taken, but the rewards would be worth it all. The urgency of the situation demanded that they move instantly and act on certain plans within the next week. The two men went with Elliad to his office and together they wrote up documents and made heart-chilling plans.

Elliad perused the papers from Frencolia with care, seeking to formulate his next plans. He was pleased with Cormick regarding his possession of the border castle. He had made inroads into Frencolia; Chezkovia and Proburg were secure. Was there anything he could not do?

The letter Luke carried from Jobyna to Konrad was of great interest to Elliad. He had received the news of Konrad's ascension to the Reideaux throne, and it intrigued him now to think of Konrad's desire for Jobyna to become queen. He was filled with violent jealousy as he read her letter to the new king. Jobyna was his; by all rights she would be dead if he had not paid the traitor Sleven to care for her! Konrad's interest in his "treasure" made her all the more desirable to the deceiver. Yes, he thought, he would be prepared to give up this Luke of Frencolia if he could get her back, and Reideaux would be his as well as Frencolia, eventually. She may be queen one day, but it would be to him! No, not queen—czarina. Yes, Czarina Jobyna!

"You will write a letter to your sister telling her to exchange places with you!" Elliad commanded Luke who stood, bone-weary, thirsty and hungry, his hands and feet chained to rings on a post in "number six."

"I will write no such letter!" Luke declared. "You may as well kill me! I will not be the reason for returning my sister into your hands, Elliad."

Elliad punched Luke's face with all the force he could muster. The blow caused the lad's nose to bleed. As he staggered against the chains, a punch with Elliad's other forceful fist split his lip and for a moment, Luke wondered if he had knocked out some teeth. A third resounding whack bruised his jaw, and a fourth his cheek, causing the lad to fall, stunned, to the stone floor.

"I am Czar Kievik! You will call me by my correct name!" Elliad's voice was strained. Grasping the handle of a lead-laden whip, he ordered the Chezkovian guards to remove Luke's tunic. Tasting the blood from his nose and lip, Luke prayed for courage and braced himself as the men unceremoniously cut and tore his tunic from his body. Hauling him to his feet, they threw him across the post, the top of which dug into his chest. The metal ring and chains felt as though they would puncture his ribs! Elliad stalked around the pole flicking the whip, a murderous gleam in his eyes.

The charlatan suddenly stood stone still, his vision filled with the sparkling jewels embedded in the seal swinging from the young king's neck. Dropping the whip, he grabbed at the medallion with both hands. The heavy gold chain pulled Luke's face close to his and the boy gasped at the extra pressure he felt in the pit of his stomach.

Elliad's eyes had alighted for the first time on the cursed seal! This medallion should have been his! He barked at the guards and Luke found himself thrown and held on the stone floor, his hands still shackled. With a sudden stroke of an axe, the chain was smashed just inches from the young king's head. Elliad uttered more orders. Taking the seal to the kingdom of Frencolia with him, he left the room. The guards collected up the solid gold chain, divided it into smaller fragments, and shared them around in glee.

Luke was consigned to a lonely dungeon, deep down within the dark depths of the palace. He shuddered as he thought of the flogging he could have received; such a flogging would have torn both skin and flesh off his back and rendered him unconscious. "All things . . ." he murmured as he knelt to pray. "All."

11

A little over a week after Prince Dorai left for Reideaux, a messenger arrived, mid-morning, from the eastern border. Chezkovian soldiers had delivered a small package to the border guards, addressed to "The Princess Jobyna, First Princess of the Kingdom of Frencolia, care of Prince Dorai, Crown Prince of the Kingdom of Frencolia." It was from the "Czar of Chezkovia," and sealed with the imperial czardom seal.

When Ruskin was given the package, he broke the seal without hesitation. Reading the letter twice, he sat staring at the object which he had unwrapped from black velvet cloth. Some minutes passed before the knight managed to pull himself together. Lord Farey was summoned, as were the older counselors and senior knights who had remained in Frencberg. After much deliberation, they decided to show Princess Jobyna the letter before dispatching the package to Prince Dorai in Reideaux.

Jobyna took the letter with trembling hands and read:

My dear Princess Jobyna:

I find myself in possession of your brother, Luke Chanec, but would much rather it were you instead. My anger was stirred greatly by your departure from Chezkovia. I am prepared to pardon you if you return to me in exchange for the life of your brother. Frencolia will have its king and I will have my treasure.

One week is all I can wait for your reply which must be from your own hand.

The note was signed simply, "John."

Ruskin gently handed Jobyna the remains of the seal to the kingdom of Frencolia. The jewels had been pried out, and the K.F. on the face was barely legible. The gold chain had been removed. Jobyna was horrified at this proof that Luke was indeed in Elliad's hands. She saw her distress mirrored in Ruskin's eyes and knew that he also remembered the time she had come to his house with a sketch she had made of the lost seal. Here it was, now, the seal to the kingdom of Frencolia, ruined, defaced, destroyed.

Ruskin finally spoke. "We have here, in this communication, complete proof that the czar of Chezkovia is a fraud. If only we could take this to those who matter in the Chezkovian council! But a miracle would have to be performed before any communication would get past Elliad's men." He informed the tearful princess that a company was ready to leave to carry the letter and seal remains to Prince Dorai at Kelsey Castle.

"How do you know my uncle will not want me to obey the request of the letter? We are dealing with my brother's life here, Ruskin . . . the life of the king of Frencolia!" Jobyna looked into Ruskin's eyes and as he stared back silently, she continued, "It will take more than a day to reach Kelsey Castle, then time to consider the plan of action, and if I am to write a letter to Elliad . . ." her voice trailed off. The point was well made. Ruskin asked her to wait in the foyer while he conferred with Lord Farey and the other men. It was only minutes later that he called her back and Ruskin asked that she have Princess Minette and the servants help her prepare to leave for Reideaux.

The young aunt was upset to see Jobyna packing and explaining she was leaving for Reideaux. Minette rushed immediately to appeal to Ruskin herself. She knew what Dorai, her husband, had ordered before he left: "The Princess Jobyna must remain in the confines of the castle walls!" Ruskin reopened Elliad's letter, allowing Minette time to read it and absorb the dire warning of the contents. Minette sat down heavily and put her head in her hands.

Jobyna arrived at the castle office dressed in the Proburg soldier's uniform she had worn when she had escaped back to Frencolia. Her braids were tucked up under the bearskin hat and she looked like a very handsome young soldier. "I saved this as a keepsake," she said to Ruskin. "It would be better and easier to travel like this, I think, than as a princess."

Minette flung her arms around her niece, sobbing out all the reasons Jobyna should not be going to Reideaux, acting as though it was be the last time she would ever embrace her. The aunt calmed down a little when she saw the large company of mounted soldiers waiting to escort Jobyna. Sabin, who arrived in the courtyard with an extra company, announced that he was riding to Reideaux as well.

Jobyna asked Minette to kiss the children for her and remind them to pray. God would bring Maia and Luke back, she was sure. On later reflection, Minette remembered she had not mentioned herself.

Ruskin took both Jobyna's hands, kissing them more affectionately than was the custom. The back portcullis was raised and the moat bridge lowered especially for the group, and they cantered away. Jobyna was excited to be moving closer to Luke; she also felt confident that Konrad and her uncle would work out a rescue plan of some kind. Whatever tomorrow held, she must do all she could for Frencolia to have Luke returned safely.

At the border castle north of Leroy, the reality of the departure from Frencolia struck Jobyna for the first time, and as they moved through the gates she remembered her tearful traverse from the eastern border over a year ago. It was dark and late when they arrived at Gerold Castle to change horses and rest until morning.

Jobyna patted Brownlea affectionately. Sabin heard her say, "I'll be back for you Brownlea, you'll see." She laid her cheek against his nose and would have stood there for some time longer, but Sabin urged, "It's so late, Princess Jobyna, and you need to sleep so we can leave at first light."

Prince Dorai was awakened before dawn. Riders had continued on through the night and arrived at Kelsey Castle with the letter from King's Castle in Frencberg. The pouch was addressed to Prince Dorai, but King Konrad had also been called, and he accompanied Dorai to the office. The prince read Ruskin's letter first, then with trembling hands passed it to Konrad and opened the letter from Elliad.

The seal to the kingdom of Frencolia was unwrapped from the black velvet cloth, and Prince Dorai was speechless to see it. The symbol of power in Frencolia, worn by kings for over 200 years, was now a defaced golden disc dismembered by the murderous deceiver.

Konrad read Ruskin's letter which informed them that the Princess Jobyna was traveling to Reideaux and would not be many hours behind this communiqué; then he sat watching Prince Dorai's face, noting the set jaw and the unspilled tears of anger and sorrow. Dorai, placing the seal on the desk, handed Elliad's letter to Konrad. The new king of Reideaux rose suddenly on completion of reading the letter from the "czar" and told Dorai he was leaving right away to ride out and meet Jobyna. The ride and the fresh air, he said, would give him time to think of ideas and plans about what could be done to rescue Luke without having to involve his sister.

Konrad spied the Frencolian party before Jobyna saw him and his soldiers. When she did see him, several hundred yards in the distance, it was to behold a blue hat being hurled in the air. Leaving it to land where it would, Konrad galloped his horse at breathtaking speed ahead of his men. He knew it was her—the only brown uniform among the green and gold. Sabin wore his simple servant's clothes, and his face broke into a wide smile when he saw the Reideaux king, wearing a blue soldier's uniform, drawing nearer. Konrad reined his horse in with the front shoulder level with Jobyna's mount, and reached across for her hand. Kissing it affectionately, he smiled his stunning smile. Still holding hands, they each told the other how glad they were to be together again.

Jobyna's face clouded as she said, "I am . . . devastated by the news that Elliad has Luke." She hung her head, then looked back up at Konrad. "My brother carried a special letter to you, Your Majesty. I accepted your offer; I . . . I said much more. . . ." She blushed as her green eyes locked into the blueness of his gaze. "The letter is in our enemy's hands; he will know how I feel about you . . . about our betrothal." They both stared at the other, a somber silence between them. Thoughts of Elliad's demand hung like a black thundercloud ready to burst.

The Frencolian soldiers were dismissed to return to Frencolia where they would remain to take care of developments there. Sabin continued on to Kelsey Castle with the silent, pensive King Konrad, Princess Jobyna and the Reideaux company.

Prince Dorai met the group as they rode into the courtyard at Kelsey Castle. He helped Jobyna from the horse and hugged her close to him. Unspoken words lingered in their minds as they entered the castle foyer where Kenrik descended the stairs, hurrying to apprehend Konrad.

"There are more problems. We must talk!" Kenrik told Konrad, bowing briefly to Jobyna, "I have our counselors waiting."

Doctor Sleven and Brenna greeted Jobyna affectionately. "Come with me," Brenna said, and Sabin followed carrying the princess' pack.

Konrad, spying Jobyna move off, left Kenrik's side and rushed to her, taking her hands. He kissed both cheeks before saying fervently, "I am so glad you are here, Princess Jobyna."

12

The small conference room at Kelsey Castle was packed full with foreigners, counselors and officials. Representatives from Danzerg and Bavarest had traveled together to report the incredible news of practically simultaneous kidnappings from both countries. Within hours of the abductions, written counter-mandates had been delivered from the said "czar of Chezkovia."

Shaking his head, King Konrad spoke the thoughts that were on all minds. "News of these kidnappings is hard to accept. How could the offenders—though working for the despotic Elliad—engineer, and succeed with, such diabolical crimes? Why hadn't the kidnappers been apprehended before exiting over the border of the victims' countries? Such well-timed abductions must have been masterminded by ruthless experts!" Asking the names of those abducted, Konrad also requested that the counter-mandates be passed around for comparison and perusal.

Crown Prince Haroun, son of King Jarvis, had been kidnapped in a scene of bloody violence and murder from Bavarest. Two little girls, Princesses Zandra and Yvette, daughters of King Thurlow and Queen Saline of Danzerg, had been snatched from a carriage in the capital city, leaving 11 people dead. Both counter-mandates were the same, demanding the said country cancel their part in the Frencolian-based mandate against the czar, to accept that Elliad John Pruwitt was dead, to send their troops home and to sign peace treaties in return for the lives of the royal hostages. A ransom of 1,000 gold pieces for each life was demanded.

Discussions and deliberations took place in one solid session over the next night and day. Ambassadors arrived from Zealavia. The spokesman told the sober group a kidnap attempt was made on King Dionysus and his son Prince Dietrick, but was detected by a man who overheard the plot being finalized in the square; it was foiled by knights and soldiers who were warned just in time. The criminals were overpowered, swiftly and mercilessly killed.

A written counter-mandate was found on one of the bodies, with a blank space apparently left to write in the name of the victim. (The identity of this criminal proved to be Welby, who was originally from Zealavia.) King Dionysus had received surface wounds and several soldiers were badly injured, but so far Zealavia had suffered no fatalities. That the royal victims were chosen when convenient was now obvious.

The atmosphere at Kelsey Castle became increasingly despondent as the great lengths this enraged Elliad was prepared to go to became clearly evident.

When King Willem from Strasland was announced to the room, everyone visibly held their breaths. Prince Dorai had become deeply depressed with the whole affair and he now shook as he stood to greet his royal neighbor. "Queen Anstice?"

Her name came involuntarily from the prince's lips.

"She is safe!" King Willem told the attentive people congregated in the room. "It is my grandson, Louis. He is the only child of my son who died from the black plague. Louis is 12 years old and heir to the throne. He was out in the fields, riding his horse. . . ." His voice broke and the king handed the counter-mandate to Konrad, whose face was gray.

There was silence in the chamber for some time; the only sound was the scratching of the quill with which Konrad wrote. He was compiling a list. On completion of the rows of names, the Reideaux king stood to speak. "It is beyond my understanding how this Elliad has managed to triumph against us all; his brutal tactics have taken us by surprise. In the name of the czar of Chezkovia, Elliad is holding the power of life and death over a multitude of innocent people. He holds supreme power in Chezkovia as czar. On this day he holds the greatest balance of power in Proburg, and one Frencolian border fortress is in his control.

"These are the prisoners the insane Elliad is holding as hostages:

"The Grand Duke Kedar and Czarevna Cynara of Chezkovia. My parents, the monarchs of Proburg, Prince Gustovas and Princess Rhaselle. My eldest brother, Crown Prince Gustav and his wife, Princess Helena. Their children—Prince Gustav Junior, Prince Gunther, Princess Fleur and Princess Irma. My brother, Prince Warford, and his wife, Princess Marianne. Their three sons—Prince Melvyn, Prince Guibert and Prince Conroy. My brother, Prince Mayer."

Pausing as the room broke into sympathetic murmurs, Konrad waited for silence before continuing. "The list is extensive, please bear with me.

"King Luke Chanec of Frencolia. Crown Prince Dorai's daughter, Princess Maia, also of Frencolia. The two princesses from Danzerg, Zandra and Yvette. Crown Prince Haroun of Bavarest. And Grand Duke Louis of Strasland.

"This is a total of 22 souls."

Konrad strode between the well-worn chairs and around the wooden benches, speaking as he moved. "I have not had the opportunity to officially welcome you all here and it is with great sadness in my heart that we meet under these grave circumstances. Tomorrow morning, in a very brief ceremony, I must entomb my predecessor, the previous king of Reideaux, King Kelsey. This ceremony is being brought forward due to the great stress of these days—the declaration of war. We must all work in our minds to think and pray for a way in which we can retrieve our loved ones without causing death."

Konrad stood in front of Kenrik, who sat with a bowed head. The king continued, "The czardom of Chezkovia is not what we fight against, but against the power of one man, Elliad John Pruwitt, and his control of it. You all know he has taken over Landmari Castle in Proburg, where one of his men sits upon my father's throne. I believe this man is a Chezkovian named Brian Napole, who has been in Elliad's pay for 10 or more years.

"Kenrik's and my own troops, joined with those we are amassing from Proburg, are planning to move closer to the capital there. We hope to be able to confine Elliad's men to the castle itself and gain control of the border. Our maneuvers are designed to retrieve total control over Proburg, but we regret that this will not happen without bloodshed and, very likely, the loss of many lives."

Konrad paused as one of his official messengers strode in through the door. They had been commanded to deliver any messages immediately to whom they concerned in the conference room.

A leather satchel was handed to Kenrik and silence reigned in the room as the czarevitch stood and opened it. Extracting a lumpy parcel of black velvet, tied securely with red ribbon, Kenrik placed it on the table. For a moment, he stared at the odd shape. Then, as he cut the ribbon with his dagger and unfolded the cloth, gasps rose from all around the room, and people stood to view the grisly contents. A small hand, severed evenly at the wrist, was revealed.

Kenrik shook his head, sitting heavily. He reached into the satchel again and drew out a sealed scroll which he opened automatically. His eyes read the words over and over, but they seemed not to see the paper. The moments passed by and still Kenrik said nothing.

The czarevitch finally stood, reached for the paper and pushed it to Konrad. "The writing . . . it is the same as my . . . my father's hand." Kenrik sat again and his head dropped into his hands. He rubbed the back of his neck and cried, "My father . . . he would never do such a thing, or . . . or write such a letter!"

The king of Reideaux read out loud,

> Kenrik:
>   This is written to you to urge you to stop advances being made by troops in Proburg and to clear the border. You have until noon on Thursday to surrender the Chezkovian and Proburg troops under your control to me or your brother Kedar will be executed. This is Kedar's hand. I will be sending his head next time. Your reply is to be sent to Jydanski Palace. Tell Konrad that Prince Gunther will be next.
>   (Signed)
>   His Imperial Highness, The Czar of Chezkovia.

The room was so quiet, the rustling of parchment sounded like thunder as Konrad rolled it once more, passing it back to Kenrik.

The king announced, "We will break for refreshments. Dinner will be served for those of you who can manage a little sustenance. We will meet again after that. I have a plan of action forming in my mind. It will be understood if some of you wish to retire to rest and pray."

Kenrik left the room with Doctor Sleven, Michael and Adolf. Doctor Sleven carried the black velvet and its gruesome contents; he would ascertain whether or not it could be the hand belonging to a nine-year-old.

Konrad sought Jobyna out. The distraught king felt greatly refreshed to view her smile and the warmth of her emerald-green eyes. He took her hand and they walked together up the castle stairs to the battlements. Moritz trailed casually behind as they walked along the rampart. The sinking sun sent deepening shadows across the fields. Flapping flocks of birds flying to their nests formed changing patterns in the coloring sky. Shades of orange reflected off billowing gray clouds and lit the surrounding countryside with warmth and a golden illumination gave the appearance of fantasy.

Konrad unfolded the list for Jobyna to view, telling her about Kedar; she cried softly on his shoulder, trying hard not to see a vision of the child's hand being amputated.

"I have the formation of a plan in my mind, Jobyna, which will require your help, but I am not sure if we can save Kedar." Half to himself, and half to Moritz, he murmured in his native tongue, "It may already be too late for Kenrik's brother!" Then in Frenc again, "We must take the castle at Landmari. The castle itself will not be hard to take. Brian has been unable to secure all the entrances to the city. Two wall towers are still being held by Father's men; these give us access into the city. This is what Elliad is afraid of and is concerned about." He turned her face to look square into his eyes. "From what you know of this Elliad, he would follow through with his threat regarding Kedar,

111

wouldn't he?"

Jobyna nodded, her face full of fear. She then shook her head, trying to dispel the thought of Elliad beheading a mere child. The sun had disappeared and she shivered in the dimness of the twilight. The beauty all around was lost in chilling remembrance of Elliad's perverted enjoyment of torture and bloodshed.

Konrad continued, "We are certain that Kedar is a prisoner at Baltic Castle. Do you think Elliad might go there himself for Kedar's execution, or would he stay in Jydanski?"

Jobyna answered that she did not know; he was unpredictable, but to her knowledge, he was usually present for executions or any other display of violence. It was likely that he would have Kedar sent to Jydanski, as it was his usual practice to have the prisoner brought to him, not stooping to go to his captive. He felt his power and authority vindicated by his presence at an execution. She shuddered to think of it, asking Konrad why the troops could not be held back to save Kedar.

Konrad shook his head. "Kenrik knows he cannot save Kedar. Elliad would fill Proburg with Chezkovian troops and then it would not be long before he advanced on Reideaux, then Frencolia. We have the Proburg border at Chezkovia practically secure and I am going to ride tonight to the border near Baltic Castle to see if and when Elliad goes in person to Baltic Castle. Kenrik will come with me, and when we are sure Elliad is in the castle, we will secure the exit road from a safe distance . . ." The king looked up in surprise as Jobyna interrupted him.

"Why don't you work it out so that he thinks you are complying with his demands? Surely you could humor him, agree to do what he wants, make him think his advances into Proburg are successful, continue to keep his mind on the hostages instead of on the troops. You could send troops that you could trust that would pretend to be loyal to him—after all, the man is insane! He obviously thinks the hostages are the key to it all. Maybe the

112

gold pieces should be sent; Kenrik should send 2,000 for his brother and sister. Elliad would be exultant to receive such a sign of Kenrik's submission. . . ." Jobyna blushed at her interruption and missed the look that Moritz and Konrad passed between them. She had learned that Moritz could understand the spoken Frenc language, but was unable to speak it himself accurately enough to be understood.

Konrad spoke to Moritz in German. "Yes, we could manipulate our men in such a way that Elliad would still think he is in control. It is about time we worked to outwit him at his own game; how about deceiving the great deceiver!" He switched back to Frenc. "That is a marvelous idea. I am sure we can work that into our plans. Anything, other than surrendering, would be worth trying if we could prevent Kedar's death!" Konrad was speaking now for Jobyna's benefit. "Once Elliad is secure in Baltic Castle, I am going to recommend to Kenrik that he take the majority of his troops and ride to Jydanski. There are plans at foot in the capital which can only be carried out when Elliad has left."

The king sighed and stared out into the darkness of the distant hills. "I will not be here to bury King Kelsey." He took her hand again. "Will you represent me at the ceremony tomorrow?"

Jobyna knew Konrad was trying to give her something else to think about. *This is what he meant when he said he needed my help*, she thought, and she nodded.

He kissed her hand and said casually, "The other matter is that I would like you to write to Elliad, telling him you will exchange places with Luke."

Jobyna drew in a deep breath. Torn in two as to whether or not she could do such a thing, she was surprised to hear Konrad suggest it so indifferently, as though she would be going to visit a friendly neighbor! His tone sounded so final, discounting any thought of discussion.

Konrad's blue eyes searched deep into hers, as he said earnestly, "I am fervently hoping and praying that you will not have to make any such exchange, but we do wish to take the letter . . . in case we have to send it. However, if you exchange places with Luke as Elliad requests, I then plan for your stay in Baltic Castle to be very short."

He faltered, then continued to explain. "We need a diversion, a lure, something that will take this man's mind off the murder of innocent people. We have two plans, and if Kenrik sends the ransom, that will be a third. If Kedar is transferred from Baltic Castle, we will intercept the group and attempt to rescue him. If Elliad does not move to Baltic Castle within the first deadline, we will send him your letter. We hope he will be drawn to his lair by your submission to his demand."

The young king paced away from her, then back again. "I am in a quandary to know whether we should attempt a rescue on Baltic Castle first, or to try and secure Elliad there. . . ." Taking her hand, he looked at Jobyna, and she felt he was measuring her against Elliad's hostages. She hung her head as he spoke again. "We dare not suggest it to Elliad, because we hope to confine him once he moves to the castle, but it is obvious that the exchange with Luke would be more convenient at Baltic Castle. Elliad can then instantly safeguard his 'treasure.' "

Jobyna pulled her hand from his; the thought of being a "lure" made her feel sick. "I am not Elliad's 'treasure,' Konrad!" Her reddened eyes filled with tears. "Please don't say that!" She wished he would tell her that she was his, but he was too preoccupied. Taking a deep breath she said, resignedly, "I will write the letter to Elliad, Konrad. When do you want it?"

"Tonight, before I leave. Give your address as 'Kelsey Castle, Reideaux' and say you expect both Luke and Maia to be released. Tell him that you must see Luke and Maia well clear and free before you will go. That way, he will realize that Baltic Castle would be the best location for such an exchange."

"What if Elliad won't let Maia come?" Jobyna asked.

"He probably won't; in fact, I don't know if he will release Luke when the final moment arrives. I don't think we should expect him to. . . ." He stood closer to her so that he could see her reactions in the deepening dark. Konrad noted the concern on her face and said, "But it will be all right. We will set them free later. Your idea was to get his mind off our forces, and I am sure that . . ."

Konrad stopped as he perceived her disdain, the knowledge in her eye that she was being used as bait. The king, however, did not ask if she wanted to back down. Instead, he instructed, "If—and when—you get in the castle grounds, I want you to detain Elliad in the grounds for as long as you can. Stall him; talk about the hostages, talk to the soldiers or servants. Once you are in the castle, try to keep him downstairs. Say that you are hungry, anything. Maybe he will celebrate and get drunk."

She looked horrified at the thought of being anywhere near the great persecutor again.

"Trust me, Jobyna." He kissed her hand once more, saying, "I care for you more than for anything else on earth. I would not ask you to take this risk if I was not sure of my plan to end his charade once and for all . . . and to save you from him."

He suddenly bowed his head, "If you can't trust me, then trust God to work it out, for if He does not, then it is over for all of us."

Strangely, Jobyna felt reassured by these words by which Konrad acknowledged his own weakness and the fact that they had to trust God. Surely God was strong and powerful enough to trust! But she still wondered just what it was that Konrad was planning. Maybe he had knowledge of secret passages. She did not ask, realizing the truth of the matter. If she did not know, there would be no information for Elliad to pry from her.

Hanging her head in submission, Jobyna felt deflated; her hopes of speaking to Konrad about their betrothal were completely squashed. Konrad's mind was entirely absorbed with the war against Elliad and the planning of a rescue for the hostages. Pandering to her hopeless desire for autonomy, she suddenly wished Konrad were a farmer and not a king; she wished she were a peasant girl and not a princess. Oh, to be far away, in Frencolia, in her secret valley, among the lilac lilies beside the laughing stream!

Noticing the faraway stare in Jobyna's green eyes, Konrad took her arm in his and they walked silently down to the dining room, where some of the guests had already begun to dine. No announcement was made as they entered and the tense, quiet atmosphere made Jobyna fearful. Konrad seated Jobyna beside Brenna. Whispering that he must have urgent discussions with Kenrik and Dorai, Konrad left the room.

After the meal, Jobyna wrote the letter and Konrad came to accompany her to the conference room. It was now late in the evening, but representatives of each kingdom were still gathered. Prince Dorai took Jobyna's hands. "I should have sent you home! It is against my wishes that we bargain like this with a maniac."

"It is because he is a maniac that we are able to bargain. Even if it's worth nothing else, I feel Luke and Maia's lives will be worth it all," she said quietly, handing to her uncle the letter she had written. Reading with a blank expression on his face, Dorai then gave it to Konrad and left the room. Jobyna sensed the emotion he needed to express, but was unable to do so in front of company. She realized again how much her uncle loved her.

Konrad passed Jobyna's letter to Kenrik then stood and addressed the group. "I have outlined briefly my plans regarding taking Landmari, the negotiations in Jydanski, and the securing of Elliad in Baltic Castle. You are asked to mobilize your troops as Kenrik has outlined. The czarevitch will be taking care of the messages that will filter to Elliad's men and also those who will be taken captive by the enemy for the purpose of passing on the false information. Large numbers of loyal troops will be sent to join with those in Chezkovia, swearing their allegiance to the czar. This idea has come to us from the wise lips of Princess Jobyna!" He paused to bow to her and they all applauded quietly, discussing this strategy.

When silence took over again, the king continued, "I say farewell to you all, asking you to pray for us. Pray especially for those men who will need vigilance as they cross sides into the enemy's territory; the game is a treacherous one. I pray we will all meet again and that there will be peace at last." He moved around, shaking hands with those present. Kenrik gave Jobyna's letter back to Konrad and left the room, unable to speak to anyone.

Jobyna followed Konrad out into the courtyard. Moritz and Vincenz walked ahead to fetch their horses. In the darkness she heard men's voices, soldiers being brought into line, and there was the clip-clop of many horses' hooves upon the cobblestones.

Kenrik grasped her hand and kissed her cheek. His voice was strained as he murmured, "Thank you, Princess Jobyna. May your God be with you and help you."

Konrad's voice whispered in her ear, "Elliad will believe your note and come to Baltic Castle. He has to! If he were to stay in Jydanski, it would be impossible to capture him, and Kenrik will not have the opportunity to regain the capital and the palace. Once Elliad is in the castle and occupied with your arrival, Kenrik will, we hope, secure Chezkovia. The troops that are there will be invaluable to him.

"We are sure our plans to enter the castle will be successful, so do not fear, my love. Wild horses will not prevent me from rescuing my princess from the dragon. Do not breathe a word to anyone about our entering Baltic Castle. Kenrik and your uncle are the only ones who know our second plan regarding Baltic Castle. There may be treacherous ears around and we cannot risk failure." His lips brushed her cheek. She turned her face toward his, but he was moving away.

"Konrad!" she called plaintively.

"Yes?" He was back by her side.

Lifting her head toward his ear, she whispered, "I love you; please kiss me." He pulled her toward him and held her. His lips gently touched hers and his hand momentarily caressed her hair, then he stepped a pace back from her as though in great turmoil and pain.

"I must go before I change my mind," he said, but she held his hand tightly.

"Why would you change your mind?" she asked.

"I love you so much, I cannot bear it. I have you now; we are together. But if I go . . ."

An overwhelming sense of how deep his love for her was pulled her back into the reality of their situation. She knew they must not waver. Her voice broke into the thoughts he was expressing.

"Go, please go! I will pray for you every moment!" Jobyna released his hand, thinking of Luke, Maia, Cynara, Kedar, Konrad's parents; the list went on and on.

Backing further away from her, Konrad turned suddenly and mounted the horse brought to him by Vincenz. He rode off into the night with Kenrik, followed by numerous knights, emirs and soldiers.

13

Luke had been transferred to Baltic Castle the second day after his arrival in Chezkovia, hogtied as before and lying cramped and uncomfortable in a carriage. Driven swiftly through the five gates, the carriage came to a halt in the courtyard by the stables. Julian was waiting to welcome this prize prisoner. He cut the ropes from Luke's feet with his sword, then released his arms and hands. Using the sword, the knight pointed the way toward the castle, and Luke, weak from having been tied for so long, began the tedious walk up the many stairs, paths and walkways.

Jobyna had described Baltic Castle to Luke and he remembered her explanation of this long walk. She had told him that each step she took had filled her with dread. He was suddenly thankful that it was he and not his timid sister who was treading this tiresome path. Pushed unceremoniously into a tiny prison cell, Luke viewed a stone-walled room with no windows; he was now incarcerated under the soldier's quarters of Baltic Castle. A stone slab was the only furniture; there was no bed, no rug or pillow, no table or chair, no wash bowl, just a small drain in the corner, a "long drop" into the castle drains which emptied into the Baltic Sea.

For two long, lonely days Luke was confined in these murky, miserable, damp conditions. A plate of food with no utensils was brought to him, but (for the first time in his life) he had no appetite. However, he sipped the cool well water from the pitcher left inside the door. Pacing around the small cell, Luke remembered Jobyna telling him how she had quoted Scripture when imprisoned. Words from the Bible came to his mind, but fears replaced them as he thought about his sister, his uncle and aunt, Frencolia, Maia and . . . Elliad! Prayer seemed oceans away, covered with the stormy waves of turbulent rapids.

"Lord, help me! I can't even pray!" Luke muttered, and this confession made him realize his tremendous weakness in the face of adversity. Words from the crevasses of his memory spoke. He almost heard the sweet sound of his sister's voice, reverberating from the uneven stones of his prison walls. It was a portion of a verse she had read from a volume of the Bible Konrad had sent: "When I am weak, then am I strong" (2 Corinthians 12:10b).

Dropping to his knees, Luke prayed fervently, "God, thank you for being here; I can feel your presence with me, and that is enough." Heartened, he continued talking to God. "Please give me the strength to keep trusting; help me to have faith." Luke realized for the first time in his life that it was one thing to pray for someone else in trouble, but a whole new feeling to pray for oneself when help was far away.

How strong Jobyna's faith must have been to have maintained her through a whole year in captivity, he thought. *I wonder if it is our faith that keeps us, or our God, our very great God, who gives us our faith!* He murmured, "Lord, thank you. Work out your plan,

God, and help me to increase in your strength and faith!"

On the morning of the third day, Julian entered the cell flanked by two soldiers. With his sword extended once more, the knight indicated Luke to follow. The soldiers marched behind.

A bathtub had been placed in one of the soldier's rooms and a fresh change of clothes was set out. Luke ignored the audience on guard and felt some of the tension relieved from his body as he soaked in the warm water. After he had dressed, he was ordered to sit on a chair. Some 20 minutes passed before Julian reentered the room.

"King Luke Chanec of Frencolia," he addressed him in a monotone. His voice was high and raspy as he said, "You are a prisoner belonging to the czar of Chezkovia, a hostage in his Baltic Castle. There is no escape from this fortress. We have other prisoners here and you will be allowed to join them during the daytime. If you make one suspicious move or speak in whispers, you will be thrown back in the cell and left there for the rest of your stay here. Remember this warning; it will not be repeated!"

Luke was escorted to the castle dining hall where an assortment of people—all ages, all sizes—were sitting around, some on chairs and couches, some at the tables; a few children were sitting listlessly on the floor. Ten or 12 soldiers stood along the walls and guards were on duty at the three doors. Julian nodded to the knave and Luke was announced. "King Luke Chanec of Frencolia, hostage of the czar of Chezkovia."

Walking toward the group, Luke wondered who they all were. Strangers stared at him silently; an older man stood, but a face Luke recognized instantly—Maia—was there before the stately prince could speak. She wrapped her arms around his waist, sobbing. He knelt down and she clung to him, unable to speak. With trembling fingertips, Maia gently touched Luke's swollen split lip, his bruised nose, cheek and jaw, but she did not ask how the injuries had been inflicted.

The older man pulled a chair out for Luke and grasped his hand. "I am Prince Gustovas of Proburg." He turned to the lady sitting beside him. "This is my wife, Princess Rhaselle." Luke, with one arm still around Maia, reached for the princess' hand, but she was staring into space, not speaking. Gustovas turned to a young man about 20 years old who had stood to his feet.

"This is my son, Prince Mayer." He waited while the two acknowledged one another. "There are two of my other sons here in the castle—Prince Gustav, my eldest, and Prince Warford—but they have been confined to the dungeons."

At the sound of her sons' names, Princess Rhaselle sobbed noisily into her kerchief. Gustovas walked to two other women sitting on a couch. "This is Gustav's wife, Princess Helena, and Princess Marianne is Warford's wife." He beckoned to his grandchildren and as they came he spoke their names, introducing them one by one to Luke.

"I met your son, Prince . . . er, King Konrad. He had been staying with me in Frencolia before he went to Reideaux." Luke ingested the strange look that Prince Gustovas gave him, and he realized the father would not have heard of Konrad's appointment. Luke looked across at Cynara and Kedar, who sat silently staring at him.

Prince Gustovas moved to introduce them. "Czarevna Cynara and the Grand Duke Kedar, children of Czar Kievik." He spoke the czar's name in undertones.

Luke took Cynara's hand and she stood, but did not curtsy. Her haughty "royal" face and eyes were accusative. "Your country is to blame for all this, Luke Chanec!" Snatching her hand away, she sat, a wooden look captivating her classical features.

Placing his hand on Kedar's shoulder, Luke told the boy,

"Your brother Kenrik was with me in Frencolia before I was brought here, and we had good discussions together." Luke faltered; aware of the soldiers in the room, he remembered Julian's warning that he was not to whisper. "Kenrik is with Konrad and I am sure everything will work out." Luke moved to sit by Gustovas.

Prince Gustovas described to Luke his visit to Jydanski, admitting how much of a fool he was not to have listened to Kenrik. He told Luke he was finding it difficult to come to terms with the actions of this depraved, vindictive man Elliad. He now fully expected to be executed with his family, and they had all resigned themselves to such a fate.

Luke gently reminded the prince how Frencolia had communicated warnings to Proburg, even sending a contract against Elliad which had been ignored. Two soldiers moved closer and stood behind them when Luke carelessly spoke the name "Elliad."

Swiftly changing the subject, Luke pretended he had not seen the soldiers approach. He spoke casually about Frencolia, his cousins and his sister. At the mention of Jobyna's name, Prince Gustovas' eyes lit up. He recounted their meeting at Chezpro Castle over a year ago. Luke would have told him about Konrad's interest in his sister, but one of the soldiers was so close he was sure he could feel the man's breath on the back of his neck, so he turned the conversation to Gustovas' grandchildren, who were all sitting on the floor, listening wide-eyed to their grandfather and Luke conversing in Frenc.

Some of the children spoke broken Frenc, and Luke squatted on the floor among them, exchanging words and attempting to speak in German. They soon broke into laughter at his attempts and Kedar left his sister to join them. The boy was fluent in both languages and joined in the fun of "teaching" King Luke, who was making deliberate mispronunciations to make them laugh.

Luke noted that the soldiers had gone back to stand guard against the walls.

The day dragged by slowly. Maia sat constantly by Luke's side, poking in questions about her mother and father, Jobyna, Elissa, Charles and Doralin. Luke informed Maia that they were all safe in the King's Castle in Frencberg. He privately hoped that it would stay that way.

Speaking once more with Gustovas, Luke informed the prince of King Kelsey's death and Konrad's subsequent appointment as king of Reideaux. When the delighted father interpreted Luke's news for his wife, Luke saw the princess' delicate brown eyes light up. Luke remembered Konrad telling him that his parents (particularly his father) were not proud of him, their fourth son. He expected that now they might change their minds about his worth! He sighed as he thought of Konrad, such a true friend; even if he had not been a prince or a king, Konrad was a great person!

Borrowing one of Princess Helena's slippers, Luke invented the playing of a game called "magic slipper." By folding the lambskin inside itself (the heel inside the toe), and throwing it like a ball at one of the children, the child it landed upon was then the "slave," and as slave of the slipper, it was their turn to throw it at another, until the magic of the touch made the next victim the slave of the slipper. Maia joined in, reluctantly at first, when Luke placed the slipper in her limp hands. Soon the room was filled with screaming, running children trying to keep away from the "dangerous" slipper. When their cheeks were red from the exertion, Luke returned the slipper to the princess, who had been watching the children with an interested light in her eyes.

Helena watched as the young king planted himself down in the middle of the floor, gathering the youngsters around him. Maia rested her elbow on his knee and Irma climbed on his shoulders. He told them stories as his father had done when

Luke had been a child. The king of Frencolia became an elephant, a camel and a horse, giving the smaller children rides around the room until he collapsed in exhaustion and laughter when Maia took a turn, sitting sideways on his back. Returning to the less stressful pastime of storytelling, the children became quiet as he told them about the shepherd-boy David who killed the lion, the bear and the giant, and then became king over Israel.

"The Gospel Book says that God appoints kings and princes." Luke had uttered these words without really considering their effect in such company. He dared not look up at Prince Gustovas or Czarevna Cynara. Instead he began telling the story of Moses and he encouraged Maia to act out the part of Miriam with the baby in the bulrushes. When one of the small children entered into the story and screamed, "Look out! Hide the baby! The soldiers are coming!" Luke completed the story quickly and began to relate another, choosing to describe Jesus' first visit to the temple in Jerusalem when he was a boy of 12.

Julian strode into the room to see the children all sitting on the floor, gathered around Luke. When the knight directed servants to bring the evening meal, the children all stood, sullen-faced, waiting fearfully. That they expected to be poisoned was obvious to Luke. However, hunger was paramount and to Luke food had never tasted so good! There were no utensils and they all helped themselves from the same bowls, eating with their fingers. A variety of bread—loaves and rolls—was available and Luke, remembering his home life at the manor house in Chanoine, broke a bread roll and wiped his fingers on the inside.

Kedar, who was keeping close to his new friend's side, laughed and followed Luke's actions, wiping his mouth with a piece of bread. "It's better than my sleeve!" he chuckled.

The moment the meal was complete, they were escorted, one

by one, from the dining room. Maia clung to Luke when the soldiers called her name together with Cynara's, and Luke kissed his cousin's cheeks, pushing her away saying, "Tomorrow, Maia. I'll see you tomorrow."

Back in the small cell, Luke hoped he would be allowed to be with them the next day; the time with Maia and the children had lifted his spirits and he knew they had been encouraged.

The next morning, Luke was escorted once more to the dining hall, this time for the light breakfast provided there. Eight children crowded around him instantly, but Luke was concerned when he could not see Maia. He drank some orange juice with his eyes toward the entrance doors. Relief flooded his face when she entered the room with a happy expression lighting her fair features. In her arms she carried a large, leather-bound Gospel Book.

"This is the one you sent to Jobyna when she was a prisoner here. Remember, Luke?" Maia prompted.

Luke took hold of the book with tenderness.

Maia explained. "The servant Boey, who is looking after Cynara and me, brought it to our room last night. She said it was in the room where Jobyna stayed, with Doctor Sleven and his wife. I asked that Julian man this morning if I could bring it here and when he took it away, I thought I wouldn't see it again. Then he came back and gave it to Boey and said I could bring it with me."

Luke turned the Book to the inside of the back cover, noting the missing pages. He well remembered the time he sent the Book to his sister. Yes, she had been a prisoner here, too. In her loneliness, the Gospel Book had been a wonderful comfort. Doctor Sleven and Brenna had also read from it.

The routine at Baltic Castle was the same each day, but since King Luke Chanec's arrival an entirely different atmosphere filled the dining hall chamber. Luke's words, "While there is life, there is hope, and if we dwell on hope, we will be free from fear," had encouraged them to stop dwelling upon being executed.

Cynara's angry disposition changed noticeably and she looked forward to listening to Luke's pleasant, commanding voice, reading and telling stories to the children. Mayer and Prince Gustovas joined in some of the games and together they thought up new ideas to occupy the time. The Proburg monarch racked his memory to drag forgotten boyhood games from years well gone. Princess Rhaselle switched into the reality of the dining room space and viewed the situation with a new attitude.

Luke told Gustovas of Konrad's proposal to his sister; he said that Jobyna had accepted their son's offer of marriage. Details of the betrothal and announcement date were yet to be decided. Princess Rhaselle was greatly cheered to think of Jobyna as her daughter-in-law. Luke saw her smile at her husband as she told him in her lilting German tongue that they had come together without his help! Luke then remembered Gustovas' offer to "buy" his sister from Elliad so that he could give her to his fourth son. Luke had not told Jobyna about this and he wondered if Konrad knew of such bargaining! He sighed. How good it was to think of his sister as being safe in King's Castle in Frencberg!

Kedar questioned Luke persistently about the deeper meaning of the words in the Gospel Book. The smaller children became restless when he asked questions, but the older ones listened attentively. Luke ignored the adults and the soldiers and told Kedar about the God of the Gospel Book, reading verses when Kedar asked another question.

One day Kedar commanded Luke, "Show me how to believe in this God of the Gospel Book! I want to know Him too, the same way as you know Him!" Luke gave his whole time to Kedar that afternoon, explaining the gospel message and praying with the lad. They were both oblivious to the listening ears around them.

"Jesus Christ is God's Son. He gave His life that we may believe and have eternal life with God in heaven. By placing faith in God's Son, we become blameless before God, forgiven by Jesus through His sacrificial death." Luke tried to explain in simple terms; then he read verses from the Book.

"That whosoever believeth in him should not perish, but have eternal life. For God so loved the world, that he gave his only begotten Son, that whosoever believeth in him should not perish, but have everlasting life. For God sent not his Son into the world to condemn the world; but that the world through him might be saved" (John 3:15–17).

Kedar fervently commanded that Luke pray with him and in turn, teach him how to pray to God. The boy, verbalizing a faltering prayer in Frenc, asked God to save his soul and take him to heaven when he died. Two soldiers, who had moved closer as the voices of the praying pair dropped lower, shifted uncomfortably from foot to foot. Both these burly men knew the czar's orders for this child, having been received that very morning.

Kedar's whole countenance changed in the joy of his new found faith. Questions came readily and Kedar drank in all of Luke's answers from the book. Before the evening meal, they prayed together once more.

For several days after this, Kedar was missing from the dining hall and no one knew where he was. Luke cautiously questioned one of the soldiers who did not seem so formidable, but he was told by the man, in no uncertain terms, that he was not to speak to the guards or they would both be imprisoned! As Kedar's absence continued, Cynara was fearful and withdrawn.

Twelve days had passed since Luke arrived at Baltic Castle when the dining hall door was flung open and the announcement made, "Princess Zandra and Princess Yvette of Danzerg, captives of the czar of Chezkovia." Luke and the children solemnly welcomed them and began introductions. The two girls stopped sobbing and calmed down. Zandra was almost Maia's age, 10, and Yvette was seven. Luke met Prince Gustovas' and Mayer's eyes; the older man had a stricken look on his face, the younger prince shook his head in amazement.

The next day, the announcement was:

"Crown Prince Haroun of Bavarest, captive of the czar of Chezkovia."

Luke noted the prince was bruised and limping. He was perhaps 22 years old. Mayer and Gustovas joined Luke to listen to Haroun describe his abduction. He told them he was over-powered and drugged somehow. At the beginning, he thought he was being transported in some kind of box, like a coffin. Later he was transferred to a carriage. Every time he had revived, he fought his captors in spite of his bonds. They had further restrained him and he had been beaten. No, he had not met the czar. On arrival at Baltic Castle, he spent three nights in a dungeon without food. Prince Haroun told Luke he was warned that if he made one move, put one foot in the wrong direction, he would be incarcerated in the cell again.

Luke told the prince that they had all been given the same warnings. There was no escape and they must accept their captivity until some negotiations were made or help arrived. The freedom of the dining room must be preferable to imprisonment in a small cell! Prince Haroun could not understand Luke's acceptance of the situation and he felt strangely warmed and calmed to hear and watch this Frencolian king read to the children and play with them.

"The Grand Duke Louis of Strasland, captive of the czar of Chezkovia."

A 12-year-old boy, standing tall and proud, entered the dining hall. He displayed an attitude of dislike when introduced and sat apart from the other royal prisoners, glancing furtively around the room at the soldiers and guards, fidgeting and fuming. Luke tried to befriend him and told him to accept the captivity; there was no escape as yet. To fight the situation was to hurt himself. Louis told Luke in no uncertain terms to mind his own business and went off to sit on his own.

He inched his way nearer the door, squatting on the floor, watching the children play. The slipper landed near him and he snatched it up quickly, throwing it at one of the guards. Caught completely unaware, the soldier raised his hand to stop the slipper in flight, and Louis raced through the door, followed swiftly by three or four soldiers. Louis did not come to the dining hall again, and the children were banned from playing "poisonous, magic slipper." It was a sober warning that Julian had meant what he had dictated.

Kedar returned to the room the next day. His heavily bandaged arm and wrist were strapped to his chest. His thinner face was drawn and dark rings circled his eyes. Cynara rushed to him, but he shook his head and held his free hand out, firmly indicating that she keep a distance away.

"You must not ask questions! I am only allowed to be with you if we do not speak about it!" Kedar cried to his sister before moving over to Luke, who was eating breakfast.

"Read to me, Luke. From the Book!" Kedar commanded, flopping back on the couch, completely exhausted. A soldier who had closely escorted Kedar stood behind the couch, watching and listening. The children thought Kedar had suffered an accident, and not one of the adults dared to imagine what else could have taken place.

Two nights later, after the evening meal, Cynara and Kedar were checked out of the dining hall first. They had been gone for over five minutes and not another prisoner had been called to leave. Luke wondered at the change. Cynara usually went with Maia, and Kedar with Gustav Junior. Since the boy had sustained his unspeakable injury, he had been closely guarded all day and escorted at nights to sleep in a room on his own.

Luke thought of Elliad and his charade as the czar; maybe the so-called czar planned to make an entrance and did not want a scene from his "daughter" or "son." An announcement confirming Luke's mental prediction came to his ears, and all in the room stood to their feet in shocked silence.

"His Imperial Highness, Czar Kievik of the Czardom of Chezkovia."

Elliad entered the room, dressed in glittering robes with the incredible crown of the czardom on his colored hair.

Prince Gustovas hissed at his grandchildren, telling them to bow and curtsy as the czar came past.

Mayer, from the side of his mouth, said quietly to Luke, "Yes, we had better grovel, or . . ." He did not dare complete the statement as he saw Elliad moving closer. Julian introduced the captives, one by one. When he finished, Elliad commanded Julian to continue escorting the "guests" out of the room; one by one they were called out as usual.

Elliad stood near Luke, with a knight on either side. The despot gloated, loud enough for all in the room to hear (his eyes were upon those of Prince Gustovas'): "You are to be released tomorrow, Luke Chanec. Your sister requests that she take your place." He turned to Luke who had stepped toward the pretend czar. The two knights moved forward to each grasp a struggling arm as Elliad continued, "I wouldn't look at the czar like that! Your sister would prefer Frencolia to receive you back in one piece! This is your farewell, Luke Chanec, and remember, it is Jobyna's idea that she exchange places with you. It seems she prefers the company in Chezkovia to that in Frencolia . . . or even, perhaps, to the king of Reideaux?"

Later, Luke was thankful that the two soldiers had firmly restrained him (he had bruises to prove it), for he was certain he would have punched Elliad's face if his arms had been free! At the time he had felt that to lash out at the sneering face would have made a whipping well worth it!

As he was escorted to his cell for the night, Luke tried to quell his fears for his sister. His angry thoughts growled, "I won't allow her to do this! She will make such an exchange over my dead body!"

14

Elliad, the keeper of Baltic Castle, sat in his office, celebrating. The letter from Jobyna lay in front of him and he gloated over it with a tremendous sense of victory. He was not bothered by her lack of warmth; to him, it just served to make her all the more desirable. *What was a victory worth*, he thought, *if there were not a battle?* It was strange, his twisted mind ran, how the gaining back of his "treasure" meant more than all the riches in Chezkovia. He had power and wealth and yet it had not brought him the peace of mind or the security he had expected. There was always more to strive for, more riches to attain, new borders to cross, people to use and crush in his path toward supremacy. But even in becoming "imperial," he found he coveted more. Elliad perused her flowery handwriting again.

Dear John:
I remember another time you gave me a choice and I

showed you the way to the treasures of Frencolia. There is far more at stake today than gold and jewels. One can dispense with a necklace or even a crown, but human lives are irreplaceable.

Therefore, I plead with you for the lives of all your captives. With all my heart, I beg you to reconsider and accept the ransoms that have been sent, as you requested.

I will make the exchange if you release my brother Luke and my cousin Maia. I must see for myself that Luke and Maia are free from all likelihood of recapture before I will come.
(signed)
Jobyna Chanec, in care of Kelsey Castle, Reideaux.

His reply letter read,

To Jobyna Chanec:
The exchange will be made on Friday at noon. I will release your brother Luke and cousin Maia. You are to be on the road outside Baltic Castle on your own. Your brother will ride a horse in front of a carriage from the gate when you, alone, are in close view. Maia will be in the carriage. There will be no further bargaining.
(signed)
The Czar

Elliad turned to the other documents on his desk. Kenrik had agreed to his demands, stating that troops were returning to the "czar's control." The ransom of 2,000 gold pieces was enclosed, in payment for the lives of Kedar and Cynara. The czarevitch begged "the czar" to spare the life of his brother, Kedar.

The great deceiver had been successfully deceived himself and believed numerous false reports that Proburg was still in his control. Some of Brian's chief men had switched sides and swiftly conveyed false reports to Elliad's men across the Proburg border—although a few true reports seeped through that Brian was having to remain in siege to maintain the Landmari Castle.

Elliad was also pleased that Danzerg, Bavarest and Strasland had agreed to his demands on the counter-mandates. Two countries had stated they would pay the 1,000 gold pieces for each prisoner upon their release. Bavarest had sent 500 gold pieces; the balance, they said, would exchange hands upon Crown Prince Haroun's release. All of this success in the demands of his counter-mandates caused Elliad to feel confident enough to make the journey himself to Baltic Castle and be there when Jobyna arrived. He intended to threaten Kenrik into surrendering himself, using Kedar and Cynara, but the impostor was still considering the details. So far, all was working out for his good, or so he thought. He was not certain whether he would release any or all of the prisoners; he felt his security was in the possession of his hostages. Unable to be trusted himself, he could not bring himself to accept that the kingdoms in question would not move in war against him if he turned his prisoners over to them. He had offered their lives for the ransom and so far, their lives would carry on. However, Elliad decided, he would be the keeper of those lives!

Oblivious to the military changes occurring both in Proburg and Jydanski, the keeper of Baltic Castle was not aware that he, in fact, was now a prisoner in his own fortress. He placed so much value upon his possession of the royal prisoners that he believed all around would bow totally to his demands. The keeper was now also being kept without knowing it!

Konrad, with his men hidden strategically along the roadside to Baltic Castle, had considered attacking the company of soldiers when they passed by late in the afternoon; only 30 men were counted. Against Moritz's will, Konrad held the men back.

Within 15 minutes, a larger group of over 2,000 knights and soldiers rode by with a vehicle recognized to be Czar Kievik's imperial carriage in their midst. This is what they had been waiting for!

Again Moritz would have attacked, but Konrad warned him that they were grossly outnumbered and even if Elliad were killed, this would not save the prisoners in Baltic Castle. If Elliad did not arrive at the castle as planned, his men would likely panic and massacre the captives. Konrad prayed he was making the right decision. Prince Dorai had warned him of Elliad's craft with the sword, that it could take several men of great skill to take him. If they had attacked and Elliad managed to gain the safety of Baltic Castle, there was no knowing what the enraged maniac would do next! No, they must have patience to hold back and follow through with their carefully laid plans.

When the czar's carriage had entered the gates to Baltic Castle, over three-quarters of the cavalcade turned back, returning along Baltic Road. Konrad felt like giving a loud cheer. He met Moritz' eyes and knew he now had his friend's approval. Moritz had felt sure they would have had the whole 2,000 to contend with when they gained access to the castle.

When the returning company was out of sight, Konrad and his men retraced their movements to rendezvous with their hidden troops. Kenrik was with them, having been physically restrained from attempting a suicidal attempt on Elliad's life. Konrad motioned the troops to take up their unseen positions, ready to capture anyone leaving the gates of Baltic Castle. The young king issued the command that anyone now moving on Baltic Road was to be taken prisoner. The capture was to be made out of view of the castle. Konrad had seen the letter from Elliad to Jobyna and knew there would be no more negotiations on that matter. Elliad expected Jobyna to turn up at noon tomorrow. She would now be traveling to Walden Castle in

Proburg, to be on hand the following day to meet the noon deadline of the exchange. Konrad had reluctantly dispatched the letter from Elliad to Prince Dorai, together with a note from himself. Messengers brought word that Elliad's troops returning from Baltic Castle had divided; half had crossed the border into Proburg and the other half rode to Jydanski. Again, this was a victory which proved that Elliad believed he was in control of Proburg. Both groups would be apprehended within hours.

Czarevitch Kenrik rode with Moritz, Doctor Sleven, and his Chezkovian troops to the Jydanski capital where they were met by several thousand men—emirs, constables, captains and sol-diers—all part of the Chezkovian cavalry. When Kenrik heard their findings, brought to him by a man called Valerian who, unknown to Elliad, had recently escaped from the palace dun-geons, the elder son of the czar began to feel he was being vindicated. The supposed body of Elliad John Pruwitt had been dug up from its crude grave; there was difficulty in ascertaining whether or not the remains belonged to the said traitor. The second difficulty would be to find out what had happened to Czar Kievik. Many of the emirs believed he was still alive and a prisoner somewhere in the palace.

The rest of the evening was spent in establishing to the Chezkovian emirs, who held leadership in the czardom, that the body under examination was not Elliad's. The testimony of Doctor Sleven, who had stitched Elliad's severe battle wounds just over a year ago, was conclusive; there were no such injuries in the decomposing remains. The body buried as Elliad proved to be that of the czar's personal servant, Nikolo, dressed in a green and gold Frencolian knight's uniform. Other bodies buried in the past four months were exhumed without the discovery of Elliad's or Czar Kievik's body.

Kenrik thought of his stepmother, Czarina Terese. The czarevitch argued that she must know exactly what had happened to his father—she was his wife! He commanded that she be found and brought for questioning. A message arrived that Terese was under heavy guard in her own apartment at the palace, a prisoner herself at the orders of the so-called czar!

A number of impressive documents were presented and a large group of the cavalry, led by 25 emirs, finally gained permission for Terese's release from the palace.

Many of Elliad's men, hoping to save themselves from capture and interrogation, fled from the palace at the appearance of the emirs with the official documents. Confusion reigned freely now, but Terese herself was quite composed. She had been expecting Elliad to end her life and each hour had been filled with fearful fretting.

Midnight had struck when the czarina was conveyed in a carriage to the Jydanski Cavalry Cheka Hall where Kenrik waited impatiently. Upon entering the Comitia Chamber, her face showed great relief when her eyes beheld Kenrik.

"Kenrik, my son!" Terese would have rushed to him but was restrained by Sleven and his nephew Moritz. She shrugged off the doctor and Konrad's bodyguard, trying to push Moritz away from her, but Kenrik ordered that they restrain his faithless stepmother.

"Do not pretend, Terese!" Kenrik would have said much more, but he desperately wanted to know about his father. He demanded, "What did Elliad do with my father, Czar Kievik?"

Sensing that the farce was over, Terese tried hard to work out how much she should say, who she could blame to save her own skin. Her silence was too much for Kenrik.

"Woman, do we have to get this out of you in other ways?" In his anger, he pulled his sword from its sheath.

"Mercy, Kenrik!" she cried, falling to her knees.

The czarevitch was beside her in an instant, trying to drag her to her feet, waving his sword.

"What mercy has been shown to the czar?" His saliva splattered her upturned face. Any previous self-control had now vanished. The czarevitch yelled, "What mercy was shown to the czar's son when he was thrown in prison and flogged?"

Kenrik's voice became hoarse as he screamed at her, "What mercy is being shown to the czar's children incarcerated in the fortress of a madman? Don't tell me you did not know that your dear stepchildren are waiting to be further carved up to satisfy your beloved's depraved campaign for power!"

Kenrik's men grappled with him, preventing him from striking and killing her there and then.

Moritz wrestled the czarevitch's sword from his hand. "Your Highness, we must find out where your father is! Let me deal with her."

Kenrik's shoulders drooped and he walked to a chair. Sitting down heavily, he put his head between his knees. Massaging the back of his neck, he tried to shake off his overpowering fury, to quench the consuming desperation he had to know about his father's fate.

Moritz walked to Terese who had fallen to the floor, in a heap of very realistic sobs. Taking her by both hands, he pulled the czarina to her feet, leading her to a bench where he drew her to sit beside him. The emirs came closer, forming a semicircle around the two. Sleven and the others stood by Kenrik.

Moritz quietly commanded Terese to tell them what she knew—the truth. "Elliad the pretender is our prisoner in Baltic Castle," Moritz informed Terese, watching her flinch at the sound of Elliad's name. "It is over, Terese. You must help us now, by telling us the truth about Czar Kievik!"

Terese, relieved to know that the pretend czar would not be returning to finish her off, blamed Elliad completely. She said that she had only accommodated him because he had threatened to kill the czar's children. Kenrik, knowing this to be a lie, would have rushed over to challenge her, but again was restrained.

Moritz asked Terese to explain just what Elliad had done to the czar, and in a voice barely audible, Terese answered, "He poisoned him!" Kenrik did not hear her reply, and moved closer, two Chezkovian emirs supporting him on either side.

"Who then was buried as Elliad John Pruwitt?" Moritz asked.

"The servant Nikolo, who tasted the wine first." Terese's voice was barely a whisper. All emotion was gone as quickly as it had been produced, now replaced by a strange breathlessness between each statement. "It was a slow-working poison."

A gasp came from Kenrik, then a deathly silence reigned as Moritz waited for her to speak again.

The czarina's voice was a faint rasp. "The czar died two days later."

The emirs turned to help hold Kenrik, who ground his teeth and fought them speechlessly, overcome with anger and sorrow. Somehow he had hoped his father was still alive. He moaned incoherently and surrendered himself to be held.

"Where did you put his body, Terese?" Moritz had no doubts as to this woman's involvement in this murder. He controlled his tone and struggled successfully to keep his deep voice soft and even.

"I did not see my husband. . . . Elliad ordered him to be buried in his stead outside the city wall, where criminals are buried."

The czarina's voice suddenly grew to the pitch of a wail. "He is my husband, and I would not have him buried like a common criminal!" She rocked back and forward on the bench, whispering suddenly, "But I was so afraid!" The room was quiet once more.

Moritz repeated his question. "Where, Terese?"

"I paid some of Elliad's men to switch the bodies and they said . . ." She became breathless. "They said it made no difference because . . . they were both dead."

"Where? Tell us where, Terese," Moritz saw a spaced out look in her eyes.

"I ordered two of the czar's servants to take the body to the bottom dungeons of the palace and embalm it. I thought no one would look there." She suddenly switched back into reality. "I hoped one day he could be laid to rest in the manner of a czar." She pulled herself to a regal sitting position, repeating, "He is my husband, the czar of Chezkovia, and I could not allow him to be buried like a common criminal."

Even as Terese completed these statements the emirs were moving away from her. She yelled at them, "It was I who saved Valerian from being killed. Elliad would have murdered him too! My servants helped him escape. . . ." Her voice wound down to a whisper. "Oh, where is Valerian? Even he has forsaken me."

Moritz moved to Kenrik's side. He placed his hand on the motionless czarevitch's shoulder. "Go with them to the palace and take care of your father."

Moritz noted that the Chezkovians were escorting Terese from the chamber, and he pushed Kenrik's sword back into its sheath. "The Cheka Council will, I trust, take care of Terese. You must be grateful that she had a part in preserving your father's body from a shameful grave. You must go with the emirs and take care of the czar."

"Come with me, Moritz." Kenrik had treated Konrad's friend as a joke in the past. Now the situation had changed dramatically, and he appreciated Moritz's calm, collected ability to handle the tragic situation.

Over an hour passed before the Chezkovian cavalry gained control of the palace and were able to enter the deepest dungeons to search for the body of Czar Kievik. The keeper of the prison was hesitant to give the emirs the keys. Only when they threatened his life did he submit. When challenged as to his knowledge of the czar's body in the dungeon depths, he said there was no such body, Czar Kievik was still alive. Upon further questioning by Moritz, the keeper remembered some of the czar's servants taking a "prisoner" to the lowest dungeons and for a fee (which proved to be considerable) he had surrendered a duplicate key to them. The prisoner had been unconscious, he thought.

Czar Kievik's body was laid out on a slab in a crude dungeon cell. Three elderly servants were taking turns watching over the body at the command of two of the czar's higher ranking servants—commissioned to do so, they said, by Czarina Terese.

The door was unlocked. Squeaking loudly on its hinges, it swung open unwillingly. Moritz stood back for Kenrik to enter. Four emirs followed the czarevitch, each carrying a cresset, which lit the small chamber with brilliance. Doctor Sleven stood with Moritz. Before retiring, Sleven had been the doctor of the royal family, and could identify Czar Kievik if a witness was needed besides Kenrik.

A lone candle burned on the floor by the slab, its light now unnecessary due to the cressets that the emirs placed around the chamber. Sickly odors from embalming spices, oils and herbs permeated the room.

Kenrik stepped closer. He could see the outline of his father's profile lit up by the flares. Numbness overtook him and he stood frozen to the spot. There would be no need for further identification; he was looking upon his father, anyone could see that.

The emirs moved nearer, staring at the form, waiting. Kenrik had not prepared himself for this moment. In his heart and mind he had hoped. . . .

Thoughts of his mother's death, three years ago, filled his mind. The tears unable to be shed for her began to run from his blurry eyes, down his cheeks, into his beard.

Finding himself kneeling beside the slab, the czarevitch placed a trembling hand toward the cold brow, pulling it away abruptly as his fingertips contacted the rock-hardness of the skin. He sobbed uncontrollably. All thoughts—of who he was, of where he was, of Chezkovia, of Elliad—were forgotten in these moments of lonely grief. He was a son who had lost his father.

Remembering Jobyna's words, he cried unrestrainedly, thinking of her soft voice: "We each only have one flesh and blood father. Elliad has taken mine away; I pray he has not taken your father from you."

Moritz stood at the door with Sleven, behind the emirs. All were like statues in a cemetery, waiting for a sign to turn them back into real flesh and blood creatures. The hours of the early morning were more than three, but time did not exist for these statues.

Kenrik stopped sobbing suddenly. His mind focused on the way his father had died, and who was responsible for his murder. He sniffed deeply and rubbed his cheeks, then his eyes, with the backs of his hands. Moving his hands to the back of his head, his deep-seated anger was giving him pains which seemed to shoot down his neck. He rubbed the back of his head and neck. Turning to the emirs, Kenrik stood unsteadily and commanded, "You will take my father to the Oval Crown Room. I have another matter to take care of."

Coming alive once more, the emirs tried to detain Kenrik by reminding him of his responsibility to the throne. "You are now the czar of Chezkovia! You must stay in Jydanski and take care of the crown!"

"There is no crown in Jydanski! I must avenge my father's death and retrieve the stolen crown from the traitor's head! Every person who worked for the Frencolian traitor must be exterminated!" He met Moritz's eyes, and his own were still blurred with tears of sorrow as he said, determinedly, "We will ride now! I will go with Konrad at noon!"

15

The reply from Elliad had arrived early in the morning at Kelsey Castle. When Prince Dorai reluctantly took it to Jobyna for her to read, her mind was filled with doubts and fears. She could not believe she was so important to Elliad that he would release both Luke and Maia. Her Uncle Dorai had read the communication with much hatred on his face. He had no trust, no faith in such a bargain, and he was worried sick about Konrad's plan. That his niece should become the captive of Elliad once more filled him with fear and pain. He wished there had been a different way to lure Elliad to Baltic Castle, but if she did not follow through now and go, he knew it would surely mean the loss of Luke and Maia and possibly the lives of other prisoners. In his deep, relentless anxiety, Dorai longed, for the first time, that he could pray like Luke.

Prince Dorai did not show Jobyna the communication from Konrad, but determined to tell her only the things Konrad had asked of him, just before she parted from him to go to Baltic Castle. The letter had read:

Prince Dorai:

I have sent soldiers to accompany you and Princess Jobyna to Walden Castle today. Further instructions will be waiting there. Proburg is now securely in the hands of those loyal to my father. Elliad's men who were holding Landmari Castle have been dealt with in a permanent manner. Brian did not escape the sword. All men of questionable nature have been detained for interrogation. This great victory must draw our hearts to thank God.

Do not tell Jobyna about the taking of the Landmari Castle. We are sure Elliad will not know about his loss of the Proburg throne as no one has been allowed to cross from Proburg to Chezkovia unless we are sure of their loyalty. We are still conveying false information to some of Elliad's men, and hopefully this has reached him and assured him of his preeminence. It will be better for Jobyna when she is questioned by Elliad if he still believes his positions are secure. Jobyna must be told "Konrad is fighting for Landmari and that casualties are heavy." This she can tell Elliad, and truthfully say she does not know any more.

Czarevitch Kenrik and Doctor Sleven will ride to Jydanski as soon as Elliad is secure in Baltic Castle.

I reviewed our task with Doctor Sleven, who knows Baltic Castle's every detail from the inside. I find it challenging, but conquerable. We will begin preparations immediately after sunrise. Pray with us that we will not be thwarted by the weather or the enemy. We will seek to take Elliad first as we feel sure that his men will surrender once we have captured their leader.

(Signed)
My kindest regards, Konrad.

Jobyna had spent the past days with Brenna and the women servants at Kelsey Castle making white and cream tassels and sewing them on the sleeves of the Frencolian and Chezkovian soldiers' uniforms. Fabric was cut into ribbons long enough to tie around the upper part of a man's arm. Konrad had commanded that the tassel be worn as identification to show which men belonged to which side. Even in Proburg, some of the men had been fighting for Elliad, who they believed to be the czar of Chezkovia. Such a confused state of affairs meant that soldiers were changing loyalties as they learned the truth! There was no telling which way a man in the red and white Chezkovian uniform would go. The Frencolian uniforms in Elliad's possession meant trouble for those loyal to Frencolia. Many men were eager to attach the identification band when they learned which side was winning. The announcement of the discovery of Czar Kievik's body brought the greater section of the Chezkovian cavalry in line, loyal to Kenrik.

Elliad's men, escaping in the Chezkovian uniforms, striving to go to Baltic Castle for refuge with their leader, were apprehended along the way. Those who made it to Baltic Road were killed or captured. Prisoners were sent back to Jydanski for questioning. In the 24 hours after Elliad arrived at Baltic Castle, the highest toll of casualties was taken.

Elliad never found out that Landmari Castle had been regained by Proburg troops, that the Proburg border now was completely sealed off. The Bavarest border was also well secured and there was no escape west or south from Chezkovia.

Jobyna left after dawn from Walden Castle in Proburg, heading toward the northeast border and Baltic Castle. A company of 300 Frencolian soldiers rode with her, the same number as the day before, and they arrived at the border two hours before noon. Just two miles of road lay ahead before Baltic Castle would be in view. Konrad had mapped out the route for Prince Dorai to take with Jobyna and the way had been carefully cleared of all troops.

Jobyna was surprised she had not seen Konrad and asked Prince Dorai, "Isn't Konrad supposed to be here?" Her voice was filled with fear. The horse she rode was unfamiliar, and she was sure he sensed her feelings of trepidation. Brownlea had been brought to the stables at Kelsey Castle, but Jobyna refused to ride him any further for fear of losing him. She determined she would ride Brownlea when she journeyed back to Frencolia.

"Konrad has to take care of his men. Remember, I told you there have been many casualties in Proburg. Konrad fights for his father's throne." Dorai's doubts were beginning to show in his voice.

"Is Konrad back in Proburg? I thought Konrad had a plan, Uncle!" Jobyna was disturbed; she could sense her uncle's unspoken fears.

"My dear Jobyna, it is better you do not know of any plans. Konrad wants you to be able to answer any questions Elliad asks truthfully."

Jobyna and her uncle rode the rest of the way in silence. The Frencolian soldiers stayed behind when the formidable Baltic Castle loomed ahead of them. The sun was directly overhead and Jobyna felt hot and faint. Her cloak hood shaded the sun from her eyes, but the thick wool felt unbearable. Several hundred yards from the gate they waited. She pulled the cloak off, rolled it up and handed it to her uncle. They could see movements of guards in the battlements and on the towers. Prince Dorai drew his horse close to Jobyna and they kissed one another, not speaking. The huge gates were opening and the grinding noise of chains could be heard, indicating the raising of a portcullis.

Jobyna rode the horse, walking him as slowly as she could, closer, closer. She could see horses in the barbican. Nearer and nearer she drew, her heart in her mouth as her eyes searched for Luke. The horses were moving out slowly and she could see a carriage behind the four animals. She reined her horse to a standstill. Luke sat on one of the horses close to the carriage. Jobyna could now see that her brother was gagged; a thin piece of leather around his face was visible. His hands were behind his back, and she guessed they were bound. When she saw the carriage moving away from the gate, she urged her horse on. Her brother was shaking his head furiously at her.

Jobyna had not expected him to agree with this exchange. Ignoring his negative reaction and his indecipherable grunts, she drew alongside him. Luke tried to push her horse away by kicking his foot at him. Peering up into the barbican, Jobyna felt relieved that there was no one hiding there.

"Luke, is Maia in the carriage?" Jobyna asked. Reaching over, she stretched her hand out, hoping to release his gag. He was still shaking his head, pulling away.

The sound of her voice was a cue; it brought an instant response from the carriage. The doors flew open and four soldiers clambered out. Aware now of trickery, she urged her horse forward a few paces so she might slap Luke's horse on the backside.

Jobyna screamed at the creatures, "Yah! Yah! Go! Go!" She pulled hard on her horse's reins, making him shy and whinny. Try as she might, she could not pull the horse around; the soldiers, all four, prevented her. The red and white uniforms were grabbing at the reins, at her horse's bridle and at her. The commotion urged the four terrified horses to bolt, and at the same time, Prince Dorai and the Frencolian company began to gallop toward them.

Elliad's soldiers abandoned the escaping horses and carriage. They rushed back to the gates, two of them dragging Jobyna. The other two pushed the gates closed, securing the heavy bars. The portcullis crashed to the ground and Jobyna found herself pulled through the second gates.

Prince Dorai put his hand up, halting the company when he saw the gates closing. Soldiers on the battlements had crossbows at the ready and he did not want to risk his men by going within range. He was amazed they had not fired on Luke.

The horses drawing the carriage had left the road and were hurtling across the uneven ground, toward the cliff edge. Soldiers left Dorai's company, hoping to head them off, but this served only to urge them on. Luke's eyes grew wider as he realized where they were heading. The horses were panic stricken but he knew it was possible for them to pull away before reaching the cliff edge. Horses had a strong sense of danger, but Luke was worried about the two creatures behind that could not see where they were going. He imagined them rushing straight over the cliffs, taking him and the carriage.

"Not me," Luke thought as he leaned forward, swinging his leg over the back of the horse, contorting his body with all his might. His hands behind his back, he landed heavily, winding himself, rolling helplessly down the incline.

Just in the nick of time, the two leading horses turned from their head-on course toward the cliff edge, swinging the carriage around at a dangerous pace, almost causing it to roll. One of the Frencolian soldiers arrived there. Leaping on one of the front horses, the man grabbed the reins and coaxed the horses to a standstill.

Prince Dorai flung himself off his horse, helping Luke up from the ground. Mattheus was there as fast, cutting the ropes and the gag, checking to see that his king was not badly hurt. Luke doubled up, trying to regain his wind. He coughed and spluttered and wheezed. Mattheus rubbed his back, slapping it when

Luke coughed.

Prince Dorai looked over to the carriage. Soldiers had the doors open and it appeared to be empty.

"Maia?" Dorai's voice betrayed his fears.

Luke sat heavily on the ground, rubbing the back of his neck. He panted, "The . . . swine . . . kept her." He closed his eyes, still gasping for air. "Why . . . Jobyna?"

Commanding the knights to bring the company back to order, Prince Dorai sat on the tussocky grass beside his nephew. He waited a few moments, trying to think where to begin. So much had happened that Luke did not know about. Prince Dorai kept talking while Luke recovered. When he spoke of the exchange, Luke asked the same questions and made the same statements Dorai himself had used in arguing with Konrad.

"War is not for women! Why should Jobyna be brought in to bargain with our enemy?" Luke spoke with anger and deep hurt in his shaky voice.

Prince Dorai offered the answers Konrad had given him. "It may be a man's war, but there are women involved, Son—Maia, Konrad's mother, his sisters-in-law, his nieces, the czar's daughter Cynara and others. We had to lure Elliad away from Jydanski. We wanted to trap him in Baltic Castle and this was the only way. Now we have him!"

The uncle asked Luke about Maia and Elliad's other prisoners. He was relieved to know they were being treated humanely, were allowed to be together and that Kedar had not been executed. Luke was mortified to learn that Kedar had lost his hand. He had hoped that the boy's injury had been a minor accident, perhaps a broken wrist. The thick mass of bandages had made any close observation impossible. Luke felt a wave of nausea pass through his empty stomach at the thought of Elliad's cruelty. Now the bloodthirsty despot was answerable for Kedar's deliberately inflicted amputation!

Luke learned of Konrad's plan to enter Baltic Castle and that it was in progress as they spoke. Konrad had wanted to make the entry while the focus of attention was on the other side of the castle with the exchange taking place. It was hoped that Elliad would be close at hand to meet Jobyna when she arrived. Luke told his uncle that Elliad had been at the gate when the carriage left and would possibly wait there, hoping to have both Luke and Jobyna in his grasp when she was brought in. Jobyna's quick action, yelling at the horses, slapping his horse, had been the deciding factor when the soldiers jumped out at her. They had been ordered by Elliad to capture her first, then recapture Luke only if possible; they were not to jeopardize the capture of the princess.

Dorai ordered the company to retract out of sight, join the other bands of soldiers, and help keep the castle road blocked off. They were to watch from unseen vantage points apprehending any and every person who traveled from the gates. Luke, riding with his uncle, asked about the access road to the beach, saying he wanted to see how Konrad and his men were progressing. With a dozen or more soldiers, they headed down the road and took the path to the beach.

Jobyna had told Luke how she went riding along this shore every day, the exercise giving her strength and the fresh salt air filling her lungs with health. Luke had never seen the sea before and the sight gave him an invigorated feeling. His uncle gave the horse free rein, and it galloped down the beach to the rocks at the other end.

Massive cliffs towered above, and Luke drew a deep breath when he saw the ominous walls of the castle itself, rising up like a monster from the rocky face. Three hundred horses were standing along the cliff base, in the shade of an overhang, watched by men in the Proburg brown uniforms. The men were walking the horses in turn to a nearby creek where the fresh water seeped through crevasses in the rock, forming a small pool before it flowed to the sea. Prince Dorai noticed drawn swords as they approached, but when the guards saw the white tassels on their green uniforms, the aggressive stance became relaxed.

After brief introductions and welcome recognition, the guards pointed to the rocks where the tide was lapping persistently. Luke and Dorai set off around the base of the cliffs, climbing the rocks where necessary to avoid the waves.

Konrad was now short of time to complete his arrangements. He wanted his men in the castle before Elliad returned with the soldiers he would no doubt have at the gates. They had hoped Elliad would go to the prison fortress days before the swap was to take place, and the plan may have been able to have been completed without Jobyna having to be involved at all. Hindsight was always said to be better than foresight, and Konrad could now think of other ways he might have outwitted the pretender, but he admitted to himself that if he could get his men inside the castle now, without being seen, this was still the best plan.

Konrad surveyed the castle walls rising above him as he pulled on the closest rope. He turned to look down the cliff face at the beach. His friend Vincenz perched precariously but relaxed beside him. Pitons had been driven in all up and down the rock face with rings attached. Now they were checking to make sure the ropes were secure. Noon had just passed and the simmering sun scorched spitefully down upon them. Konrad and Vincenz rappelled rapidly to the ragged rocks below where the men waited with baited breath. It was then Konrad learned of Kenrik's presence. The czarevitch was standing under an overhang, his red uniform, and those of his men, now standing out like bright red lobsters on the gray beach.

"We have ropes right up to the windows on the second floor, which is the royal suite. We will fill the two top floors with our men and move from there. Everyone has been briefed. The main object is to capture or kill Elliad without jeopardizing the lives of the hostages." Konrad listened as Kenrik told him about the discovery of his father's body. Interrupting with the deepest of condolences, Konrad exclaimed that every second's delay could mean more lives lost. Konrad was thinking now of his own father, his mother, his family . . . Jobyna.

"I'm coming up with you!" Kenrik's determined tone refused any opportunity of debate.

"I've briefed His Highness about the risks, but he would not change his mind!" Moritz told Konrad, "I believe if I work with him, we can make it."

Konrad explained that the more experienced men were to climb first. Kenrik must go back to the guards who were with the horses and exchange his uniform for a brown one. The others in red uniforms must wait there. If someone did happen to look out of the windows for any reason, the red would attract unwelcome attention. It was enough worry that the horses were in view if guards were to do a circuit of the walls! Luke, Dorai, Mattheus and the other Frencolians scrambled around the corner just as Konrad and Vincenz belted their weapons around their waists and placed rope coils crosswise around their shoulders and chests.

One glance at Luke, who had grass stains on his clothes and scratches on his face, made Konrad exclaim urgently, "That's it! We must go!" He spoke to the soldiers who would stay at the bottom of the cliff. "After Kenrik and Moritz, no one else is to ascend." He shook Luke's hand. "It's good to see you safe, brother. You are *not* coming up!" Bowing to Prince Dorai, he said, "As soon as we have something to tell, we will send someone down with word." He grasped the rope and said wryly, "We had better get going; we can't rescue anyone at the bottom of the cliff!"

"Elliad was at the gate when Luke was sent off," Dorai called at the climbing bodies. "With any luck, they should be there for a while before returning to the castle."

Konrad and his men knew they could rely on their powers of physical endurance and judgment. The only competition was the ruggedness of the cliff face; it was a situation of inherent risk. The element of extreme danger needed to be respected, but due to Konrad's experience, there was no real danger they felt unable to cope with, for he had gone rock climbing at least once a week for the past four years. The carefully placed ropes could be handled in safety by those who knew what they were doing.

Luke and Dorai watched as Konrad and Vincenz scaled the rock in a display of coordinated control and rhythm. Two by two, the selected men followed the leaders up the cliff. Kenrik and Moritz arrived back as the last men ascended the rocky face. High above them Luke saw Konrad wave. He was leaning out of the top-most castle window. Luke and Dorai waved back.

Moritz was explaining to Kenrik as they began climbing that he must not step on the pitons, but use his hands for balance and his feet for support. It was obvious to Luke that Kenrik's desire for revenge was urging him on, inch by inch, up the steep face. The czarevitch's feet faltered here and there, but Moritz was beside him, showing him where to step and taking his arm to steady him when necessary.

Luke and Dorai settled down with Konrad's soldiers to wait, knowing there was nothing else they could do. Luke knew he must pray. To his great surprise, his uncle suggested he pray out loud as he also wished to request the help of the Almighty but had been unable to find the words to express himself. This was the first time that Dorai had verbally acknowledged his own need for divine help to his nephew.

"Yes," Luke said to his uncle, "God is able to help. All things will work together for our good." Luke could already see how God was using the trials for good in the lives of many people.

16

"Let me alone, please!" Jobyna tried unsuccessfully to shake the soldiers' grips from her arms. "I'm unarmed; surely you do not think I can escape?" She turned at the sound of the next gate being opened. The road stretched out portentously between two high walls to the next tower.

Through open gates beyond the second tower, Jobyna saw Elliad step out from the shadow of the archway. The fearful girl turned involuntarily but the four soldiers stood stalwartly behind, and there was nowhere to go but toward him.

Thoughts of Elliad and Berg filled her mind each step she took. Traumatic memories of torture in Frencolia and of the brand given her in captivity caused her to become breathless. Where was God now? Immediately her mind flew to Daniel, the captive, who was thrown into a den of lions. When she was a child, the thought of a lions' den had caused her to have nightmares. She used to dream of lions tearing her body apart.

Her father had been horrified when she told him her nightmares. He had taught her about the God of love who would protect her in such dreams. God had rescued her from the nightmares, but here was the real thing! Elliad the lion waited for her and she wondered if God could save her from such an adversary. Suddenly she felt very weak and weary, as though all strength had drained from her body.

Elliad strode confidently toward his captive. Encircling her with his strong arms, he kissed her passionately. She suddenly became limp.

"She is so pleased to see me, she faints!" He exclaimed to his men, who laughed loudly at their champion's words. Smiling broadly, Elliad lifted her into his arms, carrying her the rest of the distance along the causeway, through the many open gates, under the last gate house and into the stable courtyard. He set her down on a grassy verge atop a small wall. He was panting from the heat of the piercing sun. Sitting beside her, he drank from a flask offered him by an attendant. Jobyna roused, looking up at her captor through terrified eyes.

"You've grown from a feather into a healthy morsel, haven't you?" He grinned at her as he spoke.

The sight of him so very near made her recoil, and she turned away, but he grasped her hands and pulled her closer until she was forced to face him again.

Elliad's voice was menacing as he asked, "Now, my treasure, think hard. How many soldiers did you see along the way, and what uniforms were they wearing?"

Jobyna tried to sit up, but he held her. "Let me sit up, please." He complied, slowly pulling her around to face him, his blue eyes feasting upon her hair and her eyes, looking in disdain at the plain brown dress she wore. Hating his scrutiny, she composed herself somewhat to answer his question. "I . . . I didn't see any soldiers, just the ones from Frencolia that Uncle Dorai has with him."

"You saw no soldiers? Not one?" She shook her head and he asked, "All the way from Reideaux? You saw no soldiers but the ones you rode with?"

"No."

"Then how many were in Dorai's company?" His blue eyes pierced into hers.

"There were 300."

"Even at the Proburg border, you did not see any other soldiers? Jobyna, are you telling me the truth?" His voice had a menacing tone that she remembered. He was looking through her.

"I always tell the truth." Jobyna looked into his eyes. "We both know I can't fool you, John."

He looked away momentarily, remembering but briefly. Elliad's mind was upon Dorai; he tried to project the man's tactics. Turning, he issued orders to the men behind him. "Alard, get me a quill and paper. Cole, bring me two soldiers who would like a bit of gold in return for a little adventure. Fetch two mounts. *Move*, man!"

Alard hurried to the tower office and brought the requested items, also a bottle of ink. Elliad moved to sit some distance from Jobyna and scribbled thoughtfully.

Standing close to the captive, Alard stared, mesmerized, as the sunlight reflected copper glints from her hair. He studied the beauty of her face, utterly entranced as she shaded her emerald eyes from the sun with her hand. The soldiers rode around from the stables and Elliad handed one of them the note.

"Read it out loud!" Elliad commanded. He wanted to envisage Dorai's response when the crown prince received it.

The soldier read,

If these same two men do not ride back within five

minutes to Baltic Castle, some of the precious prisoners'
heads will follow them.
(signed)
Czar Kievik.

"Yes. I have little doubt that you will be allowed to return here
within minutes. Ride out a couple of miles, say, even to the
Proburg turnoff, and I believe you will be apprehended. Give
them the paper and I feel sure you will be urged to return. Make
sure you take note of the uniforms; get some idea of the number
of troops out there."

The soldiers saluted him and rode toward the open gate. A
company followed on foot to monitor their progress. Elliad
turned toward Jobyna, who was staring wide-eyed at the departing soldiers. The pretender asked, "This Konrad, the son of
Prince Gustovas . . . when did you last see him, Jobyna?"

"At Kelsey Castle in Reideaux, well over a week ago," she
answered him, feeling thankful that Konrad had anticipated
such questions.

"And where is he now?" Elliad asked.

"He is in Proburg. At least, I think he is. . . ." She hesitated.

"What do you know about Proburg, Jobyna?"

"Uncle Dorai told me the casualties are heavy and that Konrad
is fighting for Landmari Castle."

"When did Dorai tell you that?"

"Just the other day."

"Did no one give you a message for the czar of Chezkovia,
Sparrow?" His eyes burned into hers, and she sensed he knew
something was amiss.

"No. Uncle was very upset that I came. I am sure he hoped
you would release his Maia . . . and Luke. Where . . . how is
Maia?"

He ignored her question. Noting her hesitation, he turned to

Alard and Cole. "Check the whole place. I want soldiers to go around all the walls. Just make sure there is no one attempting some sort of entry. This Konrad, the "Crazy Prince," climbs mountains, I believe." Moving back to Jobyna as the men walked away, he whipped out a jeweled dagger. She gasped, pulling away as he cut the sleeve of her dress, ripping it completely away from the shoulder.

Realizing what he was looking for, she cried, "It's on the other arm!" Burning heat from the sun, combined with the closeness of this unsavory man, made her feel sick. He promptly cut and tore off the other sleeve, examining the "E" he himself had branded there over a year ago.

"Rather nasty, isn't it? But it proves that you belong to me, doesn't it?"

Shrinking away from him, Jobyna wished fervently that she had never come. Realizing he had asked a question, she gave the first answer that came to her mind, "That is an 'E,' but you are Czar Kievik."

"Yes, I am. And Czar Kievik will have you, Princess Jobyna, for the traitor Elliad is dead, is he not?" Taking his time, he kissed her hand, then her arm before saying, "Czar Kievik will marry the Princess Jobyna and she will be called Czarina Jobyna." The terrified girl tried to free her hands, a frightened expression on her face. She turned her head away from him. Smirking at her, he spoke again and she felt his breath upon her cheek. "You see, Czar Kievik's son Kenrik is a traitor and works against the czardom." His tone became deadly serious; it was as though he was confiding a secret. "Czar Kievik wishes to have sons— heirs—to keep his czardom safe from those who have their greedy eyes on it." Dropping her hands, he swung around at the distant sound of horses' hooves.

"I have ridden a long way today, and I am very thirsty." Jobyna still felt faint. Perspiration ran from her forehead, half due to the heat and half caused by the torment she was going through. *He is more insane than I realized!* she thought.

Grasping her hand once more, he kissed it. Beckoning two soldiers, he spoke to her again. "Can you find your way to the apartment you stayed in with Sleven and his wife?" He watched for her nod. "Your slave is there waiting with a change of clothes for you. I will be along shortly." Kissing her again, he stood reluctantly, then strode away toward the gates through which the two soldiers were returning.

As Elliad had predicted, the soldiers had been apprehended, triumphantly handing over the note. Troops of every color uniform were there, encircling the two scoundrels, and their leaders had cursed themselves for falling into such a trap. Elliad's soldiers were held while their captors conferred out of earshot. Whatever they decided, they would lose ground. To let the soldiers ride back, gave Elliad the information he sought; but to take them into custody may mean the keeper of Baltic Castle would carry out his dire threat and the very events they were trying to avoid would be history. What a mistake! With extreme reluctance, they decided less would be lost to send the soldiers back to the castle. It just made the fact clear to Elliad, the keeper, that he was now being kept.

Jobyna was tempted to run and hide in the garden among the shrubs and statues, but the sound of the soldiers following behind made her realize how impossible this would be. She glanced back and saw they were a long distance behind jabbering away to each other in German. As she rounded a corner, she almost followed her instinct to run and hide. Her dry throat spoke of the great thirst she felt. Filled with a dread against stirring Elliad's anger, she climbed the steps and obediently walked around toward the kitchens and the "cottage" apartment which she remembered with a small sense of comfort. Sleven and Brenna had been good to her and had treated her with love

160

and care, like a daughter. She remembered the times they sat around the fireplace, reading from the Gospel Books and sampling the goodies Jobyna had baked in the castle kitchens.

Two soldiers stood by the door and she recognized their faces though she had never known their names. They bowed to her and one of them said, "It is good to have you back, Princess Jobyna." He took a bunch of keys from his belt and unlocked the door, holding it open for her to enter.

Trembling at the sound of the door being locked behind her, Jobyna was thinking, "I am a prisoner here! I should have hidden in the garden!"

Suddenly Ellice was hugging her and crying. Jobyna told the slave-girl, "You're the first person here that I am truly happy to see." She hugged Ellice close, looking past at the wooden bathtub, filled with steamy fragrant water. Her eyes fell on the table where jugs and goblets sat waiting. Examining the contents, she chose the fruit juice. Ellice took the goblet from her hand, then the jug and poured the juice. Jobyna drank thirstily and held the goblet for more. As she downed the second, her eyes strayed around the room.

A pale pink satin dress lay on the couch with the diamond tiara that Elliad had given her in Frencolia lying upon it. Beside the dress was a burgundy tunic covered with exquisite embroidery and gleaming jewels, on which sat the heavy dome-shaped Chezkovian crown with a jeweled pattern atop a solid gold orb. Jobyna recognized the crown as the one worn by Elliad when he sat in the Oval Crown Room on the throne of Chezkovia. Almost choking on the juice, Jobyna spun around and stared at the locked door half expecting her captor to burst in.

Scarcely thinking of what she was doing or the consequences, she removed everything off the table, upended it and motioned Ellice to help her carry the solid piece of furniture to the door. The table, on its side with the top at an angle under the door handle, would prevent anyone from entering.

Jobyna ran through the sitting room and closed the hefty shutters on the front windows, bolting them. Ellice watched her with great fear on her face.

Bathed and dried in the fastest time Jobyna could ever remember, Jobyna allowed Ellice to help her dress. The pink gown was sleeveless with narrow shoulder straps. Jobyna had never worn such a gown. It was low cut and the princess stared at herself in the small mirror with frustration. She reached for her own dress, a dusty heap, frayed and torn at each shoulder. Ellice caught her expression and whipped the desired article away before Jobyna could retrieve it. Crushing the brown dress to her, with a defiant look on her face, Ellice was well aware of Jobyna's disturbed state—but the slave was remembering Elliad's past displays of fury when he was displeased.

The rattle of the key sounded in the door. The handle was turned and the door pushed upon. The key sounded again and the door rattled once more, this time with greater urgency. Once again the key clicked around. Extra force sounded on the door and Elliad's voice came to their ears, "Jobyna, open the door or I'll break it down!" He hammered on it with his fists.

Jobyna rushed to the shutters, unbolting them. She hurried back, grabbed the Chezkovian crown, and grasped the slave girl's hand. "Come with me, Ellice. Konrad is planning to rescue me and I am praying to God he will. We will hide in the garden." Ellice's eyes were filled with terror, but she moved with Jobyna, knowing she would be in tremendous trouble in any case if Elliad found her on her own in the room. Jobyna pushed the crown down on her hair, almost covering her eyes. They both swung over the window ledge, dropping silently the short distance to the shrubs. Together, they looked up to see if the coast was clear. Holding the crown with one hand and Ellice's hand with the other, Jobyna ran down the stairs, across the terrace and around into the gardens, as far and as fast as she could, running as if a mad dog were chasing her. Reaching a low stone wall, they squatted down behind a large bush.

Minutes passed by before Jobyna regained her breath and gathered up the thoughts which seemed to be tumbling around her mind in fear. Realizing that it would just be a matter of time before they were found, the princess wondered what Elliad would do to Ellice. "Dear Lord," she prayed, "I can't think properly. Help me to do the right thing now!"

"But how can anything be right in this situation?" she asked herself as she looked at the crown, the garden, the high walls, the small stone wall with the garden seat built into it. *How to deceive a deceiver . . .*

"Ellice, promise me you will stay here until I call you or I send someone for you." Ellice's terrified eyes filled with tears. "Promise me you won't come out unless you hear me call, or someone else who says 'King Konrad has won the castle!' Look at me, Ellice! 'King Konrad has won the castle!' Promise me you will stay here until you hear those words!" Ellice nodded into Jobyna's anxious eyes. "This is the crown of Chezkovia, and it belongs to Czar Kievik. If the czar is dead, it belongs to Kenrik." To the slave's amazement, Jobyna stood, and with a carefully calculated movement, she threw the crown over the low wall, swinging it with both hands. "Hide behind this wall and look after the crown, Ellice. Remember, 'King Konrad has won the castle!' "

Jobyna left the hiding place. Joining herself once more to the path, she circled around to the front of the castle. Smoothing the dress, and pushing her hair into place, she climbed the steps slowly, moving toward the front entrance. Now, how to face the ferocious foe?

Elliad dashed around the side of the castle, followed by two knights who had called out as they caught sight of Jobyna walking up the stairs. The charlatan pulled himself up as she turned toward him. He strode toward her, wearing a thunderous countenance which seemed to send lightning flashes ahead of him.

Jobyna curtsied and hung her head, "I'm sorry, Your Highness. I forgot myself and my fears took over. . . . I lost control and ran. . . ."

He grabbed her arms, his fingers digging painfully into the flesh. He shook her angrily, but the sight of her in the gown he himself had taken the time to choose for her calmed his anger a little. However, he bellowed, "What did you do with my crown, Jobyna?"

She did not have to try hard to feign tears and terror on her face. Knowing she was not a very convincing actress, she turned her face from his. At the bruising grip of his hands on her arms, she gasped extra loudly at the pain, and cried, "I was angry with you for trying to trick me and keep Luke! And I am upset that you kept Maia!" She cried out as he shook her again, "You will kill me if I tell you what I did with the crown!" Her breath was coming too fast and she struggled to keep her mind on what she must tell him.

"What did you do with it, Jobyna?" He pulled her closer to him and supported her as she grew limp. He repeated the question, his voice becoming quieter as he realized that his captive was truly faint. "The crown! What did you do with it?"

"I . . . I threw it . . . over the wall!"

"You what?" His voice was filled with amazement. "Don't lie!"

"I don't . . . tell lies." Jobyna leaned her head against his chest and sobbed, "I threw it over the wall!" She hoped his mind would be thinking of the high walls running along the side of the garden, the ones on the south side that rose up from the sheer-sided, deep ravine. The two men who flanked Elliad gasped audibly at Jobyna's unbelievable confession.

"Which wall?" Elliad demanded. His strained voice was losing its control again, and a murderous fire sparked from his eyes. With his arm around her neck and a hand upon her throat, he forced her head backwards until she thought her neck would snap. Jobyna cried louder at the pain he inflicted. How miserable she felt. Elliad turned as Alard and Cole marched from the same direction he had previously strode. His hold on the captive slackened with the distraction.

"Sire, there are dozens of horses on the beach and Proburg troops with a few Chezkovian and Frencolian men. There are many more horses than there are men! We have checked the walls, but there are no signs of invasion attempts." Alard had his eyes on the gasping Jobyna who had been released as Elliad took in this news.

The pretender turned on her again, his voice shrill. "You knew about this, didn't you?" He shook her so hard that she was sure her neck would break this time.

Losing her self-control, she screamed at him, "No! No! I know nothing! I am nothing to any of you, I am just the bait!" A feeling of desolation overtook her as she realized that Elliad was likely to discover Konrad's plan before he had time to act on it.

"What did they tell you to say then?"

As Elliad's arm moved to encircle her neck again, she bent her trembling knees and ducked out of his reach. Stumbling to the ground, she yelled, "They deliberately didn't tell me anything, because they knew I would tell you!"

He dragged her to stand once more. With an anguished cry she repeated, "I am just the bait!" She hit out at her tormentor, her fists clenched, but he swiftly grasped her wrists and twisted her arms behind her back until she thought he would wrench them from the sockets. He pushed her away and she fell to the step, emitting a loud moan.

"What about the back wall?" Elliad demanded persistently, and Alard shot him a look of frustration. His instincts sensing trouble, Elliad ordered, "Take a look."

"Sire, it would be impossible . . ."

"I said, take a look! You will have to go up to the royal suite to look out the Baltic windows. Look for anything—ropes, men, anyone. Report back to me in the dining hall."

The two men turned toward the castle doors. "Not you Cole," Elliad snapped. He handed him a small piece of parchment. "Send two men out with this note. Tell them to stop, not quite out of sight of the castle. Leave it attached to a spear, and return here as fast as possible. The note should clear the way for us. We will leave for Jydanski immediately, with some of our prisoners. Prepare the carriages and the men. I need to find out what is happening back in my palace." He was disturbed that his messengers from Jydanski had not reported to Baltic Castle, but felt sure they would not have been allowed to pass through the troops on the road.

The possibility of having been caught in some kind of trap was slowly beginning to dawn on the charlatan. Jobyna's words in her loss of self-control made him feel sure that she had been used in some way. Bait, indeed! He stared at her. Yes, she could have been sent as the bait! They hadn't told her anything because they knew she would tell him! This made no sense to Elliad! Whose side was she on, anyway? He wondered if someone had been waiting when she had thrown the crown over the wall. Who? Kenrik? He began to wonder what madness had made him give up the Frencolian king for this . . . this . . . bait! He must have his soldiers check the walls and the grounds!

Shaking his head at the unexpected turn of events, Elliad pulled Jobyna roughly to her feet. Grasping her arm with a vice-like grip, he stormed quickly through the castle doors, up the main stairway to the dining room door. "Announce us," he ordered Julian. Elliad noticed the knight's beady eyes bulge as they beheld Jobyna's beauty.

Julian motioned for the doors to be opened and he announced, "His Imperial Highness, Czar Kievik. The Princess Jobyna, captive of the czar."

The faces in the room seemed to be a blur to the new entrant. All heads were turned her way, staring with great concern as she was dragged into the room. Maia stood suddenly and would have rushed to her, but Elliad bellowed, "Stay!" Maia froze.

Soldiers on either side, Julian right behind, Elliad's crushing grip on her arm, Jobyna felt hot and faint again. Remembering with a sudden rush Konrad's request that she detain Elliad if she possibly could, she decided it would be an opportune moment to succumb to her feeling of faintness. Elliad felt her growing limp. Julian moved forward to support her as she began to crumple.

"Don't you touch her!" Elliad caught her and carried her to the couch where Cynara sat. "Move," he commanded, placing Jobyna on the couch as the czarevna stood.

He whirled around. "Prince Gustovas! You, Cynara, Kedar, Gustav Junior, Mayer, Fleur, Melvyn and Maia will all be traveling with me and Princess Jobyna to Jydanski. Stand over by the door." Obediently, those chosen moved as ordered. Elliad saw Jobyna struggling to rise. He barked, "Not you, Sparrow! I'll come back for you!"

Princess Rhaselle began to sob as the soldiers stood between the ones who moved to the door and those staying behind. Maia looked back at Jobyna with wonder. She really was here! If only she could talk to her.

Elliad was issuing commands again. "Take them to the front room! Guard them well!"

He turned to Jobyna who sat slowly upright and spoke to him. She pleaded, "I haven't eaten anything all day; I'm so hungry! I'm sure that's why I feel so faint."

Elliad ignored her plea. He was puzzled by Alard's absence.

"Julian." The man was instantly at his side. "Get six men. Go with them, up to the royal suite. Spread out, move two at a time, make sure there is a stairway between you. Alard is up there. Find him! If you see anything unusual, return here instantly." He beckoned to one of the guards. "Armand, you are in charge here. Keep watch." Elliad strode from the room.

17

The top floor where Jobyna had been placed on her first night at the Baltic Castle over a year ago, plus all the guest rooms together with the royal suite and the spiral stairway, had been sealed off by Konrad and his courageous men. Servants were overpowered and those willing to cooperate were hustled into a room for questioning. Boey was among the women, but she refused to talk when she learned who the men were and their purpose. Another woman servant, Lora, told her captors quite willingly that the royal suite was empty. Elliad had slept on the ground floor last night in what was known as the "cottage apartment." She divulged that the "czar" planned to depart for Jydanski as soon as possible. Lora was not sure how many prisoners were being transported, or who they would be. The talkative woman informed her interrogators that the hostages were confined in the dining hall on the first floor during the day.

When Alard strode carelessly along the corridor to carry out Elliad's orders, he was swiftly taken care of.

Konrad and Vincenz gingerly descended the stairs and almost stepped to the marble of the first floor, hoping to enter the dining hall, when footsteps resounded from below. The soft soles of their moccasin boots were silent on the staircase as they hastily retraced their steps. The two leaders waved their following band of invaders back up the stairs and through open doors to hide.

The panting, portly knight Julian ascended to the second floor, two soldiers marching with him. He walked the length of the corridor, turning the corner to ascend the spiral stairway. The second pair, following Julian's path, arrived at the top of the stairs. The ringing sound of swords clashing entered the ears of the third pair as they began tramping along the corridor. Hastily unsheathing their swords, they found themselves confronted by Konrad and Vincenz. One of the men retreated, racing down the stairs, while the other momentarily succeeded in holding his adversaries at bay. The battle was soon over, and as Vincenz took care of the body and unavoidable bloodstains, Konrad ran swiftly down the stairs, interrupting his pursuit quickly when he realized the prey had escaped. Retracing his steps once again, Konrad commanded Vincenz to relay the word, assemble the men and advance down the stairs—they had been detected!

Konrad descended the stairs alone, moving stealthily toward the dining room doors. Swinging his rope, he attached it to the transom above the doors. He cut a shorter length of rope, doubling it and attaching it to one handle. Cautiously, the young king opened the doors.

Armand stood a few feet from the entrance doors, with his back to Konrad. Jobyna sat with Helena on the couch and her eyes caught the movement of the doors. Her green eyes widened as she viewed Konrad's curly fair hair growing into a forehead, then his blue eyes peering around. But two soldiers also noticed the unlawful entry! The men hollered and ran toward the doors, demanding that he identify himself.

Realizing he was well outnumbered, Konrad swiftly closed the doors, knotting and winding the rope around the two handles. Hauling himself effortlessly up into the concealment of the huge transom, he pulled the rope up behind him.

Elliad had been checking his departure plans with the soldiers on guard at the front room. He ordered them to bind the prisoners' hands. Cole strode through the entrance, accompanying the two men who had returned from the errand of placing the note.

One young soldier saluted and bowed. "We saw Proburg soldiers ride to take the note, Sire, and . . ." His words melted like butter on his tongue as the escaping soldier tore frantically down the stairs.

"Intruders! Proburg soldiers!" The red-faced man screamed, pointing his sword up the stairs.

Elliad cursed, yelling for Cole to collect all men and bring weapons to defend the castle. "How many?" he asked the soldier.

"I'm not sure, Sire . . . dozens maybe. They took Julian and the others . . . Lundy is dead. . . ."

His blue eyes wide with fury, Elliad paced back and forth, six paces one way, five the next, like a caged animal planning how to attack the predator. While his feet stomped, he issued orders as his men arrived. "Block off the stairs! Get guards on the main staircase! Secure the small spiral stairway! Seal off the corridors! Attack all intruders! Kill them! Don't ask questions!"

As men arrived, Elliad repeated his orders, screaming for every man to get up there! He sent a man to fetch all guards from the gates, and commanded that only a skeleton crew be left to guard the exits.

Elliad's soldiers began pouring up the stairs, past the dining room door, and on up to the second floor. The sound of their boots on the marble muffled the banging on the dining room doors. Konrad watched as the soldiers raced under his vantage point. He sat back, out of sight, intending to wait for his men to join him and free the prisoners.

The pretender himself reached the dining room door, just as it burst open, shattering the decorated handles in smithereens on the floor. Guards drew back at the sight of their leader, his ferocious face preceded by his swinging sword.

Storming into the chamber, Elliad demanded an explanation. "Who tied the rope on the doors?"

The answer was unsatisfactory and he ordered that all prisoners be taken to the front room with the others, telling Armand and the other guards to accompany them and lock them up. All but two were to return swiftly and defend the castle from enemies who had secretly entered the upstairs quarters.

The soldiers herded the prisoners together and filed them out of the room. As Jobyna walked passed Elliad, she did not look at him. He stepped in front of her, and grabbed one of her wrists.

"Take the rest! This one will make useful bait!" He pulled her to the door. "Hold her!" he ordered a soldier.

Swirling his double-edged sword, Elliad slashed the silk cord hanging by the door and unraveled it to a longer length. Grasping her wrists, he wound the cord round and round, knotting it tightly. She winced and shrank back, gasping at the pain, but the soldier held her firmly.

"Go with the others!" Elliad ordered the guard, and led Jobyna from the room, sheathing his sword. He stopped just feet from the doorway and tied the end of the cord through his belt, holding the cord close to her hands. Once again he drew his sword, walking toward the staircase. Her angry captor held the slack cord with his sword hand and Jobyna was forced to follow him closely.

Konrad dropped noiselessly to the floor. Running swiftly, he slashed the cord free with his sword. Pushing her, he stood between the enemy and Jobyna. With his sword extended, Konrad's stance issued a challenge. Elliad whirled around. The same instant, Jobyna, frightened at Konrad's appearance from nowhere, pulled away. She now found herself falling helplessly on the marble floor.

The clash of swords resounded! Konrad was gaining the advantage, driving Elliad back along the corridor. Sparks flew as the swords clashed again and again, thrusting, blocking, slicing, stabbing, swinging this way and that! Elliad's soldiers, with outstretched swords, rushed from behind Konrad.

"Konrad! Behind you!" Jobyna screamed. She rose awkwardly to her shaky feet and leaned on the wall for balance and support. Sick and faint from the horror of the battle, Jobyna realized that this was the first sword fight she had ever witnessed.

"I'll take him alive!" Elliad yelled, his mind having registered Jobyna's use of Konrad's name. The men slowly moved closer behind Konrad, their swords pointing at him as he continued to battle with Elliad. He turned sideways, his sword flashing against four. Elliad's sword sliced through his sleeve, down his arm, deep into the muscle. "Drop it!" Elliad pointed his sword at Konrad's throat. The king's sword clattered to the floor.

"Hold him for me!" Elliad smirked as blood flowed freely from Konrad's wound, trickling down his forearm and from his hand to the floor. The soldiers grasped him firmly on either side.

"So! Konrad, son of Gustovas! This is the king from Reideaux, the Crazy Prince of Proburg!" Elliad swirled his sword at Konrad's chest, slicing the rope, flicking the short pieces to the floor. The sword twirled so rapidly one could scarcely see the blade. The sound of the weapon cutting the air echoed along the corridor. With a malicious snicker, Elliad created a shredded lacy pattern of his victim's jacket front, and sliced fine surface wounds all over his chest. "Give him a headache!" Elliad ordered, and the soldiers punched Konrad's head and neck viciously from behind.

Jobyna ran to support the injured Konrad, and as he slumped forward, he fell heavily against her, causing her to crumple to the floor under the limpness of his weight. The soldiers dragged him away from her.

"Such a pretty sight!" Elliad exclaimed, sarcastically clicking his tongue as he lifted her to stand on trembling feet.

The front of her dress was ruby red, stained with Konrad's blood.

The gloating tyrant pointed at two of the soldiers who had now been joined by others. "You two! Carry him down to a carriage! I'm sure Reideaux will behave themselves if they know I have their king!" He pushed Jobyna toward one of the men. "Take this one to the czar's carriage and guard her well!" Snatching the short piece of cord still tied to the one of the knots on Jobyna's wrists, he then flung her mercilessly to stagger and fall once more to the floor. "I'll just help clean up the mess she's responsible for upstairs, and I'll join you."

Not knowing the number of intruders, Elliad was cocksure the unexpected battle in the castle would be brief; the victory was already won! He now had another kingdom under his feet! His men were skilled with their swords and he was confident in his own ability as the best swordsman in the world! His twisted mind was already seething with ways in which he would make this meddlesome couple suffer. Yes, he would enjoy that. It would prove most entertaining and would help appease his wrath!

Kenrik, in kamikaze style, slashed and sliced his way through the soldiers as they were confronted in the corridors. Moritz kept at his side, and together they battled their way to Vincenz and other Proburg soldiers who were cutting the advancing enemy down. Several of Elliad's injured men were trying to escape back to the central stairway, but Konrad's men were preventing their flight. The czarevitch inched past to the top of the stairs, looking for one person. Moritz defended him and held Elliad's men at bay.

At the halfway point on the staircase Elliad and Kenrik met, and though the former viewed his opponent with surprise, he displayed arrogant self-confidence.

The pretender hissed sarcastically, "The czar's son! What a pleasant opportunity to visit with him! He should have been announced! Never mind, I will make sure he is dispatched with all grandeur! I hope he did not strain himself too much, climbing all the way up the Baltic wall. . . ." His words were cut off as Kenrik thrust his sword toward the deceiver's throat.

"Your crimes . . . are too numerous to count!" Kenrik yelled between the strokes. "Prepare to answer . . . for them . . . all!"

The swords clashed, each trying to outwit the other by maneuver, speed and skill. Elliad soon realized he had encountered an adversary to match his own craft, and inwardly cursed himself for not knowing of Kenrik's experience with the sword. He had assumed the czar's son was too busy with the comforts and pleasures of life to be a skilled swordsman. Elliad drove Kenrik up the stairs, unaware that Kenrik was holding back, conserving his power and making his enemy over-confident.

Kenrik forced him back down. One by one, the stairs passed beneath his nimble feet. Within five minutes they were both perspiring profusely. Kenrik, the younger and fitter, gained advantage and drove Elliad along the corridor toward the dining hall doors. The czarevitch's determination and confidence of victory rose each step that Elliad was forced backwards. Feeling his opponent's strength and sudden superiority, Elliad, a great coward at heart, called his men.

"Guards!" he bellowed, expecting instant reinforcements.

Spying the sliced rope lying in a pool of blood on the marble floor, Kenrik changed his tactics, causing his enemy to stumble to rebalance his stance. The murderer's foot slipped on the slick bloody floor as he stepped backward. Kenrik took his moment, and with a ruthless thrust, he dodged Elliad's attack and lunged at his competitor's heart.

Screaming a death cry, Elliad fell to his knees with Kenrik's sword lodged in his chest. With a final thrust, it was over and Kenrik pulled his sword free, staggering with fatigue against the wall. Moritz and Vincenz raced to him, followed by the Proburg men swarming from behind. With several strikes of Moritz's sword, Elliad's head was severed at the neck.

"Goliath is dead!" Moritz shouted as he held the trophy up by the hair as David had the Philistine enemy. A cheer rose from the men.

Looking around, Moritz asked in concern, "Where is King Konrad?" He dropped the gory "prize" and headed for the staircase to search the ground floor.

Kenrik retrieved the trophy and followed. His mission was complete, but he would help free his sister and brother—if they were still alive—and he must salvage his crown!

18

Dragged carelessly down through the gardens, Jobyna stumbled breathlessly along the uneven walkways, down the countless steps, descending toward the courtyard. Twice she fell, and the irate soldier unsympathetically hauled her to resume the trek. (He would rather be back in the castle, he thought, winning the battle!)

Konrad was carried ahead, one soldier supporting his upper body from under the armpits and the other walking in front, carrying his legs. By the time they descended the last steps, Jobyna was limping and panting painfully. Her weak knee was throbbing from the numerous falls. Gray cobblestones merged with high walls and Jobyna would have fallen again, but a captain, waiting beside one of the carriages, caught and steadied her.

Memories from the past, of hardships this princess had suffered, the sight now of her soiled, bloodstained dress, and the anguish apparent on her face, made his blood boil. He remembered the kindness Jobyna had displayed to the children of her enemies while she had been in captivity at Baltic Castle; and hadn't she baked biscuits for the soldiers as well? He followed the merciless soldier to the royal carriage. When Jobyna was unceremoniously seized and thrust roughly backwards into the vehicle, he was no longer able to control his ire!

"How dare you treat the princess like that! What will the czar say when he sees her?"

" 'E's seen 'er. 'E ordered us to bring these two 'ere!" The soldier replied, tying the door shut with rope. Turning and saluting to his superior, he explained, "The bloody battle in the castle is 'er fault . . . Sir!"

"Then get back up there and fight, man!" the captain yelled at him. "You lot, too!" He shouted to the two who had locked Konrad in a plain black carriage. "The rest of you, get up there!" He swung around, speaking to other soldiers who were waiting with the horses. Drawing their swords, they dashed off up the steps toward the castle.

Cutting the rope with his dagger, the captain opened the carriage door. Jobyna drew back from his extended dagger as he reached for her hands. He climbed on the step. Grasping the cord, he jerked her toward him and deftly released her. The inflexible cord was so tightly knotted that it had cut the circulation from her hands. The gruff captain rubbed the grooves on her wrists with his own work-hardened fingers, massaging where the cruel cord had cut in.

Jobyna felt more numbness than just in her hands. She dared to voice her thoughts, and blurted, "King Konrad is in one of the carriages! He is badly hurt! Please help us escape!"

Dropping her hands in his sudden return to duty, the captain said regretfully, "I can't do that, Princess!" He stood back from the carriage, bowing. "I am sorry for you." He reached to close the door.

"I am sorry for you!" She shot at him as the door slammed. Spying the bolts on the inside, she shook her hands to restore the circulation, then pushed the bolts in place and lay back on the plush velvet seat.

"When Elliad comes, he will have to break the doors down to get in here," she lamented. All she could think of was Konrad, his bleeding arm and his pain. Her sense of reality began floating away.

The clatter of running footsteps on stone and the clashing of swords compounded into a riot of screams and yells. The captain cursed loudly as the invading men charged victoriously down the steps toward him. He rattled the door of the royal carriage, trying to open it, because he knew the princess would provide an excellent shield and hostage. Finding his attempts unsuccessful, he swung around with his sword drawn to face the advancing men. The Proburg men, not wasting time with one-on-one combat, finished him off swiftly.

Jobyna heard Moritz's voice yelling in German. Again the door was rattled. She heard Konrad's name and recognized Moritz's voice once more. Fiddling with the bolts and catches, hoping to open the shutters and view the obtrusive owner of the voice, she undid the wrong bolt. Moritz flung the door back in a flash and pointed his sword toward Jobyna's face. She had always felt frightened by Moritz, and now, the sight of his scowling features, drew an involuntary scream. He sheathed his sword and helped her from the carriage.

Jobyna, dazed by the bright sunlight, squinted to view dozens of soldiers swarming around the courtyard. They were entering the stables and sprinting toward the locked gate tower. The captain lay very dead in a pool of blood on the cobblestones. Moritz' name was called and he hastened to one of the carriages. Jobyna followed weakly, trying to collect her jumbled thoughts.

Vincenz came to Jobyna's side, taking her arm; he looked

concerned. In his halting Frenc, he asked, "You are hurt not, Princess Jobyna?"

"No, but Konrad is," Jobyna answered.

Moritz had entered the carriage to lift his master to a more comfortable position. He was now assessing Konrad's injuries. Unsheathing his dagger, he cut the shredded jacket completely off the unconscious king. After staring at the still form, Moritz left the vehicle and strode toward his men at the gate. He yelled at the guards in the tower, and they shouted a rude reply in Frenc.

Vincenz took over the conversation, calling, "Elliad, the impostor czar, is dead! Open the gates or you'll all be the same!"

The officer in charge of the gate shouted an obscenity back, and Vincenz leapt aside to avoid a spear which was aimed accurately at him. The Proburg men retreated to discuss this new complicating obstacle.

Jobyna knelt beside Konrad on the floor of the carriage, stroking his forehead. He felt clammy and cold. She could tell he was breathing, but faint and slow. The mass of bleeding cuts looked dreadful, but Jobyna could see they were not very deep. The gash on his upper arm, however, gaped horribly. She was thankful to see that the blood had congealed and was not flowing freely, as before.

Sliding the dagger from his belt, she wondered how such an obvious weapon had been forgotten. Its usefulness now made her feel pleased and she murmured a contradictory prayer, hoping God would understand her frame of mind. "Lord, I thought you had left me, and forgotten where I am. Thank you! Forgive me; I'd forgotten you! Please help Konrad. Don't let him die!" She awkwardly sliced a strip from the bottom of her dress. Pulling the flesh together as she wound the satin fabric, she cut another narrower piece to secure the binding firmly.

A booming voice, Jobyna recognized as belonging to Czarevitch Kenrik, came to her ears, "Where is Princess Jobyna?"

Tying the last knot, she turned as Kenrik's head appeared at the door. Next moment, he thrust his hand in, dangling the head of his enemy, suspended by the hair, for her to view.

Jobyna screamed uncontrollably as she beheld the grotesque remnant.

Kenrik swiftly withdrew; he had thought the trophy would have been much appreciated by this rescued princess. The gruesome appendage was given to another, and the czarevitch, feigning penitence, peered back into the carriage.

"How is King Konrad?" he asked, and with his eyes on her bloodstained dress, he added a second question: "Are you injured?"

With extreme effort, Jobyna composed herself enough to answer, unaware of the tears running down her cheeks. She shook her head. "He has . . . lost much . . . blood. He was knocked unconscious. He needs a doctor."

Kenrik held his hand to her. "Come! Let his men take care of him." She allowed him to help her from the carriage.

Turning her firmly toward him, the czarevitch's face was full of inquiry. "One of the Frencolians said—before he died—that you threw the crown of Chezkovia over the castle wall . . . ?" His voice was laced with intense self-control.

"Oh, yes . . . that!" She thought of Ellice. "No; it was . . . I mean . . ." She felt faint. The sight of the soldier impaling Elliad's head upon a spear made her feel sick. The great pretender was indeed dead, but the open blue eyes seemed to be staring at her still.

Jobyna's tongue felt stuck to the roof of her mouth and she felt herself shaking uncontrollably. "Let me tell you where it is." Looking up at the seemingly insurmountable climb, she wondered what the consequences would be for Ellice if someone caught her hiding in the garden, in charge of such a priceless object. Ellice was mute! She was totally defenseless!

Swaying dizzily, Jobyna tried to focus on Kenrik's face, and he moved to support her from crumbling in weakness.

"I will take you there. The crown is safe," she said in reassurance both for herself and for the czarevitch.

Vincenz appeared at Kenrik's side, explaining the difficulty to exit from the castle by way of the gates when they could not get past the first. He told Kenrik they should send men back down the Baltic wall, to take word to the troops about Elliad's death and the capture of the castle. If men could begin working from the other side, then one by one the gates could be taken, but it would be a painfully slow operation which might cost lives and take days. Kenrik targeted his mind on this new problem and the men gathered around discussing the lack of alternatives.

Jobyna returned to the carriage where two soldiers sat watching over Konrad. They shrugged helplessly at her questions, noting the missing hem of her dress now bandaging his arm.

In broken Frenc, one soldier spoke, "Nothing we can do . . . the king; he must need a doctor."

Jobyna asked if there was someone among the servants in the castle who could tend Konrad's arm and stitch it.

He replied, "All Elliad's people in castle have been slain, not no children. One man we had who could stitch . . . he dead!"

Jobyna closed her eyes, thinking of Boey . . . Lora . . . Dulcie . . . many more. Her mind flew to Ellice. With a last loving look at Konrad, she went as quickly as she could up the steps along the tedious stony inclines toward the castle.

Kenrik saw her leave and followed, overtaking her swiftly, "It is not safe yet! There are enemies still lurking around!"

Standing still, she turned to him. "Kenrik, I left your crown in the care of my slave-girl. She was stolen by Elliad from Strasland and forced to be here against her will, branded and made mute. I do not want her to be killed!" Her voice pleaded as she took in Kenrik's austere eyes. "She has been good to me;

at one time of my captivity, she was the only friend I had."

"She shall not be harmed." Kenrik stated decisively, "I shall go with you." He drew his sword and walked beside her, supporting her arm. "You are tired." He sounded concerned. "This has been too much for you."

Jobyna suddenly thought of Maia, Cynara, all of Elliad's prisoners. She halted once more, "Kenrik, what about Cynara and Kedar, Prince Gustovas . . . ?"

"They are all safe in the castle dining hall with Proburg soldiers guarding them. It would be safer for you to be there with them."

They both started as a man in the red and white Chezkovian uniform stepped out silently into their path. With sword drawn, his attitude was one of deadly defiance.

Kenrik's hand waved urgently at Jobyna, commanding, "Stand back, Princess!"

Jobyna recognized Cole, noting he was wounded. The swords clashed, and she stepped across the garden, moving in the direction of her flight with Ellice. With her heartbeat feeling like the pounding of a hammer in her chest, she climbed up several rockeries. The sound of swords clashed in her ears. Scrambling up to another level, she crawled up a bank toward the path, realizing the sword fight had ceased. Someone was close behind her!

Relief flooded Jobyna's face to see Kenrik leap to the path ahead. The bloodstained sword in his hand caused her to shudder. He took her arm and drew her to stand beside him.

"I'll never get used to . . . people being killed." Jobyna said, feeling despondent, hoping Ellice was still alive. They continued along the path and he walked beside her in silence.

"This is the wall I threw it over." She felt sure that her quick prayer had brought such a clever hiding place to her mind. "I told Elliad the truth; that I had thrown the crown over the wall!

I could not tolerate him dishonoring it again by placing it on his horrible head!" Unaware of the czarevitch's look of relief and amazement, she sat on the low wall and swung her legs over it. There was no sign of Ellice or the crown! The words she had commanded Ellice came to her mind.

"Ellice! It's Jobyna," she called into the air. "King Konrad has won the castle. It's safe to come out!"

A rustle from the bushes behind them caused both to whirl in apprehension. Kenrik poised himself in a protective posture, shouting a warning as Jobyna stooped to peer into the bush. Ellice disappeared further into the foliage, retrieving the sparkling diadem.

Speaking to Ellice, Jobyna introduced Kenrik, "The Czarevitch Kenrik." Curtsying low, Ellice then sank to her knees, placing the crown in her mistress' hands. Jobyna swiftly offered the crown to Kenrik, "Your father's crown, Czarevitch Kenrik."

Kenrik's eyes were suddenly blazing; he had lost his self-control, not to anger, but to grief. A stifling silence ensued. The czarevitch stared away into nothingness. He muttered, "My father is dead, Princess, and his body lies in the palace at Jydanski." His eyes were filled with sorrow and defeat as he said, "He was poisoned by the madman, Elliad. Even the pretender's death cannot bring my father back!"

"I am sorry. I know what it is to have my father killed by Elliad." She met his eyes with sad empathy.

"Then you are . . . *Czar* Kenrik!" Jobyna's arms were aching with the weight of the Chezkovian crown, as she continued to hold it out for him to receive.

Pushing his sword into the earth beside him, Kenrik suddenly fell on his knees before her. "It is yours to place on my head, Princess Jobyna; you have helped Chezkovia," he bowed his head, "more than you can ever know!"

Jobyna tremblingly placed the Chezkovian crown on his head, and her hands dropped weakly to her sides. Kenrik caught hold of both her hands and kissed them fervently, in spite of the dried blood stains. Then he rose and spoke to Ellice. "Stay with the Princess Jobyna, and you will be safe. I will escort you both to the dining hall."

The trek to the dining room was without incident, though dead bodies cluttered their path and the pogrom made Jobyna feel queasy. "At least life with all its horror is over for the dead," she said to herself as she thought of Konrad lying in the carriage. To be dead was to be out of pain, and she knew he would feel great pain when he came round.

Kenrik sheathed his sword as they entered the castle and saw Proburg soldiers guarding the doors.

The czarevitch took the crown from his head. Smiling, he said, "Look after it for me, Princess. I can think of no safer hands for it to be in than yours." He bowed as he tendered it toward her. As though in a dream, Jobyna reached out and accepted it. Ellice supported her mistress' hands as they trembled from the weight of the crown—and the thought of such responsibility.

Maia wrapped herself around Jobyna and clung to her, sobbing, pushing Ellice away. Prince Gustovas moved quickly to her side. Many voices asked questions. A tangle of unfamiliar faces swirled into Jobyna's vision. Children chattered, exclaiming in horror at the blood on her dress and the uneven, shredded hem. Cynara questioned her about the crown she held and demanded Kenrik's whereabouts. Jobyna met the bloodshot brown eyes of a young boy, a miniature version of the czarevitch; she noted his arm was bandaged to his chest. A jumble of two languages merged into confusion—they were all speaking at once. Jobyna finally succumbed to her overpowering desire to forget everything and sank into a deep faint.

19

Luke and Dorai stood and moved to avoid chips of stone tumbling down from above. Looking upwards, they watched as two men in brown uniforms rappelled quickly down the cliff face. Some minutes later, the messengers' feet were safely on the shore.

"The traitor is dead and almost all of his people in the castle! We have suffered some casualties. King Konrad and six of our men are injured, two seriously. Elliad's men on the gates will not surrender. We must gather the troops and work to take the gates from the outside. As many men as are able are to climb up from this side." The discussion centered on the problem of the gates and the necessity of bringing a doctor in for Konrad and the injured soldiers. How they had forgotten about the immense security of the gates was beyond them all. The men began to move along the rocky shore as they talked.

Luke thought of Jobyna and Maia, "The prisoners, tell me . . ."

"They are all safe, every one." He stood still, looking at Luke. "Your sister is suffering from shock. It has been a grim scene . . ." He went on to describe the battle—how Elliad had taken Konrad, and Kenrik's subsequent slaying of Elliad.

"Chezkovian men, chosen by Moritz and Vincenz for their experience in scaling walls, went wild, killing all the castle staff, women as well, once Elliad was dead. Only the intervention of Moritz and Vincenz prevented the slaying of the children."

The greater part of the tremendous Chezkovian army had congregated near Jydanski and was now making its way to the road of Baltic Castle. Feelings ran high and Chezkovians wanted to kill any man who wore the Frencolian green and gold. The thread holding them back was the fact that the leaders hoped to command such a slaughter in an "organized" fashion. King Luke Chanec and Prince Dorai were told (by way of a preliminary warning) that if the Czarevitch Kenrik was harmed in any way, it would be impossible to prevent bloodshed. Men had been sent to a nearby Proburg border base to fetch battering equipment. Tents were being erected all around.

Overhearing heart-chilling rumors, Prince Dorai petitioned to speak with the leaders of the Chezkovian army. He asked Luke and Mattheus to accompany him.

"I am tired of having Frencolia alone labeled with the crimes of the madman Elliad, especially when we have traveled so far to help you get rid of him!" Prince Dorai faced a group of 15 emirs. "You should find, in the late czar's records, documents sent from Frencolia warning you not to give refuge to the man known as Elliad John Pruwitt."

The men conferred among themselves. Dorai's words were translated for the four who did not understand Frenc.

"You have to face it, Prince Dorai, he was a Frencolian and Frencolia will have to answer to his crimes." Emir Weikol's monotonous voice spoke for all.

Prince Dorai noted their aggression, but stood firm. "Among the czar's records will be documents stating the background of this man, that is if Elliad, in his pretense as Czar Kievik, did not have them destroyed.

"His name was Elliad John Pruwitt. His mother, a Frencolian, named him "Elliad John" and his father's name was Provitt Klemens, exiled from Chezkovia some 30 years ago because of his treacherous acts against the czardom." He noted the look of consternation on their faces as he gave Klemens' name. Again waiting for this to be translated, he continued, "King Leopold's father, Friedrich, gave Elliad's father refuge in Frencolia. Klemens changed his name to 'Elliot Pruwitt.'

"Our king gave his cousin Alice to be Klemens' wife, and took an interest in them. King Leopold later displayed greater interest in their son, Elliad, and had him at court many times." He paused, allowing this information to sink in. "My men have documents to prove these facts, and your own records will also verify that Klemens came in disgrace to Frencolia. Later, he brought his son, Elliad, several times, to visit both Proburg and Chezkovia.

"I want you to hear me. He visited both your Czar Kievik and Prince Gustovas and both knew of his past treachery, *yet they welcomed him as a close friend!*" He paused while the men discussed this information. The air pulsated with questions and debate.

Dorai continued. "After his father died, Elliad continued with regular visits to Chezkovia and Proburg, claiming dual citizenship. Your records will show this. His mother was Frencolian, yes, but his father was Chezkovian. His crimes are as much to your dishonor as you claim they are to ours!"

Luke listened to all his uncle said, interested and surprised with the facts. He, too, had been concerned about the great Chezkovian army and he knew their own knights and soldiers were uneasy.

The emirs in the tent discussed the problem in German, throwing the truth back and forth, trying to come to a conclusion, a solution.

Prince Dorai listened to their debate, then in a silent moment he spoke to them in German, revealing he knew their language, "I do understand you and apologize that I did not reveal this before. It would be better if we leave, and you can discuss this privately. However, there is one thing I would like to add, being that Frencolia wishes for peace with Chezkovia and I am sure Czar Kenrik does also. It would be good for Luke of Frencolia and Kenrik of Chezkovia to discuss the matter themselves. I am sure our kingdoms could form an alliance that would prove beneficial." He bowed, motioning for Luke to precede in the departure.

The emirs deliberated for 10 minutes before requesting the three Frencolians to return. Emir Weikol was once again the spokesman. "We know what you have said is true. Eleven of us here knew the man Klemens and we have all met Elliad, posing as the czar. To our shame, we believed him. The likeness he created, with the royal robes and the crown was impeccable." His face reddened as he continued, "We have been disgraced by him and feelings of revenge have overcome us." Weikol looked at Prince Dorai and then at Luke. "We are going to call all the emirs and constables together and explain Chezkovia's part in the breeding of the said 'monster.' This must be done immediately, because it has been voiced that it will be just a matter of hours before the whole Frencolian army is wiped out. The Chezkovian cavalry has plans to massacre the lot of you!"

Luke gasped openly at this horrifying revelation.

"Will they believe you?" Prince Dorai asked, controlling his emotions.

"They will have to!" Weikol answered. "But it is a matter of ego. We will tell our men that they will have to swallow their pride and choose the way of peace instead. Many of the constables were fooled by the impostor and if they begin to think logically they will see their own part in the deceit. Some emirs were bribed by him, some of them knew of the pretense and to save face, they are continuing their play-acting, inciting a display of bloodshed, but the worst traitors were either with him in Baltic Castle or are being held for questioning in Jydanski." He sighed and said, "This has been a disastrous year for Chezkovia."

Prince Dorai bowed. "We must let you do the work of getting the word out."

Jobyna's eyes flickered open to look into Maia's tear-stained face. Ellice squeezed a cloth in a bowl brought by one of the soldiers and Jobyna revived as the slave-girl patted her face. She was lying on the floor where she had collapsed. Jobyna felt as though she had been unconscious for hours but Maia said her faint was recent. She tried to sit up, asking for a drink. Prince Gustovas ordered one of the soldiers to carry the princess to a couch and though she protested, Jobyna could not muster the strength to walk.

Ellice held the goblet for her while she drank thirstily. Jobyna revived a little, but allowed herself to sink back on the cushions, closing her eyes. Maia began to sob. Jobyna held her hand out, her eyes still closed, and said, "Maia, sit by me." Maia took her hand and sat on the edge of the couch.

"I'm all right, really I am. I'm sure it's just that I haven't eaten anything since last night, and the sun was so hot. . . ." Jobyna felt herself drifting off; then as the picture of Elliad's severed head came to her passive mind, she jumped, sitting up suddenly, opening her eyes wide, her hands clutching her throat.

"What is it?" Maia's voice sounded terrified. "Have you got a pain?"

Jobyna put her arms around Maia. "No. I'm all right, really I am."

Prince Gustovas stood watching and guessed that Jobyna was suffering from shock. Now shaking uncontrollably, her face was white. He pulled a chair to the side of the couch and took the bowl from Ellice. Not fully wringing the water out from the cloth he sponged her face once more and the water trickled down her neck. A faraway look dulled her emerald eyes.

He put the cloth down and shook her, none too gently. "Jobyna! It's all over! Elliad is dead! You don't have to worry any more!"

Jobyna tried to collect the threads of her thoughts. "I know." She began to cry and he put his arms around her, pulling her toward him so she could cry into his shoulder.

"I'm so afraid! I don't want him to die," she sobbed.

Prince Gustovas pushed her away so he could look into her eyes. "Elliad is dead! Jobyna, he is dead!"

She looked at him, puzzled. Didn't he know? Shaking her head, Jobyna murmured, "Konrad! It's Konrad!"

"What about . . . Konrad?" The prince's voice was strained.

"He was wounded . . . by Elliad." Jobyna looked around the room. "Hasn't someone told you . . . and Princess Rhaselle?" Prince Gustovas stood to his feet; he dismissed himself to his wife in German, commanding that they remain there and explaining Jobyna's disclosure. Faces stared in shock at the Proburg monarch as he departed. Princess Rhaselle sank back on her couch, and her daughters-in-law moved to comfort her.

"Where is Mayer?" Jobyna asked as Cynara came closer and sat nearby.

"He has gone down to the dungeons with Prince Haroun and other men to try and free his brothers, Gustav and Warford; also, the Grand Duke Louis from Strasland is locked down there. The main door to the dungeons has been locked and they are going to batter it down."

Ellice brought Jobyna more juice and a soldier arrived with a tray of food from the castle store rooms. Everyone was hungry, but when Ellice brought Jobyna a plate of food, she paused.

Cynara, her mouth half full of chicken, asked, "What is wrong? Why don't you eat?"

Jobyna answered Cynara, saying, "I have grown up thanking God for every meal I ever had. I must not fail to thank Him now! I am thankful to Him for delivering us from Elliad; and we shall yet be delivered! I am praying that Konrad will recover." She added, almost under her breath, "He has to, God; please, he has to!"

20

Tens of thousands of Chezkovian soldiers, standing behind their captains and constables, stood to attention on one side of the road. The several thousand Frencolian soldiers stood on the other side; in front of them were their captains and knights. Behind the Frencolians stood soldiers from Proburg, Reideaux, Danzerg, Bavarest, Zealavia and Strasland. The surrounding countryside was a variety of colors, a great kaleidoscope.

Facts had been laid before the Chezkovian cavalry. The most welcomed news was the czarevitch's slaying of Elliad; next, that King Konrad of Reideaux and Princess Jobyna of Frencolia both had a part in the taking of Baltic Castle and retrieving the czar's crown.

The Chezkovian cavalry were exultant that Kenrik was alive and unhurt!

Both Proburg and Reideaux were very disturbed about King

Konrad's condition, and all were concerned to rescue the royal people who, though safe from Elliad, were still imprisoned by guards holding the gates.

With embarrassed reluctance, Chezkovian constables, captains and soldiers accepted the facts about Elliad's father; many knew already, but had avoided admitting the truth. Constables and captains were ordered to investigate and quiz their ranks, sending home all who were not convinced to ensue for peace. Hundreds of men rode away toward Jydanski. Constables and captains were reassigned to accompany them and guard against an unwelcome uprising.

Prince Dorai and Luke watched as the sun began to sink in the sky. They wished the differences could have been reconciled before dark, as every minute was very precious.

Thousands of swords were unsheathed and dropped to the ground; the threatening sound echoed across the valley plain. King Luke Chanec and Emir Weikol together shouted "Peace!" Shaking hands, they kissed each other's cheeks.

An incredible kaleidoscope moved this way and that as men shook hands, hugged and greeted one another. Laughter mingled with deep voices conversing filled the air.

Shrieks of dying men rose ominously above the sound of peace. The great majority were grieved to learn that several groups of Chezkovians had insubordinately turned their daggers to murder Frencolians, and in turn, the assassins were likewise taken care of at the orders of nearby Chezkovian emirs and constables. A total of 87 men were slain. Denouncements of the killings caused men everywhere to grow silent. A reverse whirlpool, the kaleidoscope moved backwards; men sheathed their swords and returned to their ranks.

Kenrik heard the magnified outcry begin as he stood with Moritz, watching the Proburg men batter away at the gates, working under a makeshift mantelet to guard against the weapons, arrows, spears, rocks and boiling tar raining from above. The work ceased as the uproar surged to their ears. Kenrik was fearful at first that it was the sound of war. Later, his fears were allayed when the two Proburg messengers arrived from inside the castle (having climbed the Baltic wall once more), bringing extra men and written messages of encouragement and peace.

The czarevitch sat on the wall by the stables. Leafing through the documents, he read about Provitt Klemens and absorbed the facts of Elliad's history. He himself knew of the pretender's claims to Chezkovian citizenship, but had felt the man had been boasting wishfully. The czarevitch remembered with shame the parties he had held, celebrating and drinking with Elliad in jesting and frivolity. His father had treated the traitor like a brother.

Kenrik looked up sharply as Prince Gustovas, accompanied by guards from the dining room, approached.

"My son, Konrad . . . Where is he?" The prince's eyes searched the courtyard, staring at the bodies. A loud groaning sound came from one of the carriages. As Kenrik rose, Prince Gustovas strode quickly to the vehicle. Moritz, running from the carriage where Konrad lay, yelled for the soldiers to restrain the prince, but they dared not touch the royal personage.

Moritz grasped Gustovas before he opened the door. "There is a badly wounded soldier in there. He is not a pretty sight! It would be better if . . ."

"Where is my son?" Gustovas yelled at Moritz, who quickly led the way to the carriage where he had been sitting with Konrad.

Pungent vapors from the wine Moritz had poured over Konrad's chest and arm bandage filled the prince's nostrils as he climbed into the carriage. Konrad was unconscious and Gustovas sat gazing at him, listening to his son's labored breathing.

"We have been keeping him here, Sire, hoping we would soon have the gates open and he could receive a doctor's attention. Also, we do not think it good to move him about too much."

The prince's voice was thick, "How is he, Moritz?" He turned to look at his son's bodyguard, and the reservation he read in Moritz' eyes frightened him. "Tell me what you are thinking!" This was a command. Kenrik held his breath, listening for Moritz' assessment.

"I don't know, Sire. I really don't know! He has lost a lot of blood and has been unconscious for some time." Moritz glanced toward the gate as the battering noise came to his ears. The progress was painfully slow. "It may be better if we take your son up to the castle. I will call Vincenz and he can fetch a pallet. Once the first tower is captured, we will make progress, but right now we are scarcely gaining an inch."

The distant sound of a tremendous cheer, rising enthusiastically, came to their ears. Moritz hoped the cry was a signal that the first gate on the other side had been taken. While Vincenz went for the pallet, Moritz checked on Konrad once more.

Kenrik spoke to Prince Gustovas regarding the documents that had been delivered. He was still thumbing his way through messages of condolence and encouragement. Gustovas was relieved to know of the efforts being displayed to promote peace—that the armies were working together, and not against each other.

"I . . . I am an old fool, Kenrik. Can you forgive an old fool?" The prince hung his head when Kenrik did not reply. He knew he must express his apology in greater depth, and said, humbly, "I was wrong not to listen to you when you told me the truth. If I had listened to you from the start, everything would have been different. I accept responsibility and blame for believing the despot Elliad. I cannot thank you enough that you ended his charade!"

Kenrik again remembered how he himself had been fooled before Elliad took over his father's throne. He had been angry with Prince Gustovas (he still was, to a degree), but he knew his anger could not change the past. The heir to the czardom told Gustovas about the discovery of his father's body. The prince was overcome by the sorrow he knew Kenrik suffered. Kenrik thought of Konrad, injured, and the two sons of Gustovas still locked in the dungeons.

"It is past!" Kenrik declared. His deep voice softened. "We must work to free our loved ones and bring peace to our countries." They embraced each other, interrupted by the arrival of Vincenz, who was lugging the heavy pallet down the steps. Moritz hastened to assist him. The pallet was made of heavy wooden planks braced together with metal bands. While four soldiers held the pallet, Moritz and Vincenz lifted Konrad from the carriage on to the wooden receptacle. Konrad moaned loudly, flinging his good arm over the side of the pallet. He opened his eyes and struggled to raise his head before groaning and returning to his insensible state.

"That is a good sign," Moritz said, then added grimly, "but it is a bad sign if we hope to climb all the up way to the castle! He may wake up and try to get off!"

He asked Kenrik to walk with them, and where wide enough, for Prince Gustovas to walk on the other side. Just as they were starting off, a shrieking scream, diminishing rapidly, came to their ears, followed by a distant thud. One of the soldiers from the gates rushed up.

"Sir, we think the men in the first gates may be dead. They were yelling at each other. Some of them wanted to surrender, we think, and there was a sword fight. Then one of them jumped off, over the tower battlements." Moritz and Vincenz looked at each other. This is what they had been waiting for, hoping for! Ordering four soldiers to carry Konrad, Moritz cautioned them to be careful. "Take your time!"

Vincenz was already laying out pitons and unrolling rope. Trying to ignore the fact that his master was injured, Moritz began slamming the pitons into the face of the tower that was straddling the battered gate. No arrows or spears fell from above and the men worked as swiftly as possible, seeking small crevasses and footholds, threading the rope as they climbed, passing pitons, working as a team. Moritz reached the battlements after a final throw of a lasso. He stood on the top of the tower and the men below cheered triumphantly. As Moritz turned to gaze from the highest of the five towers, deep shadows caused by the retiring sun were stretching across the low-lying hills.

"I can see the armies!" He shouted to the men below. Moritz climbed the tallest turret, waving his arms in the air, throwing his hat as high as he was able! The ping of a longbow came to his ears and he instantly forced himself to drop 10 feet to the stony top of the tower. Arrows whistled by, and simultaneously, a great cheer came to his ears from the outlying troops. They had seen him! Feeling encouraged, he reached down and hoisted Vincenz up to his side.

"I thought you were a goner!" Vincenz said soberly as another arrow flew over the battlements.

Moritz tried the door to the turret. As he expected, it was locked. He uncoiled rope from his chest, tying it around the battlement. Vincenz could count four arrows from keyholes of the next tower, all aimed at them.

"That's suicidal, Moritz!" Vincenz grabbed hold of him, pointing at the enemies' weapons. They turned as their soldiers poured up the ropes behind them, and with the extra heavy shoulders taking turns with a display of brute force, the tower door was eventually smashed in. With boisterous bangings of bars being lifted and the grinding of chains of the portcullis, this secure gatetower was open!

The pallet was carefully set on the dining room floor. Konrad's mother flung herself down beside her son with her arms waving in all directions. She was afraid to touch him. Jobyna knew the mutilated web of his chest looked far worse than it actually was. Konrad's nieces and nephews gathered solemnly around, blocking him from Jobyna's view. Hearing him moan, she sat up, and took the cloth from her throbbing head. Kenrik moved to her side, inquiring as to her health.

"I had too much sun, probably," she murmured.

Cynara's voice rose, sarcastic and cutting, but it was directed to Kenrik, and Jobyna could not understand all she said. Enough was understood, however, to sense the czarevna's antagonistic attitude. Jobyna allowed Ellice to place the cool cloth back over her eyes.

Kenrik strode swiftly to Cynara and grabbed her firmly by one wrist. He motioned to Kedar and the three left the room. Jobyna learned later that the brother had told a few home truths to his siblings and ordered his sister, in no uncertain terms, to "shut up!"

Cynara returned to the chamber, red-faced, followed by Kenrik who announced in his resoundingly deep voice, "My sister, the czarevna of Chezkovia, wishes to speak."

Cynara stifled a sob and walked to Jobyna, curtsying. She said, "I was wrong about Frencolia, Princess Jobyna. I apologize for the things I have said. I will apologize to your brother, the king, when I see him." She turned to face the others. "You all heard the way I blamed Frencolia for . . . for everything. I was wrong. I apologize, and ask that you forget my ignorance." She rushed to Kenrik, flinging her arms around him. "I cannot forget that he killed Father!" To her surprise Kenrik held her close, speaking comforting words in her ear. Kedar joined them and they clung to each other. It was the first time Cynara had known her brothers to cry. The thought of Kenrik's surrender to weep in public made her sob all the more.

Mayer approached his father excitedly, but his excitement turned sour when he saw Konrad lying lifelessly on the pallet. Ellice had brought a rug from the couch and Princess Rhaselle draped it across her son's clammy body. The slave-girl sponged Konrad's face, listening to Mayer speak in undertones to his father. Ellice stood suddenly and walked to Jobyna, who had lain down again. Shaking her gently, Ellice made the motion of turning a key in the lock. Mayer stared at her while she tried to make Jobyna understand. His son's sudden silence caused Prince Gustovas to turn around to see what Mayer was staring at.

"What is you want, Ellice? To unlock something?" Jobyna could not work out what Ellice was trying to communicate.

Mayer came quickly, asking, "You understood my conversation with Father, and you know where the keys are?" Ellice, afraid of Prince Mayer, nodded timidly. "Good girl!" He took Ellice's hand, and before she knew what was happening, Mayer left the room with her.

Gustovas saw Jobyna's look of uneasiness and uncertainty, and he explained, "Mayer tells me that the main door to the dungeon has been battered down, but every other door in the place is locked. The keepers must have locked themselves in a room; the whole place is silent! Even when they hammered on all the doors, not a sound could be heard. Soldiers are working to break down the rest of the doors, but it could take all night. Now if your slave can find the keys, then that would make a significant difference!"

"I will pray she can." Jobyna murmured, trying to halt her imagination while she rubbed the kink that stabbed viciously in the back of her neck. She stared around the room. Kenrik was sitting at a table, with small notes of paper spread in front of him. He had a quill in his hand, but he was deep in thought. Kedar was looking at some of the notes. He drew Kenrik's attention to two small pieces of parchment and Kenrik spoke to him. Kedar rose and brought one note to Jobyna and one to Maia who was sitting on a cushion at Jobyna's feet. Jobyna read,

Dearest Sister Jobyna,
   We shall be together, yet. Our love and prayers are with you every second. Keep trusting.
(signed)
Luke

   I love you, dear Jobyna, and believe your nightmares are all over now. We will see you very soon.
(signed)
Uncle Dor

Cheered immensely by the note, she exchanged hers to read Maia's. Just a few words, but how much difference they made! Jobyna stood, unsteady at first. Prince Gustovas took her elbow, and as she moved toward Kenrik, the prince walked beside her.

"Can we send a note to them?" she asked eagerly.

"I think that would be a good idea, and will help you pass the time. We will need more quills, but let's hope that the gates will be clear before the notes arrive." Kenrik tried to put enthusiasm in his voice.

"I will write to Luke, too!" Kedar nodded decisively.

"Ellice may know where some quills are," Jobyna said to Kenrik. "I am so glad Ellice is still alive." She looked around at the door, hoping for her to return soon.

"You do not need to worry about your slave. There will be no more killings. The men here are feeling very subdued, Jobyna." Kenrik explained as briefly as he could Prince Dorai's disclosures about Elliad's background and his dual citizenship—facts that most Chezkovians had to admit they already knew.

"Then he is the problem of two countries!" she exclaimed. Viewing the people sitting around the room, she added quietly, "And he caused problems for many more!"

"But, remember . . . Elliad is finished!" Prince Gustovas spoke to Jobyna, noting that she no longer trembled and the dull, faraway look had disappeared from her beautiful emerald eyes.

21

Ellice entered the dining room timidly. A frightened, wide-eyed, wistful expression invaded her face. She walked to Prince Gustovas, curtsied and motioned for him to follow her. The slave-girl beckoned with the same actions to Kenrik, cautiously interrupting his writing. Jobyna stood, but Ellice shook her head and waved her hands at the princess.

"Something is wrong, Ellice?" Kenrik used the name Jobyna had given her. "You want us to go to the dungeons with you?" He turned to Jobyna. "No, Princess, you stay! I will take care of Ellice." Kenrik collected his sword from the table, sheathed it and departed with Prince Gustovas and Ellice. Princess Rhaselle, Helena and Marianne were obviously concerned about the sudden departures.

Soldiers brought more food and fluid; then mattresses were carried in. The guards explained that it was safer for everyone to sleep together in the dining room. A few of Elliad's soldiers and servants were still being sighted around the castle grounds and there was the possibility that such desperate men might attempt to take a hostage. Jobyna shuddered at the thought. She wished she had the motivation to tell the children a story, but she felt uncoordinated in her thinking; besides, they all appeared listless and tired. Sleep would come easily for them tonight, she thought. Taking Kenrik's quill, she rounded up her thoughts and wrote a note to Luke. She must not let him sense how disoriented she felt! Once the note was complete, Jobyna suggested that Maia write to her father.

The children were soon fast asleep snuggled up in the rugs on the comfortable feather mattresses. Jobyna went with Maia to the ladies' powder room and tried to sponge the stains off her arms and dress. The water only served to spread the effect on her dress making it look worse.

"I hope I can put on something decent before I meet Luke and your father!" Jobyna said to Maia as she looked in the mirror.

Maia hugged her. "You look frightful! I thought you had been hurt badly when you came in the door and fainted!"

Konrad had been groaning often, and Jobyna sat beside him on the floor. Maia, seeking security in her cousin's nearness, curled up by Jobyna.

Wall lamps flickered eerily and Jobyna thought the place looked like a refugee camp.

"Jobyna," Konrad called.

"I'm here." She sponged his forehead, noting how feverish he was now. Moaning and groaning, he moved his hand painfully to his chest, but his eyes remained closed.

Jobyna dragged two mattresses near to the pallet. As they settled down, Jobyna wondered how long it would be before Ellice returned.

The doors opened and Kenrik entered. He strode straight to Princess Rhaselle, Helena and Marianne, speaking to them in low whispers. They rose and followed him from the dining room.

In the early hours of the morning, Kenrik and Prince Gustovas returned to check on Konrad, noting that everyone in the room was asleep. They left once more, and Ellice entered the room, curling up on the couch not far from Jobyna.

Dawn had barely streaked the sky when Konrad called her name several times and Jobyna woke with a start, wondering where she was. Ellice was instantly by her side; a petrified look eclipsed her eyes. Jobyna held her arms out and they hugged. Without words, Jobyna knew something was very wrong. Princess Rhaselle and the daughters-in-law had not returned to the dining hall.

Konrad's brow felt a normal temperature this morning. He was muttering and complaining in painful whimpers and undertones, but his eyes remained closed. Ellice fetched fresh water and sponged his face, wetting his lips. Jobyna spooned juice into his mouth, pleased that he swallowed some, though the majority trickled out. Ellice sat beside him as well, mopping up the excess. As he made a great effort to cooperate and swallow the liquid, Konrad's eyes flickered open now and again. When a goblet had been drained, and Ellice brought more, they persevered with this as well until it had all disappeared.

Kenrik strode toward them; his boots echoed around the chamber. "How is he?" he asked, looking at Konrad. "Not much improvement, it seems." He squatted down, his face close to her ear. "I hate to add to the terror of the day, but Prince Gustovas' sons, Gustav and Warford have been murdered in the dungeons and the two keepers committed suicide. Prince Gustovas and Mayer are with the women-folk in a separate room where we laid the bodies. They will have to come and tell the children. . . ." He was silent, but Jobyna could not speak.

Kenrik continued, "The Grand Duke Louis had been trussed

and gagged. We think he was being kept in case they were able to use a hostage. Louis is almost out of his mind with anger and fright. I told him we would all be rescued soon, but he demanded to be released immediately. We have had to restrain him or we feel he may try to climb down the Baltic wall! He just needs some good food and drink, some rest. . . . When he sees his grandfather, he will think differently."

"How is the . . . progress on the gates?" Jobyna asked.

"We think the troops outside have gained another tower. There are just the two to go. The causeways in between are the trouble now; they are deathtraps." He paused and kissed her hand. "But we hope to be out of here today, or no longer than tomorrow!" Standing up, the czarevitch began to move away.

"Wait . . . please!" Jobyna turned to Ellice, and asked, "Ellice, were there other clothes for me in the cottage apartment?" The slave-girl nodded and Jobyna spoke to Kenrik. "There was bath water there; I would like to go and wash and change from this," she said, indicating her dress. "I don't want Luke to see me like this."

Konrad moaned and Jobyna said to the wide-eyed Maia, "Sit by him, Maia, please? Talk to him." Maia nodded, moving closer.

The door of the cottage apartment was off its hinges, and the overturned table was lying smashed in two. Kenrik commanded them to wait, and with his sword drawn, he strode through the sitting room. Looking out the windows, he fastened the shutters. Opening the doors to the bedrooms, he glanced around.

"I will send a man from the gates to wait outside for you. You must go back to the dining room immediately after you are finished."

"We will," Jobyna promised. Kenrik left, leaning the door up against the entrance. Ellice poked into a chest, pulling out several dresses. Jobyna stared at the couch, thinking of the tiara and the tunic that had been there. They were gone now; where they were was anyone's guess. Draping a dress on the couch, Ellice took the cloth from the edge of the tub and squeezed it out in the cool water. Jobyna was just going to pull the straps of her dress down when a movement from the bedroom caused her to freeze. The door swung around and she screamed uncontrollably. Two men wearing Chezkovian uniforms leaped out. Jobyna recognized them, instantly recalling their rank and names. One was Hagen, a knight of Elliad's, and the other was Frewin the spy, the husband of Lora.

Hagen overpowered Jobyna as she turned toward the exit. His large gnarled hand wrapped around her mouth. Frewin grabbed Ellice, winding rope around her wrists and he began binding her securely to a chair.

"Not another peep!" Hagen growled, listening. There were no intruding sounds. He slid his hand slowly from Jobyna's mouth.

"Please don't hurt Ellice!" Jobyna could think only of her friend. She hoped they were intending to leave her bound, not to kill her. Frewin picked Ellice up together with the chair, shutting her in the bedroom.

Hagen wound rope around Jobyna's wrists, saying to her, "We don't want to hurt anyone, but we need your help to get us out'a here!" As Jobyna struggled against his efforts to secure the rope, he added, "Look! You'd better cooperate and we won't get rough." Jobyna put her head down and pulled on the rope again. Frewin brought his clenched fist up under her chin, causing her head to jerk backwards.

"I'm tired of being everyone's hostage!" Jobyna declared. She felt herself becoming breathless.

Frewin slapped her soundly, first one cheek, then the other. "Just once more, and it'll be over!"

Hagan snatched up one of the towels. Slitting it quickly in two, he sliced the end of it into two narrow strips. He wrapped the wide piece around her neck, using the narrow pieces to tie it.

"What is this for?" she asked, light-headed. Her fears suddenly seemed far away.

"That is so we don't damage you before we have to!" Hagen's growl came to her ears once more. "And don't faint!" he exclaimed, knowing it was too late. He collected her in his arms. "Maybe it'll be easier like this."

Frewin unbolted the shutters. His darting eyes scanned the path; then he swung himself over the ledge and dropped into the garden. As Hagen awkwardly lifted Jobyna down to him, she opened her eyes and began to struggle.

Frewin let her sprawl on the garden. He squatted down beside her and clenched his fists. "Look, woman! Are you goin' to make this easy or not?"

Hagen crouched down beside them, pleading, "Just get us out o' here and we will let you go! Aye?"

"How do you think you will get past the gates?" Jobyna asked.

"Our men will join us when they see you. That's why we need you," Frewin said, then added to Hagen, "I don't know why's we's talking to this stupid wench! Let's move it!"

Jobyna thought of the gates. It would be worthwhile, for Konrad's sake, for everyone, if the gates were opened—even if they were abandoned!

Hagen stood to check the path. Frewin dragged their hostage to her feet. His fist was raised, ready to strike her.

"I'll cooperate," she gasped quickly and was pulled toward the path.

Frewin walked in front, a sword in one hand and the other holding the rope tying their captive's hands. Hagen was close behind, his short dagger-like sword drawn; he constantly turned to check that no one was following.

The three were confronted by the soldier whom Kenrik had sent to the cottage apartment. The soldier drew his sword as

Frewin sprang back to Jobyna's side. Hagen placed one arm about Jobyna's waist, the other hand held his sword with the razor-sharp blade pressing against the towel at her neck. "Back off, nice and slow, and no one will get hurt!" Hagen told the soldier. "Drop the sword and back up toward the gates."

Frewin grabbed up the soldier's sword; he now had one in each hand. The soldier was joined by others who had turned to observe the clatter.

Kenrik sat on the corner of the small desk in the first tower office conferring with Moritz. They were exhausted from the work and strain of the night.

A soldier rushed up the steps to them; his face was very grim. Stiffening, he called, "Some creeps have got the princess. . . . They're right outside!"

Moritz ordered Kenrik to remain in the office, waving him to lie low. By the time Moritz reached the bottom step, Hagen had pushed Jobyna through the open gates under the portcullis clear into the barbican then along the causeway. She was in full view of Elliad's men.

Frewin yelled at them, "Okay you lot! I'm Frewin! Remember me? And Hagen? We got Princess Jobyna, your passport to safety, so why don't you open the gates and let us through? We can all get away safely!" Hagen had backed over to the wall with Jobyna in front of him. She was an easy target for both sides.

"How far do you think you'll get?" Moritz cried, stepping from the shadow. He knew his protests would serve to authenticate Frewin's story.

An arrow flew at Moritz and he leapt back. It smacked the wall at his side, and clattered to the cobblestones. A nervous archer could send one like that at the princess! Moritz shouted from the safety of the archway, "You'll need horses and a carriage! There are thousands of soldiers out there! The Chezkovian army will never let you through!"

Kenrik approached from behind Moritz, but the big bodyguard waved him back.

"They'll never give them passage!" Kenrik hissed to Moritz, wondering as well how they could prevent the princess from being slain.

"I have an idea; just back me on it, Moritz, and we'll have the lot." Kenrik stepped to stand beside Moritz.

"Then get us the horses and the carriage!" Hagen yelled.

"They still won't let you through!" Kenrik called stepping out further and watching the battlements of the tower ahead.

Hagen moved uneasily. "Then if you can't help us to get through, we will finish it here." His threatening was so earnest that Jobyna felt the pressure of the sword through the towel, and though she held her breath, she felt powerless to stop the light-headed feeling surging through her like an engulfing wave.

Kenrik glanced briefly her way, then he stepped back, shouting, "Wait!" He told Moritz to bring the royal carriage and make sure it was empty. Any attempt to capture Hagan and Frewin would be a bloodbath for the captors, the captive and the attackers. Nothing would be gained as far as the gates were concerned. Kenrik called from the archway, "How many horses do you need for the men on the towers?" He waited while the message was relayed. The answer was 12; Frewin ordered them to bring an extra two. Kenrik told Moritz to bring 14 horses.

"Hey! Pretty boy! Kenrik!" Hagen hollered.

The czarevitch stepped from the shadow. The arrows were no longer pointing from the keyholes. Kenrik stepped closer.

"Why don't you come along, too?" Hagen twisted Jobyna's arm viciously until she cried loudly from the pain.

Kenrik thought, *I intended to.* But he replied, "Why should I?"

"So you can be sure we will let the pretty lady go." He twisted her arm harder and she went limp, causing him to drop the sword for fear of damaging his hostage. He released Jobyna, allowing her limp body to fall on the cobblestones.

Frewin leapt over to her; one sword was extended toward Kenrik, and the other pointed at Jobyna. His stance was very comical, like a court jester in the middle of a tragi-comedy. Kenrik saw that the point of one sword was dangerously close to Jobyna's face, but the eyes of this simple man were upon the czar's son.

Feigning defeat, the czarevitch casually dropped his sheathed sword. With a deliberate, exaggerated action, he threw down his dagger. "You will have a chance to get past the troops if you take me, but with her alone, you'll all be cut in little pieces!"

Hagen retrieved his sword, leaving Jobyna lying on the cobblestones. He held the sword at Kenrik's throat, walking around him, amazed to think he had captured the czar's son, the great Kenrik.

"Mind you, Hagen, the troops will want to see that I am alive and well." Kenrik said as he folded his arms. He was holding himself back, trying to veil the amusement in his eyes and the twitching of his mouth.

"Oh, I intend for you to be alive and well! My word, I do!" Hagen could not believe their luck. "Get the girl!" He commanded as the sound of horses' hooves came to their ears.

Kenrik obeyed, turning with Jobyna in his arms, to see the six matched horses pulling the royal carriage through the archway.

Hagen kept his sword pointed at Kenrik's throat. "Check the carriage, Frewin," he called, and Frewin, with both swords extended awkwardly, pulled the door open. His amateur action caused Kenrik to smile. The sound of the gates opening came to their ears and they were rapidly joined by four of Elliad's men, all brandishing swords. One guard also carried a coil of rope.

"Put her in there, pretty boy! On the floor! Back down nice and easy-like, no tricks!" Hagen pointed his sword toward the carriage.

"The emirs and constables will have to see that I am with you, Hagen, or they won't let you through!" Kenrik wanted to make this very clear or he knew they would be jumping from one cauldron to another. He placed Jobyna in the carriage on the plush red carpet. Wishing he could have moved on the plan formed in his mind, Kenrik felt the tip of the sword pressing on his back and decided to wait. He backed out of the carriage, slowly. One of the guards began to bind Kenrik's hands behind him, his arms to his sides, round and round with the rope. They pushed him up into the carriage and threw the rest of the rope in beside him. Frewin climbed in with Kenrik holding both swords in one hand.

Hagen urged the horses through the gates, across the bridge and into the next causeway. Four soldiers brought the rest of the horses. Two standing by secured the gates behind them. No sooner were they out of sight than Moritz and Vincenz were laying out pitons and pulling rope coils from their chests.

Two of the six men on the next tower descended to parley; they looked in the carriage at Jobyna and Kenrik. Chezkovian men had battered one gate down and were working on the middle portcullis, prying up the cobblestones.

"There are thousands of them! And I mean thousands!" one of the soldiers exclaimed. They peered again at Kenrik, ordering Frewin to wake Jobyna. She did not respond and Kenrik wondered if she had banged her head when she fell. He did not need to wonder for long. She sat up slowly, trembling; her green eyes grew wide as they took in Kenrik and his bonds. The czarevitch saw her bruised, swollen forehead, cheek and chin; also her blackening arm. There was silence except for the heavy pounding sound of the men working under a mantelet chipping persistently to release the portcullis.

"You will have to put me at the front and announce to them that you have Czarevitch Kenrik," Kenrik said, "or they'll trample us all into the cobblestones!"

They looked at him and he knew they were dangerously desperate. He commanded, "Go and yell from the tower that you have captured the czarevitch!"

"Better still, take him up there with us!" One of the soldiers reached in, grabbing the rope binding Kenrik. "Her too!" he told Frewin, who pushed Jobyna from the carriage after Kenrik. They stared at her, noting the satin dress with the bloodstains, her bruises and the uneven, fraying hemline of the silky gown. One of the soldiers drew his dagger and cut the towel from her neck. Tying it to his spear, he motioned for the group to follow him. Up the circular steps Kenrik and Jobyna were pushed, pulled and shoved.

The captain, Bodmin, waved the "flag" back and forth, back and forth, out through the keyhole, until he heard a voice calling: "Do you surrender?"

This was the cue and he waved the other men to bring the captives. Cupping his hand, Bodmin yelled, not revealing himself. "We have the Czarevitch Kenrik and Princess Jobyna!"

The constable in charge on the ground waved his men to hold their fire. He did not believe the claim, but his face changed quickly as he stepped backwards a few steps—placing himself at great risk—so he could view the enemies at the top of the tower.

Jobyna looked over the battlements at the red and white uniforms below. Her eyes blurred and the red and white merged with the gray paving stones. The three towers in the middle were the lowest and she could not see past the walls and tower of the entry gates. Shutting her eyes made her head spin away from her body. When she opened them again, it was to focus upon Chezkovian soldiers who stood on the tower battlements ahead, pointing crossbows their way. Kenrik stood beside Jobyna with Elliad's soldiers behind them.

Bodmin raised the spear as though to throw it, but Kenrik hissed at him urgently, "Don't be such a fool! They're not even sure who I am yet! I could be a hundred other men."

Bodmin kept the spear raised, but he was listening to the

czarevitch's plea:

"Elliad dressed up as the czar and fooled them! They probably think I'm a Frencolian in a Proburg uniform! Put the spear down and I'll talk to him!" Bodmin conceded. He leaned the spear on the battlement, crouched down and waited for Kenrik to speak.

The czarevitch leaned over the battlements, yelling to the constable in German, "Constable Ulmar! I am Czarevitch Kenrik Theodor Kievik Vladkov. I know you well! You taught me to sword fight when I was six; you were 20 years old and had just been promoted to captain. You celebrate your birthday one day before mine. Your wife is named Maraline. You have five children and I can give you their names if you wish."

The constable waved his hands up and down at the men on the tower and they lowered the weapons.

He turned to face Kenrik once more, "What can we do to help you, Your Imperial Highness?"

Kenrik breathed a sigh of relief, thankful that it was his father's friend, Karl Ulmar, who was leading the men that day. "Clear the way for us to come through! If you let these 14 men leave in safety, they have promised to set Princess Jobyna and me free once they are on their way!" Kenrik voiced the latter swiftly composed sentence, knowing the men had not planned anything as yet. They were all petrified, expecting to be killed any moment. Such fears created a situation of grave danger for Jobyna and him.

"It will take time, Your Highness!" Ulmar called. "I will have to come back to tell you when the way is clear."

Bodmin, who had taken leadership of the desperate men, leaned over to speak in broken German. "Then be quick as you can! We have no patience up here! I want every Chezk out of sight! If you've got anything to tell, then you come back and tell it alone!"

214

22

Luke's eyes were glued on the gates, his hand shading the early morning sun rising persistently in the sky. He had read the note from Jobyna and explained to their uncle the problem of the frequent fainting spells Jobyna had experienced as a child.

"She used to work herself up into such a state that she would hyperventilate and faint. It puzzled Father, and he called doctors who diagnosed and prophesied all kinds of maladies; one even said she would die young! Finally, a doctor told us that she did it to herself without knowing. Whenever she was afraid or upset, she would begin breathing too fast and get light-headed. If one of the family were around at the time she began the strange breathing, they told her to take a deep breath and hold it as long as she could and this would usually avert the fainting. She grew out of it some years ago." Luke looked at the letter again, feeling sure as he comprehended her wit, that she was well.

Dearest Brother Luke,

Thank you for your note. It cheered us up just to see your handwriting and to know you are safe. Maia and I feel safer now, and I haven't fainted for several hours! I have been wishing you were here to remind me about my breathing. It has been like living through a nightmare, yet knowing it to be real. I don't think I will ever have another bad dream—I may never sleep again, either!

It is bad news about the gates and we are praying that God will speed our freedom. Konrad needs a doctor. Although he seems to be improving and has taken in some fluid, he is still unconscious.

I could talk on and on to you as it helps fill in the time, but the note would end up too heavy for the men to carry down the wall.

Uncle Dorai, I look forward to being at home with you and Aunt Minette and the children. Maia is excited about seeing you today. I love you very much.

(signed)

Jobyna (with love to you both)

Chezkovian red and white soldiers began pouring from the entrance gates, abandoning their mantelets and battering rams, marching down the road.

"What's going on up there?" Luke asked, and Prince Dorai looked up from his discussion with a group of Frencolian knights. They were talking about the horrifying news received from messengers at dawn of the murder of the Proburg princes. Now they turned to watch the unexpected exodus.

Close to the entry gates, the Chezkovian army had set up tents, with emirs and constables occupying them to spearhead the operation of taking the gates. Doctor Sleven and a team of doctors and aides were on hand waiting for the final gates to be opened. A line of carriages awaited to be used to transport all the freed prisoners back to the palace at Jydanski where the royal relatives had been escorted.

Prince Gustovas and family would return to Landmari Castle; companies of Proburg troops were standing by to escort them. The capital was currently in a state of "operation mop-up." It depended on the doctors' decisions as to whether Konrad would be moved from Baltic Castle or how far. Jydanski was the closest capital to Baltic Castle. The released hostages would obviously need to be given sanctuary as quickly as possible, away from the emotional torment of the Baltic fortress and its traumatic memories.

Luke and Dorai watched with intrigue as Chezkovian leaders exited from a tent and walked toward the entrance gates. A large group of emirs and constables waited while one man entered alone. After a time, five emirs slowly followed.

Jobyna slouched back against the battlement with her eyes closed. Her head and back ached and the rope on her wrists was cutting in. Like a sudden surge of comfort, she remembered her faith. As Jobyna prayed, she relaxed and felt suddenly at peace. Words from long ago came to her mind, "Peace is not absence of war, or mere silence . . . it is a fragrance God gives us, filling our hearts and minds with tranquillity no matter what the circumstances around us are!" Her father had said these words when he had resigned as a senior knight! He had repeated them to her many years ago after she had rescued him from abductors.

Frewin broke the silence, "What's taking them skunks so long?" he snarled at Kenrik.

"There's a whole army, several armies, out there! They can't disband them in five minutes." Kenrik shot back.

"Well, they better not take too long! How do we know they won't trick us?" Bodmin spoke up, looking through the keyhole at the gate entrance.

"Czarevitch Kenrik!" A voice called and Constable Ulmar stepped through the archway.

"I am here!" Kenrik turned around, standing in the gap so he could be seen.

Ulmar stepped closer. "There are five emirs here who have to identify you and then the word will be sent out to dismiss the armies; but it has to be verified that it is truly you, Your Highness. There will be no trickery! We will not play games with the life of Czarevitch Kenrik!"

"Tell them to get it done with quickly!" Bodmin called, looking down at Ulmar, his voice resigned.

The constable disappeared briefly, returning with the five emirs who moved cautiously through the archway behind Ulmar. Kenrik expected them to demand him to give their names and answer some questions. He narrowed his eyes and scrutinized each face.

Ulmar stood in the middle of the causeway. "We want the czarevitch to send his czardom ring to us."

"The czarevitch does not 'send' his ring, he presents it!" Kenrik corrected.

"The czarevitch is to present his ring!" Ulmar commanded.

"I am bound, Ulmar," Kenrik answered, remembering the ritual of the ring he had received on his 16th birthday. The ring was the symbol of his right to the czardom.

"Then they must unbind you!" One of the emirs spoke. His face was expressionless and his voice hard.

Kenrik turned to Bodmin, "Just one hand, my right; you can tie the other."

Bodmin did not move. He doubted the whole escape now.

"I just have to say some words and throw them my ring, and they will let us go! Believe me!" Kenrik implored.

Jobyna, though she did not understand all Kenrik's words, noticed a different pleading in the czarevitch's voice that she had not heard before. She turned to Bodmin, "There's nothing to lose! If you kill us, they kill you. Why don't you do what they want?"

Hagen moved up from behind. "She's right, man! There's no other way out o' here. We can't go back! The Pros are right on our tracks! Do as they say!" Hagen held the sword at Kenrik's chest as Bodmin sliced up through the rope.

Kenrik turned slowly, and Hagen's sword moved with him. "You have to be patient. I must get this right, or it's curtains for us all." He hissed at Hagen. "Just shut up while I work through this for you!" Turning, he pulled a ring off his right hand, thankful they had not stolen his jewelry and had set both hands free.

"The Czarevitch Kenrik presents the ring!" Kenrik held the ring up with his right hand, saluted and dropped his hand to his side. The sun caught the gems in his many other rings, sending shafts of color shooting in all directions.

"Present the czarevitch's ring!" One of the emirs called out.

"The Czarevitch Kenrik presents the ring to the czardom." Kenrik held the ring up with his right hand, again saluting and dropping his hand quickly, still retaining the ring.

"Present the czarevitch's ring!" A third emir shouted.

"The Czarevitch Kenrik presents the ring!" This time Kenrik did not hold it up, but kissed it, aimed carefully and threw it hoping his ring would land at their feet. He instantly saluted, waiting. The ring hit one of the emirs on his chest, falling with a tinkle to the cobblestones; not quite the usual way the ring was parted with by the heir to the czardom, but they knew for certain he was Kenrik, son of the late czar. The emirs were surprised, for they had been sure it was not possible, and they had used this method to expose an impostor.

"The emirs receive the ring from the Czarevitch Kenrik." The five emirs saluted and one of them retrieved the ring. They disappeared back out through the archway, followed by Ulmar.

Kenrik sank to the floor. The thought had never crossed his mind that they would be so hard to convince! He knew who he was! A public display of one of the czardom secrets had been demanded to convince them! He stared around at the waiting soldiers, realizing that when this drama ended, there would be none of them left to tell, anyway. Just the princess! Kenrik looked across at Jobyna and noticed the bright, interested set of her face. Even with her limited knowledge of German, she had followed what had transpired, the sequence of words and actions. She was now looking at the gates with triumph. Kenrik tried to imagine what was making her so happy. He thought of Konrad and he knew.

Frewin interrupted his thoughts, "What now? They's gone again! Too long, if I knows anything!"

"They'll be clearing the way for us!" Kenrik told them. "When we leave here, there won't be a soldier in sight! Just give them time to do it!" He was thankful they had not tied him again, but he knew his reprieve was brief.

Luke and Dorai watched as Chezkovian soldiers rode toward them. They dismounted and the captain explained to Dorai that enemies in the tower had captured the Czarevitch Kenrik and all troops were to be moved into obscurity until the royal carriage had passed by. The uncle related the captain's message to Luke. Turning back, Dorai asked how many men would be escaping. The number of 13, or 14 at the most, came to his ears.

"How on earth did they capture the czarevitch?" Prince Dorai's voice was filled with amazement, thinking of the man who had killed Elliad, now a captive? How was it possible?

Closing his eyes in the realization of his inappropriate blunder in front of the Frencolian king and prince, the captain saluted, "I'm very sorry, Your Highness." He hesitated; looking at Luke, he began to speak in broken Frenc, "Forgive me, Your Highness!

They have another hostage as well . . . the Princess Jobyna!" The captain did not wait any longer, but quickly mounted, riding along to the leaders of the other armies to order them to move away from the road, out of sight, and wait until the carriage had gone by.

Luke surveyed Baltic Castle with fear on his face. Gradually the fear changed and a different light appeared in his eyes. "You know what this means, Uncle?" He turned to Dorai, whose face was gray. Luke answered his own question. "The gates will be free! The doctors can enter and tend those who are injured!"

"I just hope this wasn't engineered by your sister! It's not a game we're playing here!" Prince Dorai doubted Jobyna would give herself up like this. He dismissed the idea when he thought of Kenrik; the czarevitch would never give in to a bunch of Frencolian traitors! Whatever was going on, it sounded very dangerous for his niece and the heir to the czardom, if it were truly him!

"Move out! Flatten every tent!" The captains shouted as they rode back toward Baltic Castle.

Prince Dorai issued orders to the knights and they moved off. Luke hurried to the dell where the horses were grazing, trying to take in the mind-boggling events. He mounted a horse, held at the ready for him. A sea of colors was moving before his eyes—tents flattened and abandoned, men moving across to the road. He hoped tempers would not run high, that swords and daggers would stay sheathed.

Luke's eyes beheld a great number of Chezkovian guards riding down from the castle, drawing the carriages. Captains filed off sending their soldiers before them clearing the way so no one would remain to challenge the carriage when it departed.

23

Twitching and shaking, the simple Frewin was becoming uncontrollably jittery. His very breathing was vibrating with spasms of nervousness.

Bodmin was savagely biting his nails—so savagely that on some fingertips he had begun chewing off skin, drawing blood.

Hagen waved his sword and stomped around impatiently.

The soldiers lined the tower battlements, some watching behind, and the others looking toward the empty, open archway, grinding their teeth, waiting, waiting. . . .

Kenrik slouched over the parapet with his back to Hagen's coming and going sword.

Jobyna sat on the cobblestones praying and thinking of Konrad. "If you save us out of this, Lord, I'd like to go home for a while to Frencolia. Then I will marry Konrad," she determined.

Ulmar's voice finally came to them. He could see the soldiers and Kenrik looking down at him. "The way is clear! Tell us which way you will go after leaving the Baltic Road, and we will see you have a free passage."

"South!" Bodmin called back before anyone else could make a squeak.

He turned and muttered, "Well, here goes nothing!" Pointing at Kenrik, Bodmin ordered, "Tie him up, and we'll move out."

Obviously the men had not imagined they could escape, so they had no ideas for the future now that they were being released. The rope that had bound Kenrik lay in pieces on the stone floor and the soldiers scavenged desperately to gather enough to bind him successfully. Removing his rings one by one, they tied his hands behind his back with the strips, ordering him to lie on the floor of the carriage. Bodmin bound his feet. Kenrik felt the length of rope under his body as he wriggled himself across the carpet toward the other side of the carriage, and he was thankful they had not discovered this. He tested the ropes on his wrists. The many tight knots were a work of art, and would prove difficult to untie, but he made an inconspicuous start.

Jobyna, trussed up tightly, was bundled on the floor by Kenrik's feet. Frewin climbed in, this time sporting a dagger. Kenrik realized Frewin would be far more proficient with his dagger than with the sword. The glint in his darting, beady eyes gave him away as a petty thief. The small simple man sat, twisting and turning the gold ring he had been allotted, blowing on it and polishing it on the velvet.

The carriage began to move. Jobyna expelled a sigh of relief trying to conceal a smile at the crashing sound of a lowered drawbridge. The sound of gates opening came to their ears. Finally, the portcullis was raised. The carriage wheels sank momentarily in the ditch that was being dug to free the portcullis. The clatter of the horses' hooves following was echoed by the sound of the chains lowering the portcullis once more.

Jobyna frowned knowing that time would be lost in opening the portals again, but she was glad no lives would be lost as previously.

The only lives at risk now were Kenrik's . . . and hers. Jobyna wondered, *would the escapees really leave Chezkovia alive, as free men?*

One man controlled the reins and guided the horses which pulled the carriage. Six soldiers rode their horses in front. Hagen and the six others brought the extra horses behind. The entrance gates had been irreparably smashed.

The desperate escapees rode out, down the narrow castle road and out into the open countryside. Not a soul was in sight! Flattened tents and upturned tables lay here and there. There was no sign of anyone hiding anywhere, no obvious raised hiding places.

Once the carriage and horses passed, eyes looked furtively from under the flattened tents, waiting until the carriage was out of sight. Thoughts were turned toward the final taking of the castle.

Moritz was already scaling the walls of the middle tower. Many men were close behind, hurrying to lower the drawbridge, open the gates and raise the portcullis. Running through the causeway to the entrance gate, Moritz met Constable Ulmar who recognized him immediately. They saluted each other, jubilant but sober.

"The doctors are on the beach road waiting to be called back when the way is clear," Ulmar explained.

Moritz began walking with Ulmar toward the castle. "Vincenz here will take you to the castle. You'll need men to go over every inch of the castle and grounds. Enemies may still be in hiding. I am going to take a horse and follow the royal carriage."

"You won't need to," Ulmar said as Moritz increased his pace. "Troops have been detailed to ride on ahead, and a large company will be following at a discreet distance. You won't get through!"

"I'll try anyway!" Moritz said determinedly. He grabbed the reins of the horse he had left in the second causeway and swung himself into the saddle.

"I'll send some of my men to accompany you!" Ulmar called after Moritz. Turning to Vincenz, he asked for directions to the stables. Having sent Ulmar's men in the right direction, Vincenz and Ulmar headed off up the steps. Troops following spread out shoulder to shoulder across the gardens, slashing off bushes and plants level with the ground, turning over statues and investigating every nook and cranny.

Luke and Dorai headed their horses toward the castle some 15 minutes after the carriage had disappeared. Chezkovian soldiers poured through the gates ahead of them. All were monitored as they entered. The carriages moved slowly in the same direction, and Luke knew Doctor Sleven was in one of them. Other than the commissioned troops and the doctor with his team, only direct relatives of Elliad's prisoners were allowed to enter the castle gates.

The vista of the courtyard with its dead bodies revealed to the Frencolian King Luke and Prince Dorai some of the carnage of the past hours. The spear had been pushed firmly into the ground, displaying the impaled head of the impostor to all who passed by. Luke and Dorai paused momentarily before ascending the steps, gazing on the gory spectacle.

"No wonder Jobyna fainted!" Luke turned to his uncle briefly, then gazing back at the pretender's head, he said, "He had everything: riches, treasures, castles, power, a czardom at his feet, a captured kingdom, royal hostages; yet what does he have now, what is left in his memory?" Looking earnestly at his uncle, Luke murmured, "He gained so much with the power of his sword! For all he stole, he has nothing! I pray even the slightest memory of him will die fast.

"It would surprise me if anyone finds his sword, yet it would have been the last possession he had within his grasp. Elliad John Pruwitt . . . he gained the world, yet, as the Gospel Book says, he lost his own soul! He who lived by the sword has died by it!"

The path to the castle was guarded by Chezkovians who ordered everyone to "keep to the path!" Luke knew the way already; how could he forget? Soldiers were digging a mass grave in the garden. Others were bringing dead bodies and piling them beside the diggers: dead knights, emirs, constables, captains, soldiers, servants, slaves, men and women. Shaking his head, Luke thought, *This is a nightmare!*

They were detained in the castle foyer as an officer recorded their names and that of "the Princess Maia." A constable escorted them to the dining hall.

Doctor Sleven arrived and examined Konrad. He looked in his eyes, listened to his heartbeat and poked and prodded. With help from his aides, he changed Konrad's position, laying him carefully on one side. Ordering the attendants to carry the pallet, they left the room.

The doctor moved to speak with Kedar, who assured him that his wrist had been tended to carefully by a servant who was now presumed dead. A young doctor told Kedar he would ride with him back to Jydanski where physicians there would examine the amputation. The team was surprised to find Kedar so well and free from pain.

Maia sat watching the dining room doors which were propped open and guarded by men in Chezkovian uniforms. She could not understand what was being said, but Cynara and Kedar sat beside her, explaining the situation.

Ellice was escorted in and a constable asked if anyone knew her. Cynara told them she was "Princess Jobyna's servant," knowing that Jobyna had a strange liking for the slave-girl. Maia asked Cynara what was said. Correcting the czarevna, she informed her that Jobyna wanted Ellice referred to as her "friend." Maia asked Ellice about Jobyna, where she was, why she hadn't returned. The trembling Ellice shook her head and tried to hide her tears, moving desolately away to sit on a couch.

"Kenrik will be here soon . . . for this," Cynara said, walking toward the table where the crown had been placed beside the papers.

Emir Javik approached Cynara, followed by several emirs, "Your Imperial Highness, Czarevna Cynara." He said bowing, "Your Imperial Highness, Grand Duke Kedar." He bowed toward Kedar. "It will be our pleasure to escort you back to your home in Jydanski." He nodded toward the crown and two emirs moved forward, one to collect the crown, the other to gather the papers.

"Where is my brother?" Cynara asked.

Javik's expression gave nothing away. "The czarevitch is with Princess Jobyna. We wish you to come with us for some briefing and then we will take you to your carriage." He smiled, "It pleases us greatly that you are both in good health and are now free!"

Maia watched as they left. Looking at Ellice, she saw the slave-girl was sobbing. Maia sat on the couch beside her, patting her back, wishing Ellice could talk. Suddenly she heard a voice she recognized!

"Maia! My Maia!"

"Father?" Maia flew into his arms. "Father! Oh, Father!" He swung her off the ground, hugging and kissing her. Then it was Luke's turn. Exclamations and greetings all complete, Maia asked if they had seen Jobyna.

"She is with Czarevitch Kenrik," Prince Dorai told her.

Ellice dried her eyes. The princess really was with the czarevitch? Maybe everything was all right! Ellice had been tied up in the bedroom until Chezkovian soldiers had burst in. After they had cut the ropes that bound her, they had questioned and threatened her until she had managed to communicate the fact that she was mute. She wondered what would have happened to her if Cynara had said she was Elliad's slave. Ellice felt indebted to the czarevna.

"This is Jobyna's friend, Ellice." Maia introduced the curtsying Ellice to Prince Dorai, who kissed her hand, and then to Luke who repeated the greeting.

"I remember Jobyna telling me about Ellice, and there was Boey, wasn't there? You spoke of them, too, Maia." Luke's eyes toured the dining hall.

He swung around as two little girls ran toward him.

"Luke! Luke!" They wrapped themselves around his waist and his legs.

"Zandra! Yvette! Do you know? Your papa's coming soon!" He bent down to talk to them, pleased to see their smiles. Luke looked toward the doors. "Here he is now!"

The stately, brown-bearded figure of King Thurlow from Danzerg entered the room, accompanied by his knights to claim his two little daughters. Laughter and exclamations took some time to exhaust themselves.

Turning to Luke and Dorai, King Thurlow's voice became sympathetic; "I'm terribly sorry about Princess Jobyna. I hope they catch those dashed murderers. It's a terrible affair about the czarevitch . . ." King Thurlow's statement was cut off by Maia's high-pitched questioning:

"Father, what does he mean? Where is Jobyna?" She stared at her father, then to Luke, "You didn't tell me. You said she is with . . ." Maia stopped suddenly, hearing the silence, seeing their faces. Ellice stepped closer as Maia asked quietly, "Were they murdered?"

Prince Dorai picked her up in his arms again. "No darling! She is . . . they are . . ." He could not find an explanation to prevent a lie.

Dorai looked helplessly at King Thurlow who stuttered, "I'm so . . . sorry; I . . . I . . ." The king backed away with one arm around each girl. He said, "I'll see you in Jydanski, my friends."

Maia pushed against her father's chest and he stood her down, knowing she was much too big to hold like a child. "Tell me where Jobyna is!" Maia's voice became a whine.

Luke answered, "We are not sure where she is, Maia, but she is with Kenrik. And she is alive. We must pray that she will be safe."

"Then she's not safe?" Maia persisted. "Tell me, what happened? Please!"

Prince Dorai shook his head, beckoning Ellice to follow them, "We are going to Jydanski, in a carriage, and we will tell you about it on the way. When we get to the palace, we hope to receive word."

"But Father, I thought we would be going home to Mother! Jydanski is a horrid place. . . ." She stopped her whining as she caught the look in her father's eye.

"Maia! The roads are very unsafe and may remain so for some days, weeks even. We cannot travel back to Frencolia yet! I want you to keep quiet now and we will discuss it later."

Prince Dorai's frown was soon dispelled when Maia hugged him once more, exclaiming, "I'm so glad to be with you! Safe! We will pray, and I am sure God will keep Jobyna safe!"

Prince Dorai hoped the czarevitch would be rescued swiftly or no one would be safe! He did not share this fear with Luke who escorted the tearful Ellice as they walked down through the gardens to the waiting carriage.

24

Frewin sat on the plush seat with his boots up on the velvet. Using his dagger to clean his fingernails, he wiped it now and then on the luxuriant upholstery.

"Are we permitted to talk?" Kenrik felt he would humor Frewin by asking.

"Be me guest." Frewin waved his dagger, interested to know what they would talk about. He was an expert eavesdropper and loved to listen to gossip.

"I am told you ride a horse, Princess; is that true?" Kenrik began.

Jobyna thought, *He already knows that, I wonder where he is leading?* She maneuvered into a more comfortable position before replying, "Yes, I love riding Brownlea. He's the second horse I've had."

Kenrik sighed longingly, "There is nothing like riding a horse! The freedom, the speed."

"Speed is the name of Luke's horse, and he almost flies! Luke let me ride him just once. He is jealous of his horse." Jobyna sighed, thinking of her brother.

"When I was just a boy, I would climb out of this carriage and walk along the stepway to the seat at the front. It is easy to ride there. I hated riding in this carriage! I used to feel shut away, cooped up." Kenrik shrugged in disdain as his eyes traveled around the red walls.

"I don't mind," Jobyna said honestly. Immediately catching Kenrik's disappointed stare, she added deliberately, "But it is stuffy! We all smell of perspiration!" She wrinkled her nose, inquiring, "What is the scenery like out there?"

Kenrik looked away, concealing a smile from Frewin, knowing she had caught on. The simple spy was shifting uncomfortably in the seat, reaching to open the shutters.

"It isn't so good right now, but it is breathtaking soon. You can see the mountains on a clear day," Kenrik told her, watching as Frewin looked out at the passing hills. "Ah! For some fresh country air!" Kenrik sighed once more.

"I've never ridden in a royal carriage before! It is rather boring, compared to riding Brownlea." Jobyna issued an uncontrolled yawn, and spoke before it was completely exhaled, "I'm so tired, I think I'll go to sleep. Do you mind if I don't talk?" She leaned her cheek on the velvet edge of the seat.

Kenrik gave a head-shaking yawn, "I suppose we'll be here for hours! I didn't sleep last night. I might get some shut-eye, too." He noted Frewin trying to conceal a yawn.

The carriage was silent, but for the whirl of the wheels, the gentle movement of the springs and the drumming sound of the horses' hooves. Frewin narrowed his eyes at his prisoners, then tried to open the shutters to view the scenery. He "humphed" and sat back for a while, asking himself why he should travel in a stuffy carriage when it was far better outside, up front. He closed the shutters and opened the door hesitating as the ground flashed by his eyes. Kenrik was tempted to kick him hard, but Jobyna was in the way, and he knew the men riding behind would see Frewin's fall. He needed more time, but not long! Frewin shut the door again and Jobyna stirred, feigning a cough, spluttering and yawning all at once.

"It's so stuffy," she said, her eyes still shut; she let her head slump forward.

Frewin opened the door, climbed on the stepway, closed the door and inched along to the seat at the front. He sat and inhaled the fresh air, enjoying the view, glad he had thought of coming up front.

Bodmin drew his horse alongside the front of the carriage, yelling, "Hey! Frewin! I told you to stay back there!"

"It's too stuffy! I'd fall asleep!" Frewin shouted back, "Besides, they're not goin' nowhere. Go back to yer watchin'. I'll check on 'em 'fore long." He turned his attention to the man controlling the reins, boasting about his ring, and exclaiming as the man flaunted his. Frewin gasped at the huge emerald; he had killed for a smaller stone!

The instant Frewin closed the door, Kenrik pushed his feet toward Jobyna, instructing, "My boot! The right one! On the inside! You'll find a small dagger."

Jobyna shuffled around. Bringing her tied hands to his boot, she tried to get her fingers inside. It was tricky, but she felt the small implement. Sliding it out, she then eased it from its sheath, gripping the handle in her teeth.

Kenrik rocked himself around. Jobyna grasped the dagger with fingers from both hands and she sawed at his bonds. He winced as the blade sliced down through the rope and along his thumb, taking the top layer of skin. Once free, he deftly cut the rope from his feet and cut her hands loose. Her wrists were raw from the pressure of the rope. Bruises on her face and arms were swollen and purple.

Jobyna smiled at Kenrik. "They'll be inside Baltic Castle by now." She watched as he reached under the seat and pressed on the velvet-covered panel. Reaching into the cavity, Kenrik drew out a sheath with a short sword in it. He sheathed the dagger and gave it to her.

"Take it. You may need it," he said, his eyes looking into her serious emerald stare. He pulled out a flask, removed the stopper and offered it to her. Strong fumes rose to her nostrils, and she shook her head, but licked her parched lips as he thirstily swallowed several mouthfuls.

"Why don't we jump from the door? Won't there be some of your soldiers following us?" she asked, disturbed, knowing he was preparing to fight.

"I'd like to settle it with this lot first! I'm sorry you hate bloodshed so much," Kenrik said not a bit sorry.

"Kenrik!" she said as he pushed the bolts on the door and cut a small piece out of the shutter. "Kenrik! Look at me!" He turned to meet her eyes, and she continued, "There are 12 men out there . . . well, 11!" They both smiled at the thought of Frewin. "Hagen and the soldiers are killers! I am useless and you are one." She paused, feeling embarrassed. He had turned away. "You may fight like a hundred of them, Kenrik, but you are the czar now! Please think of Chezkovia and let your men take care of this miserable bunch!" She threw him one more plea. "Think of how great your men will feel that they helped destroy the czar's kidnappers!" Her words revealed to him that she cared more for him than she worried about shed blood, especially that of these traitors. Kenrik stared at this princess. He had never before met such a woman. She was anxious about his life! Not since his mother had anyone expressed real care toward him.

He climbed up into the back, slid a round metal piece from an aperture and peered out. Cutting a hole in the other side, he looked out, then made the hole larger and searched again. "I don't believe these idiots! I think they have all gone up ahead!"

Unknown to Kenrik, the soldier driving the carriage had caught sight of a distant red and white uniform. Frewin had agreed and claimed that he saw troops ahead. If the men had to ride ahead to check it out, then his reprieve from the "stuffy carriage" would last longer. He didn't cherish the idea of balancing his way back along the side of the carriage again. "Besides, they're sleepin' like babies—that they are!" he reassured himself.

The company ahead had been slowed down by men at a vantage point, reporting that they could now count all 14 men. The inside of the carriage must now be unguarded. Galloping the mounts ahead, the emir in charge selected an appropriate spot and rapidly prepared an ambush. They would wait until the carriage was alongside, then attack the 14, hoping fervently that no one else was in the carriage except the czarevitch and the princess. Quickly numbering the men, he delegated each of the 14 to three. The rest would surround and enter the carriage to protect the czarevitch.

Kenrik felt the carriage slow down and heard other accelerating hooves moving away.

"It's now or never! We're going to jump!" He stated to the wide-eyed Jobyna. He slashed and sliced, pulling the back of the seat away, cutting right through the padded velvet upholstery, through the linings and the leather casing. Slashing at the curved wooden slats, he hoped Frewin was too occupied with himself, his ring and the scenery to hear the muffled sounds. Kenrik placed the sheath on his belt, sheathed the sword and helped Jobyna through the gap to hang with him over the back of the carriage.

"I'll count to three; let yourself slide off. Try to relax, land on your feet and then roll over!" He did not look at her or he would have seen her terrified face. The carriage had slowed, but the surroundings still flew by at tremendous speed. Dust rose in all directions. Jobyna felt herself breathing faster.

"One . . . two . . . three!" Kenrik pushed her backward, prying her fingers loose from clinging to the torn covers; counting two more, he dropped off. Rising up immediately, he drew his sword.

Jobyna lay winded and wheezing on the dusty road. Kenrik's hands reached to her. "Are you hurt?" He was concerned as he pulled her to unsteady feet and supported her as she coughed and swayed.

"I don't know . . . oh, my ankle, a bit . . . it twisted my knee." She clung to him, trying to balance on one foot.

"But . . . we're free! What a ghastly way to escape!" She looked up at her rescuer's face and laughed, trying not to cry. She thought, *At least he didn't have to kill anyone or get killed himself.*

Sheathing his sword, the czarevitch helped her as she limped off the road. Lifting her into his arms, he carried her through the long grass, 50 yards away, into some low bushes. "If Frewin notices we're gone, then they'll be back . . . maybe." He thought for a moment, then said, "Or they'll ditch the carriage and keep riding. You're right, Jobyna! The men will feel good to claim the credit!" He looked at her. The torn, bloodstained dress was now covered with dust and grime. Her knee had gone right through the fabric. "You should see yourself!" He laughed.

"You should see what you look like! You have dust in your beard! It looks gray!" They both laughed, and the tension was relieved.

Kenrik crouched down into the bushes as horses approached. Two men rode from behind, around the bushes, through the grass. They were soon joined by two more. The pain in Jobyna's knee caused her to utter a muffled groan as Kenrik pulled her even lower and she sank to the ground. Kenrik watched through the top branches as Chezkovian uniformed men drew their horses on to the road. They began searching the roadsides.

"They must have seen us!" Kenrik hissed in her ear.

"What's wrong? They're yours, aren't they?" Jobyna whispered back, surprised.

"One thing you'll learn, Jobyna, is that you can never depend on people, even when you think you know them!" Kenrik whispered, trying to peer out from their hiding place.

"I always give people the benefit of the doubt!" Jobyna whispered back, keeping her head down.

"Shh! They're off their horses and coming this way. They've see our tracks in the grass. Stay right down! I wish I knew who they were. . . ."

Jobyna reclined on the decaying leaves and twigs under the bush. Kicking her slipper off, she rubbed her ankle, not daring to look at her throbbing knee, but knowing from past experience the extent of her injury. She was sure that her heart was pounding in her knee! Doctor Sleven had warned her of the ease in which a dislocated kneecap could click out of place again due to irreparable damage done to tendons and ligaments.

Two of the men stood talking, just out of earshot. Kenrik knew loyal men of the czardom would never point a weapon at a member of the royal family. He quietly stood to his feet, his hand on the hilt of his sword. One of the men was a soldier and the other a constable. "Identify yourselves!" Kenrik called and the constable whipped off his helmet. The soldier saluted.

"Ehren! I'm glad to see you!" Kenrik said, leaping out of the bushes toward the men.

"Not as glad as we are to see you, Your Imperial Highness!" Ehren saluted and bowed. He carried the sheathed dagger that Jobyna had dropped from the back of the carriage, and he held it out, handle first, to Kenrik. The sound of many horses came to their ears, and Kenrik beheld a numerous company of Chez-kovian troops riding from the direction of Baltic Castle in a billowing cloud of dust. The leaders drew the cavalcade to a halt. The front men dismounted and raced to Kenrik's side, saluting, bowing and exclaiming.

Ehren described the hole Kenrik cut in the back of the carriage and they laughed. One of the emirs slapped Kenrik on the back, turned and issued orders for troops to continue following the carriage. Once the criminals had been dealt with, they were commissioned to ride on to Chezpro Castle and capture this stronghold from Elliad's men. Frencolian knights and captains were being held prisoner either at Chezpro Castle or Baja Castle—men who had been captured when King Luke was taken prisoner. The emirs had decided to do the job properly and would go as far as the border castle on the Reideaux-Frencolian border to annihilate any remnant of the enemy and free all prisoners. Kenrik discussed these plans, cautioning them to be sure they did not kill the wrong people. He questioned them about Jydanski, and was reassured that loyal troops were taking care of the palace.

Stiffening suddenly, Kenrik remembered Jobyna. He strode back to the bushes and called her name. She did not stand and he pulled the branches aside where he had left her, reaching for her hands.

"I don't think I can get up," she said, and he laughed, stopping suddenly at her look of agony. He grasped both hands and pulled her to stand. Her clouded green eyes gazed past Kenrik at the large company in red and white all staring back at her. She knew she must look a sight!

In a clouds of swirling dust, Moritz arrived, having been delayed by the influx of soldiers swarming up the road to Baltic Castle after the carriage was out of sight.

The royal carriage appeared along the road, returning the way it had gone, now in the victors' charge. Kenrik lifted Jobyna into his arms and conveyed her to the opened door.

"It won't be stuffy, but it may be dusty." He seated her on the carpet, "You'll probably be more comfortable traveling in here." Kenrik shut the door, speaking to Moritz, who opened the door once more. Moritz knelt on the carpet, looking at Jobyna's ankle, then her knee. He pressed on the kneecap, making her wince and turn away with tears in her eyes.

Moritz spoke to Kenrik, who exchanged places, handing Jobyna the dagger. "Moritz says if you cut another strip off the bottom of your dress, he will bandage your ankle, which will help the swelling and give it support at the same time. He says that your knee will have to wait until a doctor can deal with it." Jobyna slid the dagger from the sheath.

"Be careful!" he cautioned, rubbing the place where skin was missing from his hand.

Speaking somewhat severely due to the pain of her knee, Jobyna commented, "Just what I need now is a gash in my leg!" Pushing the point of the dagger through the fabric, she tore it around the bottom.

The bandage secure, Kenrik tried to reassure her. "We will have you in Jydanski in no time!"

Sinking back on the red carpet, Jobyna realized fully for the first time that the nightmare was indeed almost over!

Kenrik would have mounted a horse to rendezvous with the group ahead—the ones who had obviously ambushed the enemies and sent the carriage back when they realized the czarevitch had escaped—but Constable Ehren and Emir Schonhausen told him he must ride to Jydanski, preferably with the royal carriage. Moritz agreed that this made sense. He should escort Princess Jobyna to King Luke Chanec and her uncle, who would be traveling to the palace. Riders sent ahead would proclaim the welcome news of their safety.

The Czarevitch Kenrik, wearing one of the constable's jackets, rode seated beside Emir Schonhausen on the front seat of the carriage, escorted by hundreds of Chezkovian soldiers. They were joined by others as they neared the capital. As the soldiers and crowds cheered, Kenrik was silent for the last half of the journey. His mind was churning over events of the past four months. How he had changed! Six months ago, he was a fired up, reckless, pleasure loving, carefree boy. The time incarcerated in dungeons had brought about great changes, and the spell in exile had caused him to view his life more realistically.

The carriage rattled on toward the place where he would soon be crowned the czar of the czardom and Kenrik realized the awesome task he was heading into. As long as his father had been there, autocratically strong and powerful, Kenrik had not taken the crown seriously. Now suddenly it was his. He determined to find time to think, to consider the new concepts he was experiencing. He needed to come to terms with his life and his destiny.

25

Soft, velvety carpet gave little comfort as Jobyna lay in the carriage. Tears made paths down her dusty cheeks and she moaned uninhibitedly. To be alone was to feel free to wallow privately in the misery that overwhelmed her. Not just the pain in her knee and ankle, but thoughts of Konrad injured for her sake, of dead soldiers and slain servants. Pictures of Elliad's gruesome head circled in her exhausted mind. The plush red upholstery of the carriage turned to blood as she closed her eyes and struggled to control the panic and desolation surging through her tormented emotions.

Maybe Kenrik was right! One could not depend upon people, even those close and dear. Her father and mother had been killed when she needed them most because they would not give Elliad the Gospel Books and a list of those to whom they had distributed the copies. For the first time Jobyna wondered if it truly had been worth it. With a bitterness she had never known before, she tried to imagine how her life would have been had her parents surrendered the books when commanded to do so. Elliad would have allowed them to live in the manor house. She would never have been captured by him and she would not be here today in this miserable land of Chezkovia.

Tears flowed more freely as Jobyna remembered that Luke would not have become king of Frencolia. The people in Frencolia would not know the freedom of having a God-fearing king. Cousin Leopold's body would not have been laid in the royal sepulcher. She would not have met Konrad. And finally, Elliad, the monster, would not have been brought to the end he so much deserved, freeing those oppressed by him and preventing further bloodshed and death.

Unwittingly, her depressed thoughts reversed to the former. She tried to reconstruct her life, to have her father and mother still alive, to make Elliad a wise and just person, asking, "Why does God allow killing, pain, heartache and death? If the Lord God is a God of love, why does He not step in and change people—force them to be peaceful and loving?"

Thirst became Jobyna's main enemy and she struggled to find the method by which Kenrik had triggered the panel under the seat. When it would not budge, she cried all the more, licking her hot, salty tears wishing for a drop of cool moisture to quench the overpowering dryness in her throat. Why should she have to suffer like this? Hadn't she been through enough already?

The sound of cheering reverberated in her confused mind. She heard many voices calling out words she could not understand. She recognized the name "Kenrik," the word "czar" and "Chezkovia." More cheering! The noise was surging, louder and louder. She thought, *we must be there*, but no longer cared. Freedom had lost its luster, life its joy. To bask in self-pity seemed the most satisfying comfort to the depressed girl.

Hands reached for her, voices she recognized, and Jobyna tried to rouse from a prison of total exhaustion. Her lips strove to form words. Luke's voice came to her ear, but she was falling . . . falling . . . sliding into a deep abyss, and the many terrible memories in her vivid imagination were lost in the darkness.

Dorai, Maia and Ellice watched as Luke stepped up into the carriage. Taking Jobyna in his arms, he cradled her head and gently kissed her bruised, tear-stained cheeks. The message had arrived with the fore-riders that Jobyna had injured her leg, but Luke was unprepared to find her in such a state. She clung to him and he stroked her dusty forehead.

"A drink . . . please. . . ." Jobyna's dry throat made her voice sound croaky. The brother looked around helplessly at his uncle. Luke moved to sit on the seat, allowing the doctor, Ruprecht, to examine his sister. The knee was his main concern. His prodding made her moan and cry. Luke explained that it had been dislocated once before, a year ago. The doctor issued orders and Jobyna was lifted to an elaborate litter and carried into the palace with the subdued group walking behind. Kenrik had been escorted away jubilantly in another direction.

A palace messenger arrived at their quarters with a request from Czarevitch Kenrik for the Frencolians to attend a celebration banquet that evening, and Luke sent a message back stating that Crown Prince Dorai and Princess Maia would be present, but he would stay with his sister who had not recovered from the ordeal she had been through.

Doctor Ruprecht manipulated Jobyna's knee, bandaged it tightly and helped her take in liquids laced with painkillers. Ellice sponged her face and arms, washing the dust away. Other servant women helped dress her in a fresh loose gown. When permitted to visit the patient, Luke, Dorai and Maia hovered over her with great concern. Doctor Ruprecht assured them that with rest and nourishment Jobyna would recover rapidly. She was exhausted and slightly dehydrated, but both conditions would be cured rapidly with rest and fluids. The knee and ankle would take a few days more, maybe a week or two. In spite of Jobyna's state of oblivion, Luke stayed by her bedside all night, falling asleep in the chair. She dozed fitfully on the next day. Luke helped her eat, and when she woke after a longer nap, he was pleased to see her smile at him. The room was filled with vases of beautiful flowers, all of which, Luke said, the czarevitch had sent for her.

Maia and her father were absent. They were guests in the presence of the czar-to-be. Luke was happy to have them represent Frencolia. Care and concern were shown to the brother and sister and on the morning of the third day, Kenrik, Cynara and Kedar visited their quarters surrounded by a large group of officials and attendants. Doctor Ruprecht, who had been in constant attendance, spoke to the czarevitch in positive tones.

Kenrik came to the bedside, "I am glad you are feeling better, Princess Jobyna." He bowed, kissed her hand and sat on the chair beside her bed. "You will be glad to know that King Konrad is making good progress and hopes to visit here as soon as he is well enough to travel. Doctor Sleven accompanied him to Landmari Castle and has been sending favorable reports." He nodded at Luke, saying, "I would like to borrow your brother. The citizens of Jydanski wish to greet the king of Frencolia, and we have planned to tour the city today."

Jobyna thanked Kenrik for sending the flowers, and he stood, suddenly self-conscious, indicating that Cynara sit. She was dressed in black. Kissing Jobyna's cheeks affectionately, Cynara spoke kindly to her and Jobyna felt warmed, though the conversation was trivial.

Kedar was officially introduced and Jobyna thought how much he looked like Kenrik. The boy gave an enthusiastic description of the contraptions which were being made to replace his hand. Soon he would have an artificial attachment.

He said he liked the hook; as well as being useful, it would make an excellent weapon! The boy's buoyancy in the face of his disablement astounded Jobyna. Of all her injuries, she had never suffered an amputation! Kedar lingered after Kenrik and Cynara moved with Luke to the sitting room.

The czar's young brother sat by Jobyna's bed and confided, "Your brother taught me about God when we were in the fortress. He told me of your faith, too, Princess Jobyna. Luke speaks highly of you. You must be very brave."

Jobyna returned, "You have great courage, Kedar, to accept such a loss without bitterness."

Kedar laughed, saying, "I lost my hand, but I now have a brother and a sister!" Aware of listening ears, he leaned to whisper in Jobyna's ear, "I have never been close to either, especially Kenrik. We may as well have lived in different countries, but Father's death . . . and my hand . . . changed it all!" He sat upright, his face shining. "I would rather have my life as it is now!" Switching subjects, he said brightly, "Did you know that Moritz is a believer?"

Jobyna was not sure how Moritz came into the conversation, but as Kedar chattered on, she was told that the older brother intended offering Moritz a position in his court after the coronation.

Before Kedar left, she grasped his hand and said, "Thank you, Kedar. You have helped me today! I must continue to believe that God is able to change the evil that man intends and use it for good in the lives of His children." She sighed.

⁂

Jobyna could not believe how good it felt to be soaking in a warm bath, right up to her neck in fragrant, steamy water. She sighed and closed her eyes. Even her swollen knee, sprained ankle and bruised arms felt relieved. She would have fallen asleep if it wasn't for Maia's constant questions and childlike chatter. Maia sat on the edge of the tub, pushing the foam around, explaining the sequence of events since her cousin had left the Baltic Castle dining hall that foreboding morning just after dawn. They had been resident at the palace for almost two weeks and Maia described the enshrinement of the late Czar Kievik on the previous day.

"The streets were lined with thousands of people! I have never seen so many! People were crying for Czar Kievik and at the same time cheering Kenrik." Maia stopped and sighed, trying to keep a mountain of foam on her palm, blowing the bubbles back into the bath. "It has been so hard for the czarevitch." She sounded grown up, motherly. "I do wish you could have been there, Jobyna! He never stops asking about you! He is sorry that you cannot dine with him yet. He is eager for you to be at his coronation next week; he said something about a special arrangement . . ." As though she was speaking out of turn, Maia blushed and looked away. Jobyna questioned her cousin, but Maia became tight-lipped, causing the older girl a measure of apprehension.

Doctor Ruprecht gave Jobyna a pair of crutches and encouraged her to use them. Luke was pleased to view her progress and he was enthusiastic when Ruprecht said she could go to the palace dining room for dinner tomorrow. Jobyna knew her brother enough to sense that there was something he wished to discuss with her, but was restraining himself! Again, she could not shake off her apprehension.

The view from the apartment was exquisite. Jobyna's eyes feasted on a man-made lake with fountains playing, encircled by graceful swans and ducks. Beautifully formed statues, colorful shrubs and flowers all brought a sense of peace and well-being. Jobyna had been visiting the library adjacent to their quarters, and she enjoyed reading from the extensive selection.

Ellice and a servant named Thirza sat reading with the princess in the library. Thirza rose and said she would prepare the bath. If Jobyna would come along in half an hour it would be ready. Ellice departed with her. The day was cloudy and a little cooler, and Jobyna moved with her book out on to the balcony, hoping to catch the warmth of the sun on her arms. The welcome orb came out and Jobyna soon became too hot. She dragged herself back through the doors, sitting on the floor in the light, behind the voluminous, purple-velvet drapes. The door opened and she heard her uncle's voice.

"Just a few seconds' privacy, Son." Dorai's eyes circled the room. "We simply must make a decision on this matter!"

Jobyna heard Luke's voice and was just about to reveal her presence when she heard her name. The words froze in her throat.

"I still feel we should include Jobyna in our discussions, Uncle. She seems so much better . . ."

"No, Son, we must not upset her. Doctor Ruprecht said she must be kept free from all stress. Besides, it is not for Jobyna to decide!" Dorai sat on the couch and Jobyna recoiled silently backwards, wondering whether to speak up or not?

Uncle Dorai continued his statements, "For the sake of Frencolia, we must decide to go ahead with the betrothal. It is an honor that Kenrik, soon to be crowned the czar of Chezkovia, wants to marry a Frencolian! It will bind our countries together and cement our security."

"Are you sure you feel that way, Uncle? Kenrik is quite a few years older. . . ."

"Age is nothing, Son. I am 12 years older than Minette and we are not encumbered by the difference. Such an age difference can be an advantage! I think we should give Kenrik our answer. His impatience to settle the matter is becoming embarrassing!"

Dorai slapped the back of the couch with his hand and stood decisively to his feet. "How could we dare to say no?" He laughed as though to a diabolical joke.

"You are right, Uncle! We must think of the alliance such a marriage would promote. Chezkovia has never been friendly to Frencolia, and this union will make all the difference." Luke stood to his feet. "I am sure Jobyna will understand when we explain. Anyway, it won't be for a couple of years. We'll have plenty of time back in Frencolia together. Minette will want that, won't she?"

Jobyna heard the door open and the men continued to talk as they walked away. She was sure her conclusions from their conversation were wrong and tried to reconstruct their dialogue. Who did Kenrik want to marry? Why did they not want to tell her? Why would she be upset? Surely they would not, they could not. . . . Jobyna dared not think. She pulled herself up and leaned on the crutches, watching the fountains spraying mist high into the air, seeing yet not beholding.

Suddenly, Kenrik's words returned to her mind: "You cannot depend on people, even when you think you know them." Her eyes traveled the palace gardens, then she withdrew into the library. Who could she turn to? To whom could she talk? What thoughts did Luke and Uncle Dorai have about Konrad now? Hadn't they been eager for her to be betrothed to him some weeks ago? Was a woman just something to dispose of in the way menfolk thought convenient?

Jobyna shuddered. She recalled their words: "For the sake of Frencolia" and "I am sure Jobyna will understand." Frencolia was more important to them than she was!

Ellice and Thirza entered the library just as Jobyna was wishing she could escape and flee to Konrad—to anywhere but this palace!

"We are ready for you, Princess . . ." Thirza stopped the

sentence as Jobyna turned away with tears glistening on her cheeks. "Your Highness, what is wrong?" Thirza came close. "Are you in pain?"

Shaking her head, Jobyna swayed and the concerned two tried to help her to the couch. "I'll be all right. Let's go back to the room." Jobyna did not want Luke to find her in the library; the way she felt, she hoped Luke would never find her!

She wondered when Luke was planning to break the news to her. How long would it be before the world knew she was promised to Kenrik?

"Help me into the bath," she commanded Ellice as in a daze, thinking of the imposing man who was to be the czar of Chezkovia. Kenrik was not such an awesome ogre really, but she loved Konrad. Dear, kind Konrad! She realized with a surge of tears just how much she loved him! His curly golden hair and blue eyes came to her mind and she closed her eyes, succumbing to the relaxation of the warm waters wrapping her body.

"Princess, are you sure you are all right?" Thirza's words broke into her thoughts. "I think I should send for Doctor Ruprecht."

"No, Thirza, don't! I'll feel better after the bath," Jobyna pleaded. "Wash my hair, please."

Maia entered the bathroom, bubbling over with enthusiasm. She watched as Jobyna, wrapped in a velvet robe, had her hair toweled dry. "You are going to sit by the czarevitch at the banquet tonight, Jobyna. He tells everyone that it is because of you he has the crown!" These words confirmed Jobyna's thoughts of dread.

The younger girl sighed. "Just imagine what it would be like to be the czarina! It's unbelievable!" Maia's words made Jobyna realize that the matter had been discussed with her cousin, maybe by Dorai, maybe even by her brother.

It was true! She did not know these people at all, and how could she depend upon any of them? They would consign her to another country, without even consulting her! She felt bitter, disillusioned, coldly aloof from reality.

"This isn't really happening!" she told herself. Grabbing the loose blue gown, she pulled it on and went to the bedroom, assisted by Ellice. Thirza protested; the princess was expected to dine with the czarevitch! Heedless of the murmuring women in the apartment, Jobyna submitted to a torrent of helpless, self-indulging tears and ignored Maia's compassionate attempts to comfort her. Thirza sent for Doctor Ruprecht.

"I cannot find anything physically wrong. Her knee is mending, as is her ankle." Doctor Ruprecht tendered his diagnosis to Luke and Dorai, who had been fetched by the anxious Maia. All questions asked by the doctor had been answered in tears, not words, by the patient.

"The princess is suffering from delayed shock. She is not as strong as I thought and needs complete rest and quiet for a while longer."

Luke sat by the bedside and listened helplessly to Jobyna's sobs. Her head was turned away from him.

"Please talk to me, Jobyna. Let me help you." He took the chair around to the other side of the bed, stroking her forehead.

She cringed and moaned, saying, "Please go to dinner! I just want to be left alone!" Jobyna pulled the cover over her head.

"It is not time yet. I'll sit with you." Luke turned to Maia. "Fetch me the Gospel Book please, Maia."

To Luke's surprise, Jobyna sobbed, "I don't want you to read to me, Luke! Go away and leave me alone!"

The brother ignored her and read from the Book in spite of her tears and protests. As he hoped, she became quiet and he continued reading through the gospel story.

Jobyna's mind kept up a depressing condemnation of her brother. *How could he? How could he! I could hate him!*

Maia and her father went to dinner. Jobyna heard Kenrik's

name mentioned and realized he must have entered the room. She turned her face away from the door, closing her eyes, hoping he would not come any closer. Standing to his feet, Luke moved out into the sitting room with the czarevitch. The brother returned after a few moments.

"Don't miss the dinner, Luke! Please go!" Jobyna pleaded.

Luke viewed his sister with compassion. Her eyes were sunk in rings of black, her face red from crying. He sat on the side of the bed and took her to his chest where she sobbed uncontrollably. The nearness of this beloved brother filled her with the desire to please him, to do whatever he asked of her. But she dared not talk to him about Kenrik; he would likely tell her she was ornery. As king, Luke had to arrange affairs in the way he felt best for Frencolia. He would talk to her about it when he was ready—but she hoped the moment would never arrive!

Jobyna had strange nightmares as she dozed: scenes of Kenrik and Konrad sword fighting over her, with Elliad's body-less head floating between the two men; Luke pushing her toward a throne where Kenrik sat. Such vivid pictures made her sit up suddenly in bed. A silent scream kept struggling to the surface.

Luke remained, reading to her while she tossed and turned. He was reminded of times long ago when their father would sit and read to Jobyna. Dreadful nightmares had been experienced by his sister, who had been affected by the plague yet had recovered four years ago. She would awaken wet with perspiration, crying and delirious, unable to be comforted apart from the words from the Book. Jobyna now appeared beyond all comfort, and Luke prayed silently for her.

Later in the evening, he read the part in the gospel story of the betrayal and crucifixion of Christ. Luke had almost skipped this part due to the gruesome nature of the reading, but Jobyna suddenly opened her eyes, obviously listening and absorbing the details. She remembered how the disciple Judas had betrayed

God's Son, how Jesus' friends forsook Him, how Peter denied Him; He was falsely accused and whipped, ridiculed and scorned; and finally, while nailed to the cross, He cried to His Father in heaven who had forsaken Him because of the sin He bore.

Luke read of the resurrection; the stone was rolled away from the tomb, and the Savior had risen from the dead!

"Read it again please, Luke," she whispered. "From the garden where he prayed, then he was betrayed. . . ." She closed her eyes, listening, feeling betrayed, forsaken, yet knowing her grief was not worthy of comparison.

"It isn't all that bad. Luke does love me," she told herself, praying silently, "Oh, Lord, how could I have forgotten? When will I ever learn that you will never forsake me? Jesus took my place! Even if everyone turns against me, you never will!"

She emitted an audible sob, praying in her heart, "Please, Lord, help me to be able to say 'Thy will be done,' when you know I love Konrad."

Luke, on completion of the gospel, was pleased to note that the patient was resting peacefully.

Jobyna did not stir when Dorai and Maia came in, whispering to Luke. They were pleased to see Jobyna sleeping peacefully.

Her uncle's deep voice brought Jobyna to consciousness, but she lay still, with her eyes shut, as remembrance of her predicament flooded her mind.

"It's late, Maia, you must go to bed. Your mother would have a fit to know you were up almost until midnight!" Prince Dorai kissed Maia.

"Luke, come out in the light and look at the ring Kenrik gave me," Maia whispered, looking over at Jobyna, who was motionless. "He made the announcement of our betrothal tonight. He told Father that he would wait no longer."

"How do you feel about it, Maia?" Luke kissed her cheek, placing his arm around her shoulder, drawing her into the lounge where the chambermaids waited to take Maia to her room.

"Wonderful! I can scarcely believe it is really happening to me! He is so . . . so wonderful, Luke! I know we will be happy." She held her hand out to show Luke the massive diamond set into the golden ring on her finger.

Jobyna experienced all manner of emotions, surging over her simultaneously! There was anger toward herself for jumping to wrong conclusions. There was frustration at Luke for having hidden such news from her, thus helping cause her confusion. There was concern because Kenrik had chosen such a dear child as Maia! Thankfulness toward the doctor was felt because he had not pressed her to discover the cause of her childish tears. Jobyna was glad that no one had guessed the real reason for her stupid grief. She was very embarrassed with herself! Most of all, she was truly delighted that it was Maia, not herself, that Dorai and Luke had been discussing in the library! Relief! Oh, the incredible, humiliating relief!

Luke came back to find Jobyna wide awake, sitting up, sipping juice. Her face was still puffy and eyes red, but she was smiling!

She blurted, "Tell me about Maia and Kenrik please, Luke." Jobyna was determined to learn the truth. At Luke's look of surprise, she explained, "I heard Maia talking about a diamond ring. . . ."

Jobyna decided to keep her previous feelings a secret for now. Hadn't Luke kept the news from her, she thought? *If I had attended the dinner, I would have heard the announcement for myself! How strange life is, twisting and turning as it does! It is true, I would have been ornery about Maia's betrothal to Kenrik. It may be just as well the decision was made before I could give my negative opinion!*

Jobyna felt like a reprimanded child! Maybe she would tell Konrad one day and they would laugh together!

26

"Konrad is coming! Konrad is coming!" The horses' hooves seemed to be repeating these words to Jobyna. She stood on the marble terrace in front of the great Jydanski Palace, waiting and watching. Luke supported her on one side and Uncle Dorai on the other. Chezkovian soldiers on horseback were riding in through the huge archways, lining up in formation, holding their swords high in the air, forming a guard of honor for the monarch of Proburg, Prince Gustovas, and his son, the monarch of Reideaux, King Konrad. Czarevitch Kenrik stood with Maia on one side, Cynara, Ellice and Kedar at his other. Maia was wearing an elaborate set of crown jewelry which Kenrik had given her when their betrothal contract had been signed at the short ceremony the previous day. Kenrik had wasted no time in securing his future bride.

Soldiers in the brown uniform of Proburg were now riding in, followed by the royal carriage from Landmari Castle and escorted by Reideaux guards. Prince Gustovas stepped down first, followed by King Konrad. Jobyna saw his gaunt face and gasped involuntarily. Konrad wore his right arm in a sling. He was so thin, and the dark rings under his eyes were not relieved by his suntanned skin. His eyes searched for one face and when the blue met the green, the wide smile breaking across his face transformed the weariness to joy.

"You look so pale, my princess." He was the first to speak. "You should have taken Doctor Sleven's advice, as I did, and recuperated while lying in the sun!"

"It is so good to see you, King Konrad." Jobyna gripped Luke's arm as she attempted a faltering curtsy.

Konrad bowed and spoke to Kenrik and Maia. "Congratulations to both of you."

"I am sure you will be making an announcement of your own very soon," Kenrik said to Konrad. "We will be cousins, related by marriage." He laughed and sent a wink to Jobyna who blushed at the memory of her previous mistaken reasoning.

Ellice had been presented to King Willem of Strasland while he was resident at Jydanski. They had communicated at length before he returned home with his grandson, Grand Duke Louis. Ellice had written for King Willem, her real name, Celene, daughter of Baron Randall from the village of Ranard. The king of Strasland had informed her that Elliad and his men had wiped out the whole village of Ranard, and he had left it to burn down. The only survivors were a few women and children who had hidden in the woods. Ellice's father had been killed. (Her mother had died in childbirth some years before.) Ellice had suspected the loss of her home village as she had seen most of the carnage for herself. Elliad had brutally branded her at the same time he marked her father's horses, and he himself had rendered her mute then taken her to his castle at Valdemar in Frencolia. Her recovery from the trauma had been slow, and Ellice had wanted only to die. After Elliad claimed the Frencolian throne, Ellice had been transferred to King's Castle and had worked as a slave for Elliad's woman, Ranee.

Luke told Jobyna that was as much as Ellice wished to reveal, except that her life had been completely meaningless until she met Jobyna.

King Willem had invited "Celene Randall" to return to Strasland with him, promising her a position in his palace or the freedom to seek out relatives and live with them if she wished. Luke in turn offered her a place in Frencberg at King's Castle as a lady-in-waiting to his sister. Luke urged Ellice to take time to consider and not to make a hasty decision. She was welcome in both countries and she must realize she was now free. Ellice was to present her answer in writing when she had decided.

Ellice was encouraged to do as she pleased at the palace in Jydanski. She was told she was no longer to behave like a slave, but she stayed beside Jobyna's bed with unerring devotion. Forced to accept a bedroom of her own, Ellice trembled when chambermaids treated her as equal to Jobyna and Maia. Luke had made her sit down in his presence—a task of no mean proportion—and told her it was his wish and command that she accept that she was no longer a slave; she must consider herself at the very least a lady.

Writing a letter to King Willem, Ellice thanked him for his kind offer but said she wished to live with her friends in Frencolia. A second letter to King Luke Chanec from her hand stated she would accept his offer, and would be privileged to become one of Princess Jobyna's ladies-in-waiting. Strasland did not tempt her any more; she felt only strangers would be there now, after five years away. She would correspond with an uncle she had been told still lived and inform him that she was taking up residence in Frencolia. Ellice requested that they call her by the name Jobyna gave her—Ellice—because, as the young woman wrote, "I will never forget when the princess gave me my name. She told me that she cared for me! She said that Ellice means 'Jehovah is God,' and I am glad to have a name which will bring praise to the God of the Gospel Book."

Sharing the letter with Jobyna, Luke knew his sister was very happy with Ellice's devotion to her; their love and friendship were mutual. Maia was excited with the arrangement and talked to Cynara about Ellice. Cynara turned out her wardrobe and filled trunks with beautiful clothes for Ellice. Maia and Cynara had Ellice parade the dresses before them, seeking to make her comfortable in her new role. Cynara felt strangely satisfied to give to Ellice—the first time in her life that the czarevna had delighted in someone less fortunate. She pulled out forgotten jewelry, ignoring Ellice's protests, adding daily to the new lady's collection. Maia and Cynara made her wear a particularly becoming gown, styling her hair in the fashion of a princess and decking her out with some of the new jewelry. They then presented her to Luke and Dorai.

"The Lady Ellice!" Maia led Ellice into the sitting room of the guest apartment. She took her through into Jobyna's bedroom. They giggled when Jobyna did not recognize her at first.

"So shall you be called 'Lady Ellice' from this moment on!" Luke declared. "Your king has spoken!" he commanded, as he saw Ellice's look of doubt.

Jobyna walked holding Konrad's arm. Her limp was barely noticeable, her head was held high and a smile of happiness played gently on her rose-pink lips. Luke, Maia, Dorai and Ellice gazed with pride as she stood beside them in the Oval Crown Room. This moment had been rehearsed repeatedly over the past few days.

All eyes were upon the entrance doors held open by emirs. All around the crown room, standing like silent, solid statues, were 3,000 noblemen with their wives, dressed in suits and gowns of all colors, sparkling with jewels of all descriptions. They stood beside plushly covered seats set upon long platforms, three tiers high. Their eager faces were turned toward the door, waiting for the music to sound out the entrance of Czarevitch Kenrik, to be crowned in a few moments the czar of Chezkovia. The instruments blared out the triumphant sound, and Kenrik strode through the doors. Kedar followed, bearing the crown cushioned on red velvet. Cynara walked behind. Kedar would become *Czarevitch* Kedar today. He stood beside Jobyna with Cynara at his side. Kenrik sat on the throne.

Jobyna's trembling hands took the cushion from Kedar. This had been Kenrik's request, a public declaration as to her part in rescuing the crown from the deceiver. She carried the crown to Emir Weikol who extended it up in the air held by both hands, speaking well-rehearsed words to those present. Jobyna returned to her place. On completion of his long speech, the emir knelt in front of Kenrik for some moments then stood and placed the crown on his head, pronouncing him the czar of the czardom of Chezkovia.

Dorai, Luke and Jobyna all found it difficult to imagine that one day Maia would sit on the throne beside Kenrik as Czarina Maia of Chezkovia.

Czar Kenrik rose and motioned for Kedar to come before him. Kedar knelt while Kenrik pronounced him "His Imperial Highness, Czarevitch Kedar." The new czar stated his brother would receive the ring to the czardom when he turned 16.

Speeches were long and involved, and Luke and Jobyna (unbeknownst to each other) decided they must learn this language for future communications. Kenrik was commissioning a tutor to teach Maia German, and they must try to find the time to sit in on the sessions. It was no great surprise when Luke and Jobyna conferred on the matter later and found they had both been thinking the same thoughts.

Czar Kenrik led the way up the staircase and out on to the balcony overlooking the palace courtyard. Trumpets triumphantly sounded out as he walked into view of the thousands below who cheered, applauded and waved with thunderous enthusiasm. Kedar and Cynara stood on one side and the cheers grew louder as Maia took Kenrik's outstretched hand and stood at his side, followed by Konrad, Jobyna, Luke, Dorai, Prince Gustovas and 20 emirs.

"Four kingdoms are united here today, Jobyna," Konrad whispered in her ear. "Chezkovia, Proburg, Reideaux and Frencolia."

Beyond the palace, the great sprawling metropolis of Jydanski lay glistening in the overhead morning sun. Hundreds of reflections played off the domes and spires, making a parade of sparkling hues and fantasies. All the castles and palaces in the world seemed to be represented in the panorama below, and the mass of people waving and cheering appeared to be animated decorations on a bedazzling spectacle. They clung to battlements and pillars, sat on walls and fences, leaned out of windows and were crowded on balconies. Red and white uniforms lined the arched clerestories, flanked by brown, blue and green. It was a sight never to be forgotten!

The feast that followed lasted a week. Huge oxen stuffed with game and poultry were carried into the banquet hall, placed on massive tables for carving, followed by numerous cooked white swans presented on silver platters, complete with feathers unscorched and fresh as though floating upon a silver lake. Hundreds of dishes and delicacies were served up amidst music and singing. A fountain of wine flowed freely for all to help themselves. Music, entertainment, dancing—Konrad, Jobyna and Luke, shadowed by Moritz and Vincenz, sought the contrasting tranquility of the garden to stroll, talk and pass the time.

"I'll never be able to eat another thing for a month!" Jobyna declared, sitting by the lake. "How will we ever last out the wedding feast? Cynara told me that Kenrik is planning a feast to last a month!"

"The wedding will not be for two years, and I'm sure we will have recovered by then!" Luke leaned on the back of the seat.

"We will have our wedding before Maia's," Konrad reminded her as he sat beside her, taking her small hand in his. "The question is, how soon, my love?"

"Our feast will be short, I hope; two days is enough!" Jobyna said, not answering his question, looking to see Konrad's reaction. "To me, this is just an excuse for some to display gluttony and drunkenness! I hope our wedding feast can have more meaning to it, more purpose. . . ." She turned as someone approached and rose quickly to curtsy to Konrad's father.

"Your absence is noticed!" Prince Gustovas said, ignoring Jobyna's words. He took her hand in his. "You are as beautiful as ever, Princess. You need to allow Kenrik's guests to look at your fairness." He drew her with him, but not before she had caught Konrad's look of disapproval.

Gustovas said fervently, "We hope you have a long wedding supper that will last as long as the guests can stay!" He turned to Konrad who was now right beside them, "When are you planning to announce your betrothal, Son?"

"When the feasting is over, we plan to return with you to Proburg, Father, and you shall announce the betrothal there; but I am planning to go to Frencolia for the ceremony." Konrad walked beside Prince Gustovas as they returned to the banquet hall. "We will travel with King Luke, Prince Dorai and Princess Maia."

Prince Gustovas turned to his son. "That will be an honor,

Son. Your mother will like that. Maybe we will travel with you to Frencolia; it would be good for her to have something else to consider. . . ."

Luke knew the monarch of Proburg was thinking of his sons, Gustav and Warford. Konrad had told him of the morbid funeral procession, the extreme sadness of the family, the grief, hopelessness and emptiness he sensed in the widows and children.

"Without faith," Konrad told Luke, "where does comfort come from? The Lord God is the source of all comfort, and one goes through grief so that one may be able to comfort another when it is their turn to sorrow." One day, Luke would remind him of these words.

Konrad had been well enough to travel in a carriage, sit for the brief ceremony and pray with his family at the tomb. Prince Gustovas had traveled to Jydanski with Konrad for Kenrik's coronation to escape from realities he did not want to face. Many of his trusted, loyal friends and counselors had been killed at Elliad's orders. He realized also that Konrad's life had been hanging on a thin thread when Elliad decided to keep him alive. The Proburg monarch now appreciated his youngest son in a way he had never imagined possible.

The czar of Chezkovia, his sister Czarevna Cynara and brother Czarevitch Kedar all accompanied the Frencolian-bound group to the Proburg capital, Landmari. Jobyna, Maia and Ellice journeyed with Cynara in the royal carriage. The men traveled on horseback. Jobyna was concerned about Konrad but he discounted her fears, stating he needed the fresh air and exercise to work off some of the food he had eaten over the past 10 days. Prince Gustovas rode beside his son, proud to hear the cheers and calls of support.

Cynara and Maia, now inseparable, chatted ceaselessly, and Jobyna listened contentedly. Cynara was verbally planning their wedding dresses and promised she would send the fabric to make them. Kenrik wanted Maia to wear pale green and Jobyna was amused to think of such things being decided with two years to wait. Konrad had not decided how long their betrothal would be, but secretly she hoped it would not be too long.

Kenrik had presented the stolen treasures of Frencolia to Luke and these were carefully loaded on carts to be sent, securely escorted, back to the vaults of King's Castle in Frencberg. Luke and his uncle sorted through some of the more unique treasures and offered Kenrik free choice for Maia's dowry. Once his selection was complete, Konrad and Jobyna chose a few things they could use in Kelsey Castle at Reideaux. Konrad's kingdom was very poor, and he decided to take a chest of gold bullion which he would mint for special distribution after their wedding.

When they reached the Proburg border, Jobyna transferred to the Proburg royal carriage to sit with Prince Gustovas and Konrad. Still weak, Konrad had tired of the ride and was content to sit the rest of the way in the carriage. It also gave him time to talk with his love, a precious opportunity (even though his father was listening and absorbing everything they said).

Prince Gustovas kept silent, even when he felt disturbed with their serious discussion. They took life too seriously and talked of concepts that were better forgotten in a drink of wine, he thought. He knew enough about Konrad to know he had a mind of his own. Prince Gustovas remembered the time he had the unrepenting Konrad whipped for quoting a verse from the Gospel Book at him.

The monarch had yelled at his son, "There is no God!"

Konrad had quoted quietly, "The Gospel Book says, 'The fool has said in his heart, there is no God!' " (Psalm 14:1).

Gustovas had not tolerated his son suggesting that he, the supreme monarch of Proburg, was a fool, even if it were by quoted words. The prince smiled to himself to think he had told Kenrik at Baltic Castle, "I am an old fool!" Life had a way of turning the tide on the claims one made.

"Next spring. That will give us about seven months' betrothal. What do you say to that, Father?" Konrad waited briefly for an answer but his father was involved with thoughts of his own. "If we waited until May, then we could be married on your birthday, Jobyna!"

"Yes, I would like that, or in April when my real birthday falls. Let's see what Luke says." Jobyna was happy. How suddenly her whole life had changed! Ahead was only happiness and sunshine, she was sure. She frowned. Hadn't she told herself such things before? Yes! When she had returned to Frencolia, she had thought she would remain there for the rest of her life, safe and happy. Was life ever only brightness and sunshine? No! That would be wrong; without precipitations, there would be desert and in the desert there was no growth, no life.

"What is it? What makes you sad?" Konrad saw her frown, and noted her silence.

"I was thinking of all the happiness ahead, wishing only for blessings, for no trials or sorrows. . . . But we cannot grow without the thirst-quenching rainfall upon the dry soil of our laughter and joy." Jobyna lifted her long eyelashes to look at Konrad. "So we must pray for strength from God to help us turn trials into joys. I have struggled to do this and at times the trials overcame me. Kedar's courage and faith puts me to shame!"

Konrad placed his arm around her shoulders, drawing her head to his chest. "You have had more than your share of trials, my love. The main thing is to keep on keeping on, to continue believing, not to give up, whatever life brings along. And I shall be there beside you all the way!"

27

Landmari Castle was, as Prince Gustovas had claimed in the past, a real castle. Konrad led his Frencolian guests, including the Lady Ellice, on a grand tour to every part of the huge edifice, proudly describing to Jobyna the places he had romped as a young boy.

Luke and Jobyna gazed down from the battlements where Konrad, barely seven years old, had swung on a thin rope and scared his mother almost to death. The rope would not have supported the weight of another and had been far short of reaching the ground. By the time Prince Gustovas' attendants brought piles of mattresses, Konrad had climbed back up to the battlements where his tutor began to slap him mercilessly. To escape the dreaded punishment (torture and certain death, his teacher promised), Konrad slid down the rope once more and dropped into the pile of mattresses. When the servants retrieved the young prince, his father boxed his ears and sent him to his room to be confined there for two long days.

Konrad had dabbled in rope climbing ever since, and at one time, when his parents were away, he tied rope to every accessible beam from one end of the castle to the other, allowing him to swing spectacularly, at breathtaking speed from one floor to the next, across the largest areas. Upon his parents' return, the poised young prince proudly presented a perilous performance of his precarious pastime. His punishment was great when Prince Gustovas commanded that every piece of rope in the castle be impounded, locked away from the primate princeling.

Jobyna and Luke laughed loudly at Konrad's descriptions of his escapades. Jobyna whispered in his ear, "I hope we have a son like you. It will be such fun! You can hang rope all over Kelsey Castle and teach our son to climb properly from the start!"

Konrad smiled at her; he was amazed that she verbalized such a delightful idea. "You are some woman, Jobyna, my love," he whispered back.

The throne room at Landmari Castle was of peculiar interest. The single throne graced the center of the round chamber, molded from a raised round marble slab which pivoted in any direction at the control of a lever on the throne itself. The throne was able to dominate every part of the room and Prince Gustovas could turn it to face any area he wished. Konrad told Jobyna that the throne was mostly kept stationery. The rotational effect had been created to please some eccentric predecessor who had more wealth than sense. Konrad told Jobyna in undertones that he had discovered the throne to be an amusing round-about to ride on. As a young boy (not so long ago), he would sneak there secretly and could spin it around at quite a speed. Jobyna gasped at the thought, wearing an openly shocked expression, staring at the throne of Proburg, imagining a small boy with a mass of yellow curls, an angelic look upon his face (she was sure he had one), spinning round and round. . . . She looked up at Konrad to see if he was teasing her.

"You are just beginning to find out what I'm really like!" he laughed. "Don't tell Father! That is one he doesn't know about!"

The royal apartments, the children's quarters, the dining halls, the banquet rooms, the theater, the ballroom—all were of great interest. Maia expressed her weariness and the tour group broke into two. Luke (now permanently shadowed by Kedar), Jobyna and Ellice continued on with Konrad and Moritz who showed them the military quarters and the stables.

Jobyna exclaimed with happiness when her eyes fell upon Brownlea's shining coat. "You had him brought here! Oh, Brownlea!" She kissed his nose and patted his neck.

Konrad took her hand. "Look here!" He took her to another stall. "This horse is for you. He is a gift from Father who asked me to present him to you now, on his behalf."

Jobyna gazed at the stallion with great interest. He was pure white, not another color anywhere; even his mane and tail were white. "I've never seen anything so beautiful!" Jobyna looked at Konrad, and seeing his admiration of her, she teased, "Except you, my love." She turned to Luke. "Look at him, Luke! What do you say?"

"Konrad, or the horse? I have definitely seen more beautiful things!" Luke laughed at her. "Just look in the mirror, little Sister!" He ducked as she threw handfuls of grain at him.

Luke asked, "What will you name him?"

"I shall call him 'Lightning!' You have Speed, my brother, but this horse shall flash past Speed, like lightning! See if I can't race you now!"

The banquet hall was packed to capacity that night. All the royal family members were present, including Prince Mayer and Princess Ordella, the two royal widows, all the royal grandchildren and Prince Gustovas' court. Proburg officials and dignitaries were introduced. Dignitaries from Reideaux included Count Ira and his wife Countess Celia, and Lord Jarman. The new czar of neighboring Chezkovia was welcomed, and his newly betrothed, Princess Maia from Frencolia. Czarevna Cynara and Czarevitch Kedar sat with the Chezkovian emirs who had accompanied them and with Doctor Sleven and his wife Brenna. King Luke Chanec and Prince Dorai were joined by six senior knights. Luke was pleased to greet Sir Valdre and Sir Keith, who had been successfully rescued by the Chezkovian cavalry. Konrad sat by Jobyna, with Ellice by her side.

Prince Gustovas stood to his feet before the meal was served and made an announcement followed by a request that would be remembered for a long time. "We would like to welcome you all here tonight. It is by the grace of God that we are together like this. We have much to celebrate and to give thanks for." He turned to Konrad. "We would like our son King Konrad to return a prayer of thanks tonight before we begin this meal."

Konrad gulped and looked bewildered. His father was not mocking him, not joking with him! He stood to his feet and a hush took over as he said, "Let us give thanks to the Lord God."

The meal was sumptuous; seafood was featured, presented in every way imaginable. Jobyna had never tasted shellfish before, and Konrad laughed at the faces she made when she sampled the gritty, fishy dishes. She enjoyed the mild lobster and fish fillets served with lemon sauce.

Desserts were presented with music; brightly dressed actors, jesters and dwarves brought in elaborately frosted cakes and pastries. One of the huge pastries was cut open and a flock of doves flew from the center. A huge cake shaped like a heart, frosted with pink and trimmed with fresh strawberries and red roses, was brought to the table in front of Konrad and Jobyna. The musicians began playing soft music.

Prince Gustovas stood; he clicked his fingers and the music ceased. "It is my pleasure to announce the betrothal of my son

Konrad, king of Reideaux, to Princess Jobyna, sister of King Luke Chanec of Frencolia. King Luke Chanec extends an invitation to you all to attend the ceremony in Frencolia in three weeks' time."

Mayer stood behind Konrad, and Cynara moved to stand behind Jobyna. They waited as the couple each cut a piece of cake, then they placed blindfolds around their eyes and told them they must feed the cake to their love, using one hand only. Konrad could comply because one arm was limited by the sling, but Cynara had to hold Jobyna's left arm as she raised it to feel Konrad's face (he was head and shoulders above her). Whenever the cake came near their mouths, the guests called out "too high!" or "too low!" or "to the left!" Konrad had pink frosting in his hair, on his moustache, all over his nose and down his neck. Jobyna wore the pink goo on her forehead and all over her blindfold. Both were shaking with laughter as was everyone else in the banquet room. In a final attempt to eat some of the delectable delight, Konrad grasped Jobyna's hand, finishing off the cake and licking the strawberry frosting from her fingers as the company applauded loudly.

The waiter brought towels and a bowl of steaming water, and Ellice helped sponge the couple's mistakes away as best she could. Pleased and surprised to see Ellice laughing, Jobyna realized this was a first, to hear the sound of her sparkling voice in giggles she could not control. After the delicious heart cake was cut by the cook, Konrad and Jobyna walked hand in hand among the tables, distributing the tasty pieces to their guests.

After a late breakfast the next morning, Konrad suggested they go to the stables, and Lightning was brought out by one of the grooms. "You may not be able to ride him yet, but at least you can sit on him," Konrad encouraged her. Luke helped her onto the horse's back, and she felt the animal give a slight tremor as she pulled on the reins. She trotted him across the courtyard.

"He's so gentle, so very sensitive; he moves with even the suggestion of a tug!" she exclaimed. Her eyes met with those of Konrad's father as she drew the animal round at the castle terrace. "He's beautiful, Prince Gustovas! Thank you." Blowing him a kiss, Jobyna walked the horse across to Konrad. Luke helped her down. "My knee is stiff; some riding would help to loosen it!" she declared.

Doctor Sleven examined her knee later in the day and agreed that exercise would help. He removed the stitches from Konrad's arm and told him he must use it as much as he could. The doctor demonstrated exercises which would increase the muscle strength. Konrad declared, "A good hard bit of climbing will cure me!"

At the end of the week, Kenrik, Cynara and Kedar returned to Jydanski with the emirs and their escort. Maia promised to write to Kenrik "every day" and would send the letters each time a messenger left for Chezkovia—or Proburg, where they would be rapidly forwarded. Kenrik told her he could not promise as much, but would send communications when a messenger left Jydanski for Frencberg. Cynara and Kedar promised to write and Cynara said she would tell Maia all the tidbits that a woman would want to know, "the things that men overlook."

Moritz stepped toward Konrad, embracing him fervently. Kenrik had offered Moritz the position of personal bodyguard and counselor, and Moritz had accepted, being unable to decline and thus slight the new czar. Konrad understood and was pleased for Kenrik; Moritz had a stabilizing, calming effect on those to whom he was close. Moritz said he would stay with Kenrik for two years, until the czar's marriage to Maia. Then he requested to review the situation. Kenrik gladly agreed with this arrangement.

Jobyna stepped away as Konrad bade final farewells to Moritz. At the same moment, Czar Kenrik took her hand.

"We will always be friends, Princess Jobyna, and I promise I will always give you the benefit of the doubt!" He kissed her cheeks. Jobyna would recall these words vividly one day; they would save her life!

The journey to Reideaux, the jubilant welcome there, another celebration for the sake of King Konrad's subjects—all this was secondary to Luke's thoughts of returning to Frencolia.

Halfway between Kelsey Castle and Ira Castle, Konrad ordered the company to ride on. He drew Luke aside and they left the road, followed by Sir Dorai, Mayer, Reideaux personnel and a few Frencolian soldiers. Jobyna wondered what was happening, but complying with the king's command she urged Lightning into a gentle gallop. Prince Gustovas rode to one side of her, and Ellice rode Brownlea at her other side.

Princess Rhaselle, the three daughters-in-law and the children traveled in carriages. These carriages would leave the group before Ira Castle and Prince Gustovas would travel with them to Gerold Castle. They would enter the Leroy road, and the two companies would rendezvous at Prince Dorai's castle at Leroy. This way to Frencberg, though somewhat longer, was the only suitable route from the north for the traverse of the carriages.

Not until she was married to Konrad did Jobyna learn the reason for the diversion.

King Konrad wished to build a manor house, identical to the one at Chanoine, as a wedding present for Jobyna. Luke had commissioned a large team of builders to work on his to enclose it before the snows; then the inside work was completed during the winter months when outside work was limited. It had taken a year. Luke offered to send the same builders if Konrad would supply the manpower, the masons and the lumber. It would be no mean task to complete the manor house before the wedding, but Konrad issued the commands and that day preparations were made. A new village would be built around the manor house which was to be located beside a lake. Konrad would let Jobyna name the village after they were married. He was excited with the secret and Luke shared his enthusiasm, promising to send furnishings and tapestries to grace the rooms.

They joined the group at Ira Castle later in the day. The plans had taken longer to discuss; the positioning of the house, the walls and the moat bridge had been decided. Jobyna noticed Luke and Konrad hush when she approached them in the sitting room at Ira Castle. "You're up to something, Brother!" she smiled at them. "I'll find out what it is. . . ."

Konrad stood and took her hand. "That you will, my love; I can guarantee!"

Princess Minette, Prince Charles, and the Princesses Doralin and Elissa stood with Ruskin, Sabin and Felix to welcome the travelers at Leroy Castle. Maia cried uncontrollably when her mother hugged her close and kissed her.

"I know exactly what she feels like!" Jobyna said to Luke and Konrad.

Sabin greeted them with affection. He said that amazing stories were being told of the goings-on in Chezkovia. News of all that had happened had traveled to Frencolia. Many of the reports were highly exaggerated, and it relieved their tension to be able to laugh at the incredible tales told of their escapades.

King Luke and Czar Kenrik had been pictured as totally invincible. Frencolians believed Luke had killed Elliad and then ridden out to rescue his sister (and the czar) from murderous kidnappers. That King Konrad had climbed the castle walls was incidental. He was reported to have fallen and broken his leg!

The gossips told the tale of Princess Jobyna, who had been pushed by the evil Elliad from Baltic Castle wall and had been kidnapped while trying to escape along the beach! Maia was said to have been injured when she rescued the Chezkovian crown from a mad soldier. The stories were retold, 10 feet taller and more gruesome each time. Jobyna laughed to think that others had vivid imaginations; it wasn't her affliction alone!

Recounting the true series of events to Minette and others was a very sobering experience. Konrad could see the horror on Jobyna's face. He himself expressed that he now considered himself to be mad to have taken on such a person as Elliad. Glancing at Jobyna he said that, in hindsight, he wished she had not gone to Baltic Castle! However, Jobyna, sitting between Konrad's father and mother, declared that it was well worth it! How else did Konrad think they could be here now?

Prince Gustovas joined the conversation, admitting that he had never expected to leave Baltic Castle alive. He had fully expected his whole family to have been murdered. The prince told them the story of his time in Jydanski and of the incarceration at Baltic Castle. Luke was acclaimed by Prince Gustovas and family for his calm bravery and support while they were all under such incredible pressure.

Jobyna shared with Konrad later how good it had been to talk about the ordeal at Baltic Castle. Recounting the facts helped clear her mind and brought the whole trauma into perspective; she could see how God had worked, in spite of the terrible drama created by man. "At times I wondered how God could possibly allow such things, and then I remembered that He created man with a free choice. It is not God's fault if man chooses to abuse the gift of life and the gifts of freedom and love. When man's choices affect the freedom of other human beings, then he does, indeed, have much to answer for! God's judgment will take care of Elliad now!"

Jobyna was silent then, remembering a verse from the book of Hebrews. At Konrad's query about her thoughts, she quoted, "It is appointed unto men once to die, but after this the judgment" (Hebrews 9:27).

After a while Konrad said, "We must never blame God for man's mistakes. We must trust Him like Joseph and have patience that God will use the bad that man creates to work out for our good!" Konrad looked into her serious green eyes. They would both remember these words.

King's Castle, at Frencberg, was now under inspection. Luke led the Proburg party on a tour, taking them into the secret tunnel accessed in the throne room. He promised the children he would accompany them another day through to the secret cave in the valley and tell them about the great treasures Jobyna and he had discovered there. Then he would take them to the secret treasury chamber in the dungeons which was the new domicile for the treasures.

Jobyna did not go on the tour with Luke but walked arm-in-arm with Konrad, accompanied by Vincenz, Maia, Ellice and Sabin, strolling along the rampart on the battlements.

The starry-eyed couple talked about the future, about the setting sun and about their betrothal ceremony to be held the next morning. They agreed joyfully about the goodness of the Lord God of the Gospel Book, His faithfulness and love. Together they prayed, promising to keep on with the task of the Scriptures being handwritten and distributed.

They whispered together about how much they loved each other. Then for a while they didn't talk. Jobyna leaned her head on Konrad's shoulder. The sun had gone down beneath the western mountains, and they watched the sky as it changed from its blushing hues into deeper night shades. Tomorrow, their betrothal day, would be a new day.